CW00405996

TERMINUS GATE

SURVIVAL WARS BOOK 5

ANTHONY JAMES

© 2018 Anthony James
All rights reserved

The right of Anthony James to be identified as the author of this work has been asserted by him in accordance with the Copyright, Designs and Patents Act, 1988

The characters and events portrayed in this book are fictitious. Any similarity to real persons, living or dead, is coincidental and not intended by the author

This book is sold subject to the condition that it shall not, by way of trade or otherwise, be lent, resold, hired out, or otherwise circulated without the publisher's prior consent in any form of binding or cover other than that in which it is published and without a similar condition including this condition being imposed upon the subsequent purchaser

Cover Design by Dan Van Oss www.covermint.design

Follow Anthony James on Facebook at facebook.com/anthonyjamesauthor.

CHAPTER ONE

A TINY SLIVER of the sun became visible above the edge of planet Atlantis. In contrast to the carpet of star-speckled darkness, the intensity of the white-yellow light was dazzling. The planet itself was no less breath taking than the majesty of the backdrop, covered as it was in a belt of lush green forests and deep blue oceans.

Half a million kilometres away a spaceship appeared in local space, dispersing the colossal energy from its fission drive throughout the vacuum. The signature alerted the personnel at the Tillos military base to its arrival, and the base mainframe communicated with the much quicker AI core on the spacecraft to find out its status.

Without a pause, the captain of the ESS *Crimson* fired up the gravity drive, which propelled the one-point-five billion tonne vessel onwards as if it weighed no more than a handful of feathers.

The hull of the *Crimson* was battered and scarred. There were two huge craters in the outer armour plating and the exterior showed signs of heat damage, giving its edges a blurred appearance. As well as the visible signs, there was other damage. The warship's engines leaked a vast trail of positrons and the metals of its hull reeked with an impossibly high level of radiation.

In spite of its size, the *Crimson* had not been designed to carry more than a tiny crew and a small complement of ground troops. There were only four occupants onboard and they sat brooding over what lay before them. The warship had recently accomplished a monumental victory over a seemingly unstoppable enemy mothership, so the mood should have been good. Instead, the high spirits were dampened by uncertainty over what would follow.

"Fleet Admiral Teron was as good as his word, sir," said Lieutenant Frank Chainer. "We've got clearance codes for an immediate landing."

"That's good," said Captain John Nathan Duggan. He stretched and pushed his fingertips across his scalp. "I could do with a haircut."

Commander Lucy McGlashan fixed him with a piercing stare. "That's the furthest ahead you've thought?"

Duggan shrugged. "I'm not hopeful the Space Corps will grant us anything more significant."

"I thought I was the cynical one," said Chainer.

"You are, Lieutenant," said McGlashan. "It must be rubbing off on the captain."

"It wouldn't be too much to expect a week or two of shore leave, would it?" asked Lieutenant Bill Breeze. "I think we deserve it."

"I'll have a word when we land," said Duggan. "I don't want to make a promise and then find out Admiral Teron has another one of his brown folders predicting a hundred billion deaths somewhere else in the Confederation."

"The Space Corps has more than one damned captain," said McGlashan angrily. Duggan could understand the reason for her frustration and he shared it. They were hoping to spend some time together when they landed and if Teron sent them off on another mission, they'd have to keep each other at arm's length while on duty.

"It would be lovely to think they'll give us a medal and then pack us off for a couple of weeks to one of the resorts on Atlantis," said Chainer wistfully. "It's been twenty years since I was last here on non-military business."

"Does the Space Corps even give out medals anymore?" asked Breeze. The crew joked about medals, but none of them particularly craved the recognition, though they'd each been decorated on several previous occasions.

"There was talk a few years ago in the Confederation Council that we should abolish medals," said Duggan, remembering the consternation it had caused at the time. "A couple of the council members got it into their heads that decorating only the deserving few would somehow make the other serving members of the Corps feel less worthy."

"Yeah, I think I remember," said Breeze. "I thought it was rumour."

"I'm afraid it wasn't."

McGlashan shook her head incredulously. "You're seriously telling me someone thought it was a good idea?"

"Apparently so," said Duggan. "Everyone is equal in the Confederation and there was a genuine attempt to carry that ideal across to the military."

"I wouldn't turn down a medal if they wanted to give me one," said Chainer. "I'd wear it proudly on my chest."

"You've already got five medals that I'm aware of," said Duggan mildly. "I don't see them anywhere."

"I carry them in my hand luggage everywhere I go, sir. I wouldn't want to lose them."

"What would happen to them in the likely event we get blown to pieces on our next mission?" asked McGlashan. "Shouldn't you keep them in a safe place?"

"I've got nobody to give them to - at least nobody I'd want to have them. I'd prefer my medals to be destroyed in space by an enemy missile."

"Let us turn our attention towards matters in hand, ladies and gentlemen," said Duggan. The information on his console indicated they'd soon be close enough for him to engage the auto-docking systems on the *Crimson*. Duggan occasionally enjoyed landing his spacecraft manually, but in the circumstances, he wanted to do things by the book.

"I've got Colonel Jabran on the comms, sir. He asks that we engage the autopilot at once."

"He must be worried," said McGlashan.

"It's his neck on the line if irradiated fish start washing up on shore next to the tourist resorts," said Duggan.

"Are they still pretending the damage caused by the wreckage of the *Kuidenar* and *Dretisear* was natural causes?" asked Chainer.

"As far as I'm aware, Lieutenant. In the Confederation you only hear what the Council decides you need to hear. After all, if the good citizens knew everything that went on during wartime, there might be a few more questions asked."

"Difficult questions," added Breeze. "Questions to which there might be no easily-justified answers."

"Yeah, we wouldn't want people to think there are eight-thousand-cubic-kilometre hostile enemy motherships flying through the vicinity and looking to destroy entire planets in their search for conquest and new energy sources," said Chainer. "That might cause a little bit of panic."

Duggan half-regretted bringing the conversation around to the Confederation Council. They had their failings – many failings – but it wasn't becoming of his rank to criticise them so openly. On the other hand, he trusted his crew implicitly and they wouldn't spread gossip.

"We're on auto-pilot," he said, motioning the others back to their pre-landing routines.

"Let me see what lies below," said Chainer, searching through the sensor feeds. "They've still got the *ES Rampage* in one of the trenches. Other than that, it's only going to be us."

"The *Rampage* must be more badly damaged than I thought," said Duggan. "Otherwise they'd have flown it into orbit."

"Is that some kind of emergency procedure?" asked Breeze.

"It is – the Space Corps tries to avoid cross-contamination. Now they're going to have to clean up the *Rampage* as well."

"They're going to spray us before we land, aren't they?"

"They certainly are," said Chainer. "There's a clean-up vessel inbound."

They rendezvoused with the vessel *SC Plutos* high above Atlantis, at sufficient distance to ensure no harmful emissions would reach the surface below. Duggan observed the clean-up craft as it laboured its way close to the *Crimson*. The *SC Plutos* was little more than a featureless cylinder, nine hundred metres in length. It was ancient and incapable of even the most rudimentary lightspeed travel.

"The logs show they built that thing over ninety years ago," said Breeze. "It must be one of the oldest vessels in the fleet."

"It doesn't need to do anything sophisticated," Duggan replied. He checked their speed and saw they'd slowed right down. "The Tillos mainframe is bringing us to a halt."

"I thought they could do basic stuff like this on the move," grumbled Chainer.

"They're not taking any risks this time."

For the next hour, the crew watched as the *SC Plutos* flew sedately around them, firing out high-pressure bursts of semi-liquid particles onto the *Crimson*'s hull in order to contain the radiation until a full clean could be undertaken on the ground.

"Osmium," said Breeze. "Lots and lots of it. We'll be covered in a hard shell worth a hundred billion dollars by the time the *Plutos* is done."

"The treatment doesn't come cheap," said McGlashan.

"On the plus side, we'll be the shiniest ship in the Space Corps," said Chainer.

"Until they scrape the coating off for recycling."

At last, the pilot of the *SC Plutos* decided his work was done. There were only two crew onboard the clean-up vessel and one of them spoke briefly to Chainer to advise the treatment was finished. The Tillos landing computer resumed control and the *Crimson* broke away from the second spacecraft, soon leaving it far behind.

"Technology has moved on a lot since they built the *Plutos*," said Breeze.

"I doubt it was fast when it entered service. It does what it was designed to do," Duggan remarked.

The *Crimson* established a stationary orbit, directly above the Tillos landing field. Then, it descended quickly in a straight line. The airfield below was clear of ground staff, but an army of automated repair bots clustered eagerly around trench two. They'd strip away as much of the outer shell of irradiated armour plating as necessary to make the warship safe again and carry the thousands of tonnes of waste elsewhere for treatment.

"The *Crimson*'s going to be grounded for a while," said Breeze. "I've accessed the details of the intended repairs and we're looking at a few weeks until everything's as good as new again."

"We might yet see that shore leave," said Chainer with a glimmering of hope.

Duggan grunted noncommittally. "It'll take them less than ten days for make-do repairs, folks. If they want this ship in the air, they'll skip the spit and polish."

"We're on the ground," said McGlashan, in case they hadn't realised. The auto-pilot landings rarely produced a perceptible thump.

"We'd best get our suits on," said Duggan. "We'll be in decontamination for a day or two after we disembark."

A short time later, the crew exited the spaceship by the front ramp. Duggan's helmet flashed up a series of red alerts to make him aware there was far more radiation in the vicinity than the suit could protect against. The four of them sprinted to the closest lift, which carried them to the top of trench two. Through the clear panels of the lift door, the *Crimson* appeared a glossy and shiny silver from the thin coating which had been applied to it.

"It looks like cheap jewellery," said McGlashan.

"I like it," Chainer replied. "Pimp my spaceship."

Breeze rolled his eyes and looked to the heavens. "You need to see someone from the Space Corps' Wellbeing Team, Frank. Tell them about these strange ideas you get."

"They take all shapes and sizes in the Corps, Bill. You know that."

The lift door fizzed open. There was a single vehicle waiting for them – it was a dull-grey cuboid with rounded sides and a wedge-shaped cabin for a driver to sit in. The words 'Decontamination Unit' were written across the sides in yellow, unmissable letters. There was no human occupant in sight, but a robotic voice blared out instructions for the crew to enter the vehicle through a door in the back.

Moments later, they were inside and being sprayed with a

variety of substances to scour away the radiation from their spacesuits. The vehicle sped across the landing pad towards a little-used building at the far edge of the base, wherein incidents such as this one were handled. The four of them were directed inside and told to prepare for a thorough process of decontamination and treatment.

CHAPTER TWO

TWO DAYS LATER, Duggan and his crew were given clearance to return to their duties. They took a trip in a decontamination vehicle to one of the primary base administrative facilities. The base was still on radiation alert, but they were permitted to wear their normal uniforms. The journey gave them an opportunity to view the hulking shape of the *ES Rampage*, which remained unmoving in the place it had docked after sustaining heavy damage in the recent conflict with the Ghasts.

"It's blocking my view of the *Crimson*," said Chainer, craning his neck to look.

"There won't be anything much worth looking at," said Breeze, not bothering to raise his head.

"They've got the whole base on lock-down still," said McGlashan, pointing ahead.

"Yeah."

Duggan looked where she indicated. The building they headed towards was shuttered against radiation. As they drew closer, he saw a pair of stony-faced guards at the door, carrying metering equipment.

"They're not suited," said Breeze. "They usually keep the monitoring teams covered up until the air is as clean as it should be."

"It doesn't take long to neutralise radiation emissions these days," McGlashan replied. "The base must have dropped to a yellow alert. Maybe even to blue."

"Colonel Jabran strikes me as a man who does everything by the book," said Chainer. "If those guys aren't suited, there'll be no gamma rays to worry about."

"I'll bet he's pissed at us," McGlashan laughed. "This must be the most excitement the Tillos base has ever seen."

Duggan wasn't so sure Jabran was a man prone to anger. Though he didn't get on with the colonel, he was happy to admit that the Tillos base was as well-run as most others.

"Colonel Jabran has done well in the circumstances," he said. "He has fewer resources than a main facility and he's been forced to handle a series of critical situations."

"I suppose," said McGlashan.

Up close, the two guards were as dour-faced as they appeared from a distance. They grunted surly greetings which teetered on the brink of rudeness. Duggan recognized the type – they'd been given more authority than they could handle and it had instilled an inflated sense of their own self-worth. There was no need to let it worry him, so Duggan stood for a moment as they scanned him for contaminants and walked on when he got the nod.

"Miserable bastards," said Chainer, just loudly enough for the two guards to pick up his words. They'd likely heard it dozens of times and they didn't respond, not that there was much they could do about it.

The foyer of the building was anodyne in the same manner as every other Space Corps foyer across the entirety of the Confederation. Duggan counted himself an observant man, but his eyes did their best to skate across the features of the place he stood in and fought his brain's desire to build a picture of his surroundings. Perhaps this was inspiration for the stealth technology which had served so well in recent weeks, he thought to himself.

The four of them headed towards the wide reception desk, which had been made from some type of polymer and given a finish faintly reminiscent of marble. Duggan gave it a surreptitious rap with his knuckles.

"Good morning," said the man before them. He was dressed in white and blue clothing, with his hair brushed neatly back.

"We've been in decontamination," said Duggan. "And nobody over there had a clue about where we've been assigned."

"Let me have a look at that for you, sir," said the man, efficient and polite. The security on Space Corps bases was excellent and the names of the four arrivals had been fed through to the reception consoles. "Here we are," the man continued. "Commander McGlashan, Lieutenants Breeze and Chainer, you have been returned to the personnel pool and will be provided with rooms here on Tillos until you're assigned to new vessels."

This wasn't expected and the four of them exchanged looks of confusion. A return to the personnel pool made it certain they'd be split up. The receptionist wasn't done with them yet.

"Captain Duggan? There's a transport shuttle waiting for you on landing pad two. I'm to inform you this is of the highest priority."

"Do you have any more information?" asked Duggan, knowing that the receptionist was simply passing on a message.

"Nothing, sir."

"You're sure these are confirmed orders?"

"I'm just telling you what's on my screen, sir."

Duggan was nonplussed. "How long has the shuttle been waiting there?"

"Let me see." The receptionist furrowed his brow. "A little over four hours, sir."

Duggan sighed and thanked the man. He and the others drifted away from the desk and looked at each other blankly. It was McGlashan who spoke first.

"So much for a holiday, eh?" There were layers of meaning behind the words.

"Why're they doing this to us?" asked Chainer.

"I have no idea, Lieutenant," said Duggan. He was less than pleased and would be making his feelings known as soon as the opportunity arose.

"I guess this is goodbye, then. For a while at least," said Breeze. He looked as shocked as Duggan felt.

"I'll find out what's going on," said Duggan.

"Good luck, sir," said Chainer, extending a hand.

Duggan shook it. "And to you, Frank. I'll see you soon."

He shook McGlashan's and Breeze's hands in turn.

"Best get on, sir," McGlashan said.

"Don't want to miss your shuttle," added Breeze.

"It'll wait," said Duggan. In truth, his duty was already pulling at him. He struggled against its insistence that he leave immediately, but he had no acceptable excuse for delay. With a sigh, he waved farewell and left through the door by which he'd recently entered the administrative building. He could feel three pairs of eyes on his back, but he didn't turn.

Outside, there was a row of vehicles waiting for whoever needed them. He climbed into the nearest and instructed it to take him to landing pad two. It was sweltering outside and he was grateful for the coolness within the cabin as the car swished quietly between the high-walled buildings of the base. With the contamination reduced to a safe level, people went about their business dressed in their usual clothes. Decontamination teams roved about, occasionally stopping to take readings from people or vehicles selected at random.

The landing pad was a long way distant and Duggan found

himself carried past a small research lab, numerous accommodation blocks and a large training field. There was also a vast warehouse which housed spares for the vessels which came here. Cranes and ground-based heavy lifters were visible as he passed by. In spite of everything, Duggan got the distinct impression that Tillos was of little importance to the Space Corps hierarchy. The base was adequately funded, but there appeared to be no master plan to expand its capabilities and make it a significant contributor to the Confederation's defensive shield. Even the research facilities didn't look as if they could be responsible for anything more than a few minor side-projects.

There was time enough to think about these most recent orders. Duggan wasn't foolish enough to believe there'd be a welcoming party for his return, but there should have been *something* – a formal acknowledgement of what they'd achieved in defeating the most powerful enemy warship the Space Corps had ever encountered. Instead, there was this – a completely impersonal reassignment to who-knew-where, without even the option to spend a few days recovering from the mental toils of the past weeks and months. Admiral Teron was a no-nonsense man, but he had loyalty to the people who served under him. Duggan was disappointed.

"Maybe I'm getting soft," he said, his voice so quiet he hardly heard the words himself. "I thought for a moment I might get myself a life away from all of this, only to find the hope was a lie."

The vehicle turned to the left and entered an expansive area of bare, concreted ground. The sky was cloudless and the sun beat mercilessly down, reflecting against the creamy whiteness of the surface. Duggan shielded his eyes and saw the raised landing pad in the distance. The promised shuttle waited there – it was a standard model, with a boxy shape that was as far from that of a warship as he could imagine. The Space Corps didn't usually permit its funds to be spent on beauty, so it wasn't surprising that such basic vessels as these were completely utilitarian in both appearance and function.

Duggan's car stopped the regulation distance from the landing pad. He got out and walked up the sloped sides to top. The side door of the shuttle was open and there was nobody in sight. As he approached, a man stepped into view from the inside. This man took a few paces down the boarding ramp and studied Duggan from the fifty or so metres between them. When Duggan drew closer, the man he assumed was the pilot lifted a hand in greeting.

"Captain John Duggan?"

Duggan sized up the other man. He was of a medium height and broad, dressed in a dark blue uniform. His hair was thinning and his unlined face was forgettable. "Yes. Where are we going?"

"We're docking with the Anderlecht *ES Glister*." The man shrugged. "After that, who knows where? I'll take you and the other two passengers where you're going and then I'll return for the next trip."

Duggan walked past the pilot and into the shuttle. There was nothing unexpected here, apart from the presence of the two others. There were six rows of four seats. The seats faced forwards and had grubby blue harnesses which had seen too much use. The two other men were dressed in nondescript grey and sat next to each other in the first row. There was nothing remarkable about them and they stared ahead, unwilling to meet Duggan's gaze. The pilot came up the ramp and headed towards the single door into the cockpit.

"Who are these?" Duggan asked, uncaring if the other two men heard. "I wasn't aware there would be passengers."

The pilot looked blank. "I just take who I'm told to take, sir."

Duggan didn't respond. He sat himself on the end seat of the second row and leaned back. He felt drained of energy and unhappy with the way things had turned out, and his mind drifted onto thoughts of what lay in store for him once he reached the ES *Glister*.

The hull of the shuttle buzzed when the pilot started up the engines. The pitch changed in a manner which told Duggan they'd lifted off. He kept his eyes fixed on the single bulkhead screen, in hope that the pilot would show the transport's sensor feeds. The screen remained blank, so Duggan settled himself for a boring trip.

CHAPTER THREE

DUGGAN WASN'T a man who accepted events without questioning them. After ten minutes of looking at the blank viewscreen in expectation that it would show something interesting, he got to his feet and thumped on the cockpit door with his fist. The door slid open and the pilot looked out, his expression lacking in patience.

"What is it, sir?" asked the man, his tone of voice not especially respectful.

"I like to see where I'm going. Can you turn the viewscreen on?"

"No can do - it's broken. They keep promising they'll fix it, but it never happens."

"Your own viewscreen is broken as well?" asked Duggan. There was no sensor feed into the cockpit either. External visibility wasn't necessary to fly one of the shuttles, yet every pilot Duggan had met liked to see what was happening around them.

"My screen works fine." The man laughed nervously. "I don't need it – an old superstition I have."

"Fine. How long until we dock with the *Glister*?"

"Another forty or fifty minutes, sir."

"I expected it to be sooner than that. How high are they orbiting?"

"Thirty thousand kilometres."

Duggan nodded. "Thank you."

He returned to his seat. The other two men remained quiet and wouldn't look at him. Duggan wondered who they were – their uniform wasn't standard for on-ship duty, so they weren't going to work on the ES *Glister*. That suggested the warship was going to take them elsewhere and he scratched his head as he tried to work out the likely destination. Atlantis was far distant from most of the major Confederation planets. There were a few minor orbitals that could require personnel, but no logical reason that Duggan would need to go to one of them. As an experienced officer, he expected his destination would be a place significant enough for the fleet's larger warships to dock.

"Where are you going?" Duggan asked the men.

The closest man gave a start and turned. There was something dislikeable about him – he had a surly face and no sign of the intelligence needed to perform in a technical role. "What?" he asked.

"Where are you two headed?"

The second man looked over. He had a gleam in his eyes that suggested he was the more intellectually accomplished of the two. It was this second man who spoke. "We're going to Overtide, sir."

"What are you needed for?"

The man smiled thinly. "We're nothing too technical, me and Gavs. We do bits and pieces where we're sent. We go where we're told and we don't ask why."

"You're going a long way for bits and pieces."

"Like I say, we don't ask, sir."

They lapsed into silence. Duggan wasn't the conversational

sort and his companions on this trip seemed no more interested in talking than he was. The minutes dragged by and Duggan couldn't shake the feeling that something was amiss. He couldn't quite put his finger on what it was and the feeling gnawed at him. The Space Corps employed a vast number of people and it was impossible to expect each one of them to be someone he could relate to, but the individuals on the shuttle came across as being especially peculiar.

Duggan got up and banged on the cockpit door again. Once more, he was greeted by the unfriendly face of the pilot. Duggan got the impression the man was in the middle of a comms talk with someone and didn't appreciate the interruption.

"Yes, sir?" he asked.

"I have a favour to ask."

"Ask away."

"I used to serve on the *Glister* a long time ago. Would you mind if I used the comms to speak to them? I want to see if a woman I know still serves on board."

The man grinned weakly. "You know I'm not allowed to give passengers access to the shuttle comms, sir."

"I know that," said Duggan, trying to sound friendly. "Those regulations don't apply if the passenger is a lieutenant or higher rank."

The man's smile faltered. "I'm sorry sir, but I can't let you use the comms. You'll need to wait until we're docked."

"What if I were to insist?" asked Duggan, bringing a note of command into his voice. He leaned into the small cockpit before the pilot could stop him. The information on the console showed they were travelling at a height of only one hundred kilometres. He stepped back again, pretending he'd seen nothing unexpected.

Before the pilot could respond, Duggan sensed movement from his periphery. The other two passengers were on their feet and they walked two or three steps towards him. The man who appeared to be the more intelligent of the two was short and stocky.

"You're in no position to insist on anything. Sir."

In his youth, Duggan had been an impetuous man, prone to act before his brain could intervene with a rational alternative. The years combined with the weight of responsibility had conspired to replace his tendency to the impulsive with a healthy streak of caution. Not so on this occasion. He sized up the situation immediately and realised his life was in danger.

The two men in grey had made the mistake of stepping in close, presumably hoping to intimidate. Without hesitation, Duggan smashed his fist into the nose of the shorter man. It was a crunching blow and he staggered away, shouting in surprise.

The taller man wasn't caught out so easily. He stepped back a pace and dropped into a defensive stance, with his fists clenched in front of his face. Duggan saw at once that he'd underestimated the man – the appearance of stupidity was a calculated act.

With no time to think about it, Duggan stepped in and launched a couple of hard punches. His opponent rolled to the side, suffering only glancing blows. Duggan cursed and smashed a kick into the other man's knee. The man grunted in pain and threw a fast punch in return, catching Duggan a painful strike on the cheek.

Movement to the side prompted Duggan to duck, just in time to avoid a blow from the pilot aimed at his temple. Instead, the fist caught Duggan on top of his head, adding a second pain to that from his cheekbone. The pilot came off worst and he grunted with the shock of breaking his fingers on Duggan's skull.

Rising from his crouch, Duggan evaluated his predicament in a split second. The first man he'd struck had blood streaming from his flattened nose. Even so, the injury wasn't serious and the fellow had righted himself. The second grey-clothed man stepped away another pace and begun to rummage at something in his clothing. There was a scarcely-concealed bulge beneath his uniform under one arm – certainly it was a firearm of some type. Meanwhile, the pilot readied himself to grapple with Duggan. The situation was not a good one.

The pilot hurled himself bodily through the cockpit door, his arms wide apart. Duggan threw his elbow hard into the man's face. The force of the impact was sufficient to knock the pilot senseless for a brief moment. It was just enough time for Duggan to get a grip on the man's clothing. He twisted and heaved, sending his opponent spinning away from the cockpit and headlong onto the floor.

In a flash, Duggan leapt into the cockpit. He thumped his hand firmly against the large, red button used to activate the door. A moment before the aperture closed, he had time to catch a glimpse of cold alloy as the second man drew forth a wicked-looking snub-nosed gauss pistol. Then, the door shut, leaving Duggan within and his enemies without.

"Shit," he muttered, dropping into the single, battered seat.

His eyes scanned the shuttle's consoles. It was nothing like as sophisticated as a warship and he quickly found what he needed. Firstly, he enabled the emergency lock for the cockpit door, in case one of his three opponents had a way to override the mechanism from outside. Next, he reassured himself that he wasn't becoming paranoid. The shuttle was flying at a low velocity and at a low height. Wherever it was headed, it definitely wasn't the ES Glister.

Even though he'd put the door between himself and his enemies, Duggan's position was a poor one. The shuttle's comms were locked down – probably biologically coded to the pilot. On top of that, the autopilot was engaged and there was no obvious way to disable it. He swore again. It was a military vessel so he could likely find a way past these obstacles if he was given time. He didn't expect his opponents to give him the opportunity.

There was a faint thumping noise from behind. One of the men was stupid enough to think he could knock his way through a reinforced interior door with his bare hands. Flesh would certainly fail against the metal, but Duggan wasn't so sure the hand cannon he'd seen would do so. He recognized the type, if not the exact model. The second man had been armed with a modern, high-impact pistol, used for close-quarters combat. The presence of the weapon only added to the mystery of what was happening.

Most of the shuttle's equipment was locked down, but the sensors were not. Duggan searched the local area and checked through the list of spacecraft orbiting Atlantis - a military shuttle automatically received such information. In this instance, there was no sign of the ES *Glister*, which didn't come as a shock, since Duggan was certain it was nowhere near Atlantis.

A loud bang came from outside. Duggan turned and saw a small bulge in the metal surface of the door – the bump was two or three centimetres in diameter. There was another bang and a second bulge appeared, overlapping the first.

They're trying to shoot their way inside, he thought. *How much ammunition does one of those pistols hold and will it be enough to punch a hole through the door?*

There was a series of clangs as gauss rounds clattered against the door. Even the most basic of Space Corps vessels was built to take a beating and the door didn't immediately succumb to the onslaught of projectiles. The bulge grew and Duggan was sure the alloy would soon split. The cockpit was only about eight square metres in size, so once the door was breached, it would be easy enough to push a gun barrel through and force the occupant's surrender. *Or just shoot me,* he thought grimly. *Even if I keep my back to the bulkhead wall.*

While he considered his rapidly-diminishing array of options, a series of numbers on one of the cockpit screens caught Duggan's eye. It was the flight computer telling him how long it was until the shuttle reached its destination. There were only nine minutes remaining before the vessel landed. If he somehow managed to get himself out of the mess he found himself in, there was definitely going to be a whole new one to contend with when he landed. Whoever had set this up had gone to a lot of trouble so far and there was no way they'd give up easily.

With one eye on the door, Duggan racked his brains for a solution.

CHAPTER FOUR

FOR A SHORT WHILE, the attack on the door stopped. Duggan used the quiet to help him concentrate and he scrolled through the shuttle's onboard systems in an attempt to find something which would help him. Additionally, he attempted to use his override code which should have allowed him to take control of almost any spaceship in the fleet. For reasons he couldn't fathom, the menu screen in which he needed to enter his codes had been hidden away. He was sure it was still in the system somewhere, since stripping the option out completely would have taken a high level of programming skill as well as a great deal of time. For the moment, it eluded him.

The gauss attack on the door began anew. With each impact, the inner surface of the door flexed and creaked. The noises came faster and Duggan guessed the men outside were becoming desperate in case he managed to take control of the shuttle and use it to carry them back to the Tillos base for questioning.

Duggan was also becoming desperate to find a way out. He wasn't frightened, though this situation was entirely unexpected. Amongst the clamour, his mind offered him a plan. Even in the circumstances, it wasn't a plan he wished to enact, but there was little time for him to address the moral conflict it produced – once his enemies breached the door, he'd no longer be able to do what was required.

"They've brought this upon themselves," he said angrily.

His fingers moved swiftly through the sub-menus of the shuttle's control systems. Within seconds, he found what he was after. The activation button glowed invitingly and he pressed it at once. The onboard computer refused the request as he'd expected it to do, but it did offer him a chance to enter an override command. He tapped in a code and sent it to the mainframe. Moments later, the shuttle's external door opened.

An alarm chimed in the cockpit and a red warning light flashed on and off at intervals. Additional alerts appeared on the shuttle's monitors, to let him know about a critical pressure drop in the main passenger cabin. The cockpit was well-insulated against noise, but Duggan wondered if he could just make out the sound of a scream through the bulkhead wall. He waited for a further ten seconds and then instructed the mainframe to close the external door.

It was done. The three men sent to kidnap him had been sucked out of the shuttle and into the planet's upper atmosphere. They'd have frozen to death quickly, with hardly any time to feel pain or fear. Their swift deaths were scant consolation to Duggan, who was furious he'd been forced to kill three people without knowing what they wanted from him. There was no chance of getting information from them now they were dead and tumbling towards the ground a hundred kilometres below. He swore for the dozenth time and put the matter from his head for the moment. There were only a few minutes remaining until the shuttle's autopilot set it down and Duggan didn't want to sit around passively waiting for it to happen.

While he thought, a request came through on the comms

from an anonymous source. Duggan would have dearly liked to answer it in order to hear the voice of whoever it was in charge, however he had no access to the comms system yet, so could do nothing about it. The inbound comms light winked for a few seconds, before it stopped flashing.

With two minutes left until the autopilot reached the end of its pre-programmed course, Duggan finally managed to gain full control of the shuttle. Whoever was responsible for the alterations, they had a good idea of how to make things difficult. Fortunately for Duggan, the override codes provided to officers of captain grade allowed him to get into more or less anything. The shuttle had been partially re-programmed, but there was no way the culprit could strip out the deep coding installed in the hardware.

Duggan searched through the navigational system to find the shuttle's destination. He was disappointed to discover it to be nowhere of apparent significance – the vessel was programmed to halt above a section of jungle, several hundred kilometres away from the nearest major population centre. He studied the local charts and assumed it was nothing more than a waypoint. *Or a rendezvous,* he thought, keeping the shuttle on its existing course.

The shuttle reached its destination. It stopped in the air, ten kilometres above the surface and did nothing else. Duggan watched the sensors carefully. There were no other aircraft within three hundred kilometres. The ground was dense with foliage and the shuttle's sensors were fairly low-tech, making it hard to be certain there was nothing waiting below. However, there were no roads or any other way to easily reach this place from the ground, so Duggan had to assume the intended rendezvous was in the air.

He waited for an hour and nobody showed up. He conceded that the other parties involved in the kidnapping must have been spooked when the shuttle's pilot failed to respond to the earlier comms request. Duggan was stubborn enough to wait for as long as it took, but he admitted to himself that he would be wasting his time. He took the controls and executed a tight turn. The Tillos base was on the opposite side of the planet, so he allowed the vessel's mainframe to plot the most efficient course. Soon, the shuttle was skimming across the upper reaches of the planet's atmosphere at maximum speed.

As soon as he was close enough, he requested a priority landing slot at Tillos and set the shuttle down on landing pad one, which he was pleased to find was much closer to the central administrative cluster than landing pad two. Once on the ground, he left the cockpit and spared a moment to look around the passenger bay. Anything which wasn't firmly screwed in place had been sucked out, along with the three men who had been up to no good. There was a chance some evidence might remain for the forensics teams, so he didn't touch anything on his way through. A team of security guards was waiting and he told them to keep away from the shuttle until it could be properly examined.

Fifteen minutes later and he was in the same reception area he'd visited prior to his ill-fated journey on the shuttle. The base security officers were exceptionally keen to speak with him, though Duggan managed to deflect them for the moment. He was as keen to find out what had happened as they were, but he realised that his true orders from the Space Corps were still awaiting him and he was very interested to learn what they might be. He walked to the same desk with the same gentleman sitting behind it and asked what instructions were on his file. If the receptionist recognized Duggan, he showed no sign and he checked his logging software obligingly.

"You've been given an office on the second floor, sir." He looked puzzled. "I'm not sure what's up with the system. The dates are screwed up and there's a gap in the timeline. I wonder if the IT guys have been running some updates."

"Maybe. Are there any details on how long I'm to stay?"

"No, sir. There's an office number and that's it."

"Thank you," said Duggan. He was about to go, when he had a thought. "Can you have a look at the last instructions for a Commander Lucy McGlashan, along with Lieutenants Bill Breeze and Frank Chainer?"

The receptionist took another look at Duggan, as if to be certain he had the authority to request these details. "Certainly. Commander McGlashan has been given accommodation in another building. Likewise for Lieutenants Breeze and Chainer. Someone's granted them a bit of downtime, huh?"

"Seems that way." Duggan smiled at the man and left to find his office.

It didn't take long to find and was larger and more luxuriously appointed than he was used to. There was a carpet and real wood furnishings. On another occasion, he might have appreciated the details. For now, he had other things on his mind. He sat at the desk and made a call.

"Lucy?"

She sounded confused and happy. "John? What's happening. I tried to make myself available to the personnel pool, but something must have gone wrong. I was told to go and put my feet up for a while instead. I've spoken with Frank and Bill. The same thing happened to them."

"Someone tried to kidnap me. I have no idea who it was or why. They must have inserted some fake details into the base logging system in order to separate us. The bastards were waiting for me on the shuttle."

"What? What happened?"

"We fought and I killed them. The evidence is likely gone. The forensics guys are looking and there'll be an inspection team poring over the shuttle's audit logs. I don't know what they'll find."

"I don't like this, John. Who'd want to kill you?"

A seed took root in Duggan's head, giving him an idea. He didn't speak about it yet. Instead, he changed the subject. "We'll talk about it when I've had a chance to think. Want to get something to eat off-base later?"

"You can get clearance for that?"

"I think I can manage."

"Great!" She hesitated. "Should I invite Frank and Bill?"

"They can sit this one out."

He ended the call and sat back. The faux-leather of his chair squeaked convincingly and he looked at the white-painted ceiling, lost in thought. He'd imagined that life would become simpler once the Dreamer mothership was destroyed. It didn't look as though it was meant to be.

An hour or two drifted by and Duggan found his eye constantly drawn to the comms unit on his desk. He knew he was going to get a message from Admiral Teron at some point, he just didn't know when. For once, it appeared as though he wasn't in demand.

"Or perhaps the good Admiral has decided to give me some time to myself as a reward," he mused out loud. Now the mothership was destroyed, there was no urgent requirement to micromanage Duggan's movements. Teron still had plenty on his plate – peace negotiations with the Ghasts would have the added complication of how to deal with the wreckage of the mothership. The pieces were dirty with radiation and badly damaged from the force of several nuclear explosions, but there'd still be valuable information to be gathered from the remains. Whatever was coming to Duggan could wait. Or so he told himself.

By early evening, Duggan was showered and spruced up. He headed to the reception area at the agreed time. Commander

McGlashan was waiting for him. She was wearing her uniform – like many in the Space Corps they were the only clothes she owned - and had tied her hair back in a way he'd not seen before. She smiled warmly and he smiled back.

"I've not been on a date for a long time," she said.

"Who said this is a date?" he joked. "We're going to talk about strategy and planning."

"I don't think you'd dare," she replied.

"Come on, let's get out of here."

They set off towards the main doorway. The Tillos base had originally been built far from anywhere, but the Space Corps' money always created places to spend it and there were several modestly-sized towns within a few minutes' drive.

Before they could leave, an announcement came through the building speaker system, clear and in defiance of Duggan's attempts to ignore it.

"Priority message for Captain John Nathan Duggan. Please report to Meeting Room 73 at once. Repeat, priority message."

Duggan stopped in his tracks. "I could ignore it."

McGlashan looked at him. "You wouldn't be John Duggan if you did that."

He sighed. "I suppose not. Can we postpone for an hour?"

"I don't think there's much choice, is there?"

Duggan left her alone in the reception area and hurried to the meeting room. It was empty and there were no milling crowds outside. He entered and settled himself in a chair, looking expectantly at the video screen. A connection request came through and he answered it. The screen lit up, showing the familiar image of Fleet Admiral Teron, sitting at his desk on the Juniper.

"Captain Duggan. I hope I'm not interrupting anything."

"It'll wait, sir."

CHAPTER FIVE

DUGGAN HAD ALREADY SPOKEN EXTENSIVELY to Teron since the destruction of the Dreamer mothership. During the aftermath of the battle, he'd kept the *ESS Crimson* in local space to watch over the *Archimedes* and the Ghast warship *Sandarvax* whilst they'd repaired their engines sufficiently to allow lightspeed travel. The first encounter with the mothership had been utterly devastating for the human and Ghast fleets and the enemy had also demonstrated their capability to disable a warship's engine. Since that time, the Space Corps labs had been hard at work researching a way to counter or reduce the effects of this new weapon. Their efforts were partially successful and the stranded *Archimedes* had been able to lift off after ten days, with another six days until it was capable of lightspeed.

Teron was straight to the point. "You're needed, John."

Duggan sighed inwardly. "I'd hoped to have a few days off, sir."

"I'm sorry. Truly I am. I'll let you in on a secret – I'd arranged a ceremony for you and your crew, to formally thank you for your bravery. There's a warship due to land later this evening. It was meant to bring you to the Juniper, but plans have changed."

"Has there been more conflict?"

Teron permitted himself a smile. "No, fortunately there has not. For once, your skills are required in the pursuit of peace, rather than the pursuit of war."

"What do you mean?"

"You have impressed Subjos Gol-Tur and he has asked for your presence during the final stages of the peace negotiations."

"Me?" asked Duggan. He quickly realised the response made him sound like a bumpkin, so he continued. "What does he feel I can bring that our trained negotiators can't?"

"Does it matter? One of the most senior Ghasts has asked for you to come. He might want to share war stories or he might want you to wear a top hat and dance with his wife."

Duggan briefly wondered if Teron had been drinking, since it was unlike him to be so flippant. "I'll do whatever it takes, sir, though I draw the line at dancing." A question leapt from his mouth before he could stop it. "Have you seen Gol-Tur's wife? I was beginning to think there were no Ghast women and that they were a race of clones."

Teron laughed. "You're not the only one to harbour such thoughts, John. Gol-Tur does have a wife and yes, I have seen her with my own eyes. In fact, I have spoken to several Ghast women in the past few weeks. The more familiar we become with our intended allies, the more willing they are to open up to us."

Duggan couldn't help himself. "Is she seven feet tall and built like an ox?"

"Not one bit of it. The few I've seen were in the region of six feet tall. Compared to the males, they are slender and dare I say it, exceptionally graceful. There are some image files in the Space Corps databanks if you ever want to take a look."

"I must confess to my curiosity, sir. After all these years of fighting the males, it might help me understand their race better if I were to see the other half of the population."

"You might get the chance." Teron leaned forward, his gaze intense. "This really is it. There are unanswered questions about the Ghasts, but nothing which is a barrier to lasting peace. We are on the brink of a monumental achievement – settlement and friendship instead of annihilation. After everything which has gone before, we've shown we can fight together against a common foe. The Dreamers will return and when they do, they must face two determined and united races. We'll destroy those bastards again and again, until they finally give up trying."

"Do you think they'll ever stop?"

"Does it matter? As long as we keep beating them, that's the only thing which counts."

"Eternal war."

"It won't come to that. I have no plans to die soon, but when I finally go, I want to look back upon a time of peace, not a lifetime of conflict."

"Me too, sir."

"Are you prepared to speak to the Ghasts?"

"I am. Do I have a list of goals?"

"What's the point in me giving you a list? You'd just ignore it anyway. No, John, all you're required to do is be there as Gol-Tur has asked. Speak to him and hopefully he will see mankind's strength and determination."

Duggan realised he was being complimented. "Thank you, sir."

"Your ship lands later - you'll be in command. Take your crew if you wish, though they might have to do a bit of waiting around, twiddling their thumbs."

"I doubt they'll mind."

"I thought that would be the case."

Duggan opened his mouth, wondering if he should bother

Teron with details of what happened earlier. There were security teams who could investigate and Duggan felt he was capable of looking after himself. After a moment's consideration, he decided to share the details.

"Someone tried to kidnap me today, sir."

For once, Teron had no immediate response. He spluttered, but no words came out. Eventually he managed to ask for some details, which Duggan duly provided.

"How *dare* they!" Teron shouted, crashing his fist down.

"The Tillos security guys are on the case, sir."

"That isn't enough! This is unheard of!" The set of Teron's jaw showed him to be livid. "You understand this isn't minor criminal activity? For someone to have access to the military's equipment..." He tailed off and Duggan knew he'd been right to let the Admiral know.

"They failed, sir," he said, hoping it would calm Teron.

After a few deep breaths, Teron did become outwardly calm. "If you were specifically targeted, you'll be safe once you get onboard your transport. It'll give me time to find out what's going on." He clenched his fist unconsciously on top of the table, reassuring Duggan that the consequences would not be pretty for those involved.

While Duggan wasn't uncaring about his personal safety, he suddenly felt uncomfortable at the attention. "What do the Projections Team say about our situation now the dust has settled?" he asked, knowing the question would distract Teron.

"It's...complicated," Teron replied, taking the bait.

Duggan stared at the screen.

"I'm not sure what else to say," Teron finished. "Previously, the destruction of Atlantis was a nailed-on certainty, with things looking precarious for Overtide and Freedom. As it stands, the odds have receded *somewhat*."

"The emphasis on the word contains the complication, I assume?"

"Indeed." Teron rubbed his scalp. "There is now a uniform three percent chance for each of the Confederation planets to be destroyed. The peculiar thing is, if we assume the loss of one planet, the chance of the others being annihilated climbs to one hundred percent. The fate of all is tied to the fate of one."

"If the Dreamers establish another planet-based weapon, they'll wipe us out."

"And the Ghasts. Their existence is now firmly tied to ours."

"Have you told Gol-Tur?"

"No, and I'm not sure I will. These are high-level military secrets, Captain Duggan. I'm sure the Ghasts have their own research teams. In truth, it probably doesn't matter if they know."

"There are plans, sir?"

"Yes, there are plans and they'll likely involve the *ESS Crimson*." Teron gave a genuine smile. "There! Did you see that? I managed to say it outright without keeping it shrouded in secrecy."

"Will these plans also involve me and my crew?"

"Let's wait and see, John. You're our best officer, but it's getting to the stage where I'd prefer you to be on my staff, passing on your knowledge and ideas to others. I can't keep risking you forever."

"I'll always stand up, sir."

"I know you will. The time will come when there's someone else."

"If you ever ask me to do something new, I'll listen with an open mind."

"That's good to know. We'll have that talk sometime. Not just yet, since there are things unfinished." Teron sighed again, revealing a depth of weariness. "If I ever ask you to do make the ultimate sacrifice, will you do it?"

"I've shown time and again that I'm not afraid of death. My crew as well."

"I don't mean death. Nothing so simple as that."

"What greater sacrifice could you ask?"

"We'll see, John, we'll see. I might never need to ask, but if I do, will you still stand up?"

"Yes, sir. I do believe I will."

Teron looked sorrowful, rather than uplifted by the response, as if Duggan had somehow passed a test the Admiral hoped he would fail. "Very well. My time for this meeting has run out. I'll send through the few details you'll need for your involvement in the peace settlement. Goodbye, Captain Duggan."

"Goodbye, sir."

The screen went blank, leaving Duggan alone in the room with his thoughts. After a minute, he pushed himself to his feet and left. He made his way to the reception area, where Commander McGlashan was sitting in the waiting area, looking glum. She briefly perked up when she saw Duggan arrive, until she realised how preoccupied he was.

"You're going to cancel on me, aren't you?"

"In a way. We've got a mission. There shouldn't be much risk of death – the stakes are far higher than that."

"Peace?" she asked, surprising him with her insight. "They're sending you to speak with the Ghasts, aren't they?"

"That's exactly what they're doing. There's a ship landing tonight and we'll be on it."

"Do you want me to let Bill and Frank know? I'm sure Frank will have something to complain about."

"Yes, please. This is as good a place to meet as any. Tell them to get here as soon as possible."

"What ship have we been given? The *Crimson* isn't ready to go anywhere."

"Admiral Teron didn't say and I didn't ask. There's something going on, I'm sure."

"Something which we're eventually going to find out about, only to wish we never had?" she asked with a grin.

"What makes you say that?" asked Duggan drily.

McGlashan didn't answer – something had caught her eye across the landing pad. The radiation-proof shutters had been removed at some point in the last few hours, allowing them to see outside. Duggan looked and saw the vast shape of a spaceship, descending slowly from the deepening blue sky.

"That's not our ride, is it?" she asked.

Duggan walked closer to the windows, with McGlashan following. "I doubt it." He searched his brain for the name of the ship. "The *MHL Gargantua*," he said. "I read about it recently – it's just come out of the yard. The newest heavy lifter, rumoured to have space for a Hadron inside."

The *Gargantua* came lower and lower, until its incomprehensible bulk blotted out the evening sun and bathed much of the Tillos base in cool shadow. The older heavy lifters were boxy affairs – angular and ungainly. This new addition to the fleet was the shape of a flattened cylinder, dotted at regular intervals with square outcroppings. The front of the vessel was wedge-shaped and streamlined, taking design cues from many of the Space Corps' warships.

"It's impressive," McGlashan said. "How long do you think it is?"

"Eight thousand two hundred metres," said Duggan with confidence. "I checked the specification details when I first learned about it."

There were crowds of people everywhere, each pair of eyes looking upwards at the incoming spaceship. The Tillos base rarely saw such overt examples of the Space Corps' technological and industrial might. In fact, few people in the Confederation could expect to see something so impressive unless they spent their days camped outside a space port.

"It must be coming for the *Rampage*," she said. "Perhaps it sustained more damage than they can repair here."

"Perhaps."

The *MHL Gargantua* stopped a kilometre above the surface. Duggan could see activity across the landing field as the repair teams retreated to a safe distance. For the next ten minutes, the vessel remained exactly where it was. Such was the excitement at its arrival that none of the watchers moved away. It was as though a thousand people held their breaths in anticipation of what was to come.

Then, the underside doors of the *Gargantua* slid open, revealing the cavernous interior of the spaceship. From this distance, it was hard to make out specifics – there were shapes and forms within and Duggan thought he could see rows of colossal gravity clamps.

"Here we go," said McGlashan.

Slowly but surely, the *ES Rampage* rose from its docking trench, drawn upwards by the heavy lifter's gravity chains. The warship was over three thousand metres long and weighed more than ten billion tonnes. Duggan was sure the crew on the *Gargantua* were sweating, but they made it look effortless. The lift took twenty minutes to complete, during which time Lieutenants Breeze and Chainer arrived. Neither of them spoke much beyond a quick greeting, so intent were they on what was happening.

"It's done," said Breeze at last. The *ES Rampage* disappeared into the hold of the heavy lifter. The cargo doors stayed open and the warship remained visible to the people below.

"I don't think so," said Duggan. "Look."

The *MHL Gargantua* wasn't finished. It drifted smoothly and quietly across the sky to a new location nearby.

"There's only one ship left," said McGlashan.

The *ESS Crimson* was visible in its trench, a mix of dull and shiny from the partially-removed coating of osmium. Moments after it stopped, the *Gargantua* began its second lift. The *Crimson* was heavier per cubic metre than the *Rampage*, but weighed less than twenty percent as much overall. Up it went, until it joined the Galactic class heavy cruiser in the lifter's bay. The cargo doors closed, leaving no visible seam on the *Gargantua's* hull.

"That was spectacular," said Breeze.

"They're not hanging around now they've got what they came for," said McGlashan, her finger raised in needless indication.

The shape of *Gargantua* receded gradually as it climbed towards the upper atmosphere. Duggan thought he might have just detected a vibration in the air to indicate the stresses being placed on the lifter's gravity drives. In minutes, it was gone and the crowds drifted away, talking excitedly amongst themselves.

Duggan and the others stayed where they were. Their wait was rewarded when a tiny dot appeared overhead. It grew bigger and bigger, until it was close enough for them to be sure it wasn't the *Gargantua* returning.

"That'll be ours," said Duggan. "Let's get ourselves a car and go meet it."

CHAPTER SIX

TWO HOURS LATER, Duggan and the others were cruising at a high lightspeed towards their destination on an Imposition class cruiser called *ES Castigate*. The *Castigate* had clean lines and looked like a deliberate cross between the *Crimson* and a smaller version of a Ghost Oblivion. Its appearance took some getting used to, though Duggan was sure he'd grow to like it.

"Three days until we get there at this speed," said Breeze. "If they start building these Imposition warships in big numbers I'll be a happy man."

"I'm looking through the Space Corps datafiles," said Duggan. "The *Castigate* was signed off for service only a week ago. Apparently, they're going to phase out the Anderlechts entirely over the next twenty years and replace them with an equivalent number of warships like these."

"Had nobody told you about them, sir?" asked Chainer.

"I'm too wise to be upset when I discover my ignorance of plans I have no real need to be aware of," said Duggan. "Besides, the strategic decision was only made a couple of weeks ago.

There are three Imposition class in service as we speak, each one as new as the *Castigate*."

"That's the same number as they made of the Galactic class, isn't it?" asked Breeze.

"If memory serves, it is," Duggan replied. "The Space Corps likes to trial new ideas before committing to the construction of dozens."

"We've got it all. Two thousand five hundred metres in length and bristling with more Lambdas and nukes than you can shake a stick at, as well as one medium-range disruptor and two Splinter anti-missile systems," said McGlashan. "There are eighty fully-equipped soldiers in their quarters aft, none of whom I recognize the names of. We have tanks and artillery in our cargo bay. On top of that, there's a single Shatterer launch tube and room to retrofit three additional ones."

"There are manufacturing issues on our version of the Shatterers," said Duggan. "The failure rate on the missiles is high, so we don't have enough to go around. I've been told the ones which *do* work are still a way behind the Ghast versions."

"It's better than we had," said Chainer. "Are they going to fit them on warships other than the Imposition class?"

"The Galactic class were designed with flexibility in mind, so they'll get them," said Duggan. "The Hadron hulls were always a generation ahead of their time – we simply lacked the weaponry to take advantage of the fact."

"The things money will buy you, eh?"

"Money *and* determination, Lieutenant. One without the other gets you nowhere fast."

"Is the Confederation still at total war?" asked McGlashan.

"It is. Expect that to change immediately we settle with the Ghasts."

"What happens to these flashy new spaceships after that?" asked Chainer.

"Teron's a smart man," said Duggan. "I'll bet he's managed to commit the Space Corps to long-term, legally-binding contracts to keep the warship building running as planned. By the time the Confederation Council think of a way to terminate our commitments, we'll have replaced most of the fleet."

"Is it the end of the line for the Gunners as well?" asked Breeze.

"I wouldn't be surprised if we were left with fewer than a hundred at the end of this." Duggan had a fondness for the Vincent class and he stifled a sigh. "It's for the best. Times have changed, along with the requirements for our spacecraft. We could send a hundred Gunners against a Dreamer battleship and we'd come off worst. You can't keep throwing money at obsolete equipment."

"They could put stealth modules in a few to act as scouts."

"That may be what they'll do. Remember the *ES Lightning* needed extensive – and expensive – modifications in order to run the modules." He shrugged. "We'll see."

The conversation appeared to be winding down. Chainer had other ideas. "Isn't Imposition a bit *provocative* these days? In this time of comradeship and understanding, shouldn't they have named them something a bit friendlier?"

Duggan shook his head. "I wonder what goes on your mind sometimes, Lieutenant."

"Best not to think about it too hard," said Breeze, unable to resist.

"They'll have come up with the name quite possibly several years ago," said Duggan, responding in spite of himself. "Once a name sticks, it's hard to change. And I can think of many reasons why it's important for the fleet to project a warlike impression, whether or not we're at peace."

The *Castigate* was fitted with a brutally fast AI core, which estimated their travel time to within ten seconds of the actual.

The warship exited lightspeed into an area of neutral space, far from any significant populated outposts.

"It's pretty crowded around here," said Chainer.

"Keep on high alert until we're sure everything is as it should be," said Duggan. "What've we got?"

"Hadrons *Devastator* and *Maximilian*, along with the *ES Terminus*, sir. Nice to see the *Terminus* again."

"What else?"

"There are two Space Corps VIP personnel transporters – big ones - and they look as if they've been polished to within an inch of their lives."

Duggan watched the sensor feed. "That's where the talking will take place," he said. "I've been on one of those, many years ago. They're as close to luxury as you'll find in the Corps. The Confederation's representatives must have travelled on them."

"The Trivanor is in the vicinity," said Chainer in surprise. The Ghast Oblivion had been knocked out of the sky by the Dreamer mothership. The damage had evidently not been as terminal as it appeared at the time. "It looks like shit, but the readings from their engines suggest they're right back at full power."

"I doubt the *Archimedes* is much past fifty percent," said Duggan. "The Ghasts must have discovered a better way to mitigate the effects of the Dreamer engine scramblers."

"They adapt well to change," said McGlashan.

"I've had a friendly hail from the Ghast battleship *Akstron* and the heavy cruiser *Oretsen*, sir."

"Three of theirs and three of ours," said Duggan.

"Now four of ours," Breeze added.

"I'm sure another Ghast ship will show up at some point to even the numbers," said Duggan. "That's how I'd want it too."

"Everything looks calm and collected, sir," said Chainer. "What happens next?"

Duggan grinned. "I have no idea. My mission brief is somewhat lacking in detail."

"Are we going to sit around until someone asks what we're here for?" asked Breeze.

"Not a chance," said Duggan. "I never did like waiting. Lieutenant Chainer, get me a meeting with Gol-Tur. Alone and at his first available opportunity."

"I'm on it."

Confirmation didn't take long and shortly, Duggan found himself in the cockpit of the *Castigate*'s surprisingly plush shuttle, heading towards the Trivanor. The Ghast battleship was streaked with scars and energy burns, giving it an even more threatening appearance than usual. He checked in with McGlashan to see if anyone from the Confederation's delegation had asked for him.

"Negative, sir. They know we're here, but they don't seem to care."

Duggan chuckled. "Teron's a wily old bastard. I'll bet no one knows what I'm doing here."

"And since you *are* here, they'll assume it's in an official capacity."

"I'll have to be careful I don't ruffle any feathers by going straight to the Trivanor, instead of meeting our illustrious representatives."

"I'm sure it'll work out, sir."

He docked after a short flight and triggered the exit ramp as soon as the atmosphere in the bay was sufficient to for him to disembark. Last time he'd come here, there'd been two Ghast soldiers to escort him to his destination. This time there were four, though Duggan had no idea if the increased number had any significance or meaning. Certainly, he wasn't planning to start a fight.

A walk through the Oblivion's interior followed, terminating inevitably at the door to Gol-Tur's room. The door slid aside and Duggan entered. His mind had already painted a picture of what he expected to find and the scene was identical to his mental brushstrokes, even down to the unusual species of plant which Gol-Tur kept in one corner. It was exactly the same as last time – blue-tiled floor, wooden desk, chairs, screens on the wall. The Ghost was sitting in one of the three uncomfortable seats, dressed in grey. His eyes were fixed on Duggan.

"Greetings, John Duggan."

"Subjos Gol-Tur," acknowledged Duggan. He helped himself to one of the two chairs opposite the Ghost, wondering if the creator of the seat had actively striven to make it as unpleasant a place to spend time as possible. "I am pleased to find our two species have made progress."

"That we have," said the Ghost, his interpretation module reproducing the harshness of his voice.

"Are the negotiations concluded?"

"They were effectively concluded the moment the Dreamer mothership was destroyed. What has followed is little more than details. We could sign an accord at any moment, but these things are unnecessarily complicated. Each crease in the sheet needs progressively greater attention."

"What do you need me for?" Duggan asked.

The Ghost's lined face adopted an expression Duggan had rarely seen from these aliens before. With a start, he realised Gol-Tur was smiling. "The men you sent to negotiate are not soldiers. They talk and they talk and I am weary of listening to it. I realised that if I were to understand my former enemies, I should speak to one who is like me. Someone who has experienced fighting and known what it's like to see his fellows die."

Duggan nodded. "I have seen plenty of both."

"What are your hopes for the future?"

"I am tired of fighting. In my heart I know I will miss it when it ends, but I know the time for it to cease is long past."

"Will it really end when we sign our accord?" asked Gol-Tur, his eyes never leaving Duggan's.

Duggan knew what the Ghast referred to – the meaning underlying the words. "The Dreamers will come."

"They will come, Captain Duggan. For us and for you. There is nothing we can do to stop them, so we must fight."

"You want more than just peace."

"We do. My species has suffered terrible losses in our conflict with the Confederation. It is nothing compared to what will come. We will face it, like we face every threat. This is something we do not wish to fight alone."

"I can promise you will have peace with humanity. I don't have the authority to approve a formal military alliance."

"Is a military alliance something you would personally accept?"

"I think we have no choice."

The Ghast nodded. "You are correct. Together we will lose, though we will be a much greater opponent than if we stand apart."

"You are certain the Dreamers are a foe beyond our combined resources to defeat or repel?"

"They are and I will tell you why."

Duggan sat bolt upright when he heard those words. They confirmed the Ghasts knew much more about the Dreamers than they'd previously admitted. "What do you know?" he asked.

CHAPTER SEVEN

"YOU ONCE BELIEVED we were allied to the Dreamers," said Gol-Tur. "Later, you came to ask questions about the presence of their pyramid on our home world Vempor. The reality is, we are one and the same. You refer to us as Ghosts and them as Dreamers. In truth, we call ourselves Estral."

Many questions surged up in Duggan's mind. "Why are you fighting each other?" he asked.

"There is much that is in the past. In short, there was a schism and millions of us separated from the others. It was not amicable and we came far to ensure the others would never find us again."

"How long ago did this happen?"

"It happened almost four hundred years ago. We journeyed for a hundred years, until finally we discovered a place to settle. Many years later, we encountered the Confederation."

Duggan found his hand venturing towards his head, ready to scratch it. He brought his arm down quickly. "The Dreamers are far more advanced than you," he said.

"Our empire was vast and rich with resources. We fled to a

place where we had nothing bar the ships we came on. It is difficult to begin again."

"You came on ships?" asked Duggan, wondering what monstrous vessels would have been required to carry millions.

"We did – on many self-supporting transport vessels. Our history reports several generations died and were born on the journey, until we came here. The transports were broken up long ago, and the parts used to create our factories. For a long time, we were hampered by a shortage of the material you call Gallenium. Without it, there was little we could do to advance. We overcame that obstacle and you have seen the result."

Duggan *had* seen the result. The Ghast technology had advanced with terrifying speed, until they'd been on the brink of exterminating humanity. "The Dreamers have something of a head start on you."

"The Estral empire spanned many galaxies. I dread to think what it has become."

"Why have they come now?"

"I am sure it is nothing other than random chance – our joint misfortune. They have found a way to traverse the wormhole, which has brought them close to us. If our two fleets had not been near the Helius Blackstar, the enemy might never have known how close they were to us."

Duggan opened his mouth to ask a question, then found himself asking something completely different to what he'd intended. "The Space Corps believes your technology advanced so quickly because you recovered some pieces of a broken Dreamer spacecraft – in the same way we used parts of their wreckage in the construction of the *ESS Crimson*."

Gol-Tur smiled again, showing a row of straight, white teeth. "We found a number of components which assisted our research laboratories."

"Didn't you realise you'd found parts of a spaceship built by your own race?" asked Duggan.

"We found metal, not bodies, John Duggan. There was nothing to link the two."

"What a strange situation we find ourselves in."

"It is not so strange. Everything is a circle. It was inevitable we would meet our parent race. It is bad luck for the Confederation that you will be drawn into the resulting conflict."

"The Confederation will survive," Duggan said, with unexpected determination. "We humans are a species who are content to meander until we are forced to do otherwise. Over the last few years, we have accomplished feats which I would never have thought possible. We will not accept extinction."

"You have perfected a way to cloak your warships."

"We have," said Duggan. "There will be more to come from our labs, given time."

"Let us drink to that," said Gol-Tur, reaching beneath his desk. He pulled out a decanter of the Ghast spirit Grask and two glasses. When the liquid was poured, Duggan took his glass and raised it. If the gesture confused Gol-Tur, he didn't let on and the Ghast took a sip from his own glass.

"What now?" asked Duggan.

"My time is short – I am due to attend another meeting with your people soon. Until then, I will enjoy the coolness of the spirit. Once the accord is signed, I will take the Trivanor and the other warships elsewhere."

"To look for Dreamers?"

"Not yet. The time will come."

"I will return to Fleet Admiral Teron with details of what we have discussed, and give him my recommendation that our two fleets commence joint exercises in preparation for the return of our common enemy."

"Admiral Teron is driven," said Gol-Tur.

"He is," Duggan replied. "It is rare for him to wait when there is an opportunity to act."

"Will he prepare against the Dreamers, even though their mothership is gone?"

"He will have a dozen plans in motion, I am sure," said Duggan.

Gol-Tur nodded, as if this was all the reassurance he needed. "You should return to your ship."

Within the hour, Duggan was back on the bridge of the *Castigate*, breathing in the scent of the real leather chairs and doing his best to answer questions from his crew.

"We came all this way for you to spend twenty minutes chatting to one of the Ghast leaders?" asked Breeze.

"For some reason, I feel as if much was accomplished. I don't know why – perhaps it was because Gol-Tur was willing to speak openly. On top of that, he revealed his worries about the future. I haven't spoken to many Ghasts, but that's the first time I can remember them showing what some people might call weakness or uncertainty."

"It's not really a weakness," said McGlashan.

"I didn't say it was," Duggan replied. "I heard enough to know he accepts our two races are allies."

"Should we have a celebration or something?" asked Chainer doubtfully. "We've been fighting them for more than thirty years, yet it doesn't feel right that we start the applause."

"It's been coming for so long that the excitement's gone," said McGlashan. "That doesn't mean I'm not happy, you understand."

"Maybe it'll feel better once it's sunk in," said Breeze.

"The fighting won't end," said Duggan. "There's going to be a pause, but rest assured it'll resume."

"That's probably why I'm not feeling too happy," said Chainer. "It's not really peace, is it? We've just swapped one enemy for another. One bunch of Ghasts for another lot of bigger, stronger Ghasts, who happen to have even more warships."

Breeze and McGlashan muttered their agreement and they fell quiet for a time.

"How long do we have to sit here?" asked Chainer eventually.

"Admiral Teron didn't say."

"They could take weeks," said Breeze.

"We'll be dead from boredom by then."

"Here's something to cheer you up, sir," said Chainer. "I've got Admiral Teron on the comms for you."

"Pass him through."

"Captain Duggan?" said Teron.

"Yes, sir?"

"It's done. Gol-Tur has accepted the proposals for a permanent peace between our two species."

"That's great, sir."

"You're not happy?"

"I'm too old to live for the moment. I know this is only the beginning."

Teron gave one of his gruff laughs. "A man after my own heart. Fine, I wasn't expecting you to clap your hands or anything like that." The levity faded from his voice. "Do you recall the details of our last conversation?"

"Where you asked if I would stand up for something you had in mind?"

"That's the one. The time is coming, John."

"It didn't take long."

"We've detected activity at the Helius Blackstar."

"More trouble?"

"I wouldn't be speaking to you if it wasn't."

"What sort of trouble?"

"We installed low-profile monitoring stations on the nearest planets some months ago – as soon as we were sure the coast was clear after the mothership first appeared. One of the stations detected something making a successful transit of the Blackstar."

"They were certain it was successful?"

"Absolutely. They detected a large object moving extremely quickly away from the gravitational pull. They couldn't get a solid lock on it. Whatever it was, it detected this particular monitoring station and destroyed it, though not before we received the news of this unknown vessel's arrival."

"Was it only the one, sir?"

"We can't be sure. There may have been others which slipped through. The loss of that monitoring station left a hole in our sensor net."

"Have you told the Ghasts?"

"Not yet. That's the next thing on my list."

Duggan wanted to hit something. "Nothing has changed, has it?"

"No, it has not."

"What do you want us to do?"

"You're going to rendezvous with the *MHL Gargantua*. You might have seen it recently at Atlantis."

"Yes, sir. Are they still carrying the *Crimson*?"

"They've had it three days and by the time you reach them, they'll have had it for another eleven. They're making a number of internal modifications."

"Sir, you're being evasive."

"There's a mission for you, John. For you and your crew. I thought we had more time. The arrival of our enemy through the Blackstar means I need to take a gamble. *You* need to take a gamble."

Cold, hard dread seeped into Duggan's bones. Admiral Teron

often took his time to get to the point. This was different, like he was fearful to admit what he had planned.

"Admiral, I trust your judgement. If there are extreme dangers, I'm sure the mission is a critical one."

Teron didn't answer at once, and Duggan got the impression he was steeling himself for what he was about to say. At last, he spoke.

"John, you're going to try and fly through the wormhole."

Whatever Duggan had expected to hear, it wasn't that. He looked at the other three and saw his own shock reflected in their faces.

CHAPTER EIGHT

"DO YOU REMEMBER OUR PREVIOUS DISCUSSIONS?" said Teron. "I told you that if it ever came to war again, I'd do everything I could to fight it as hard and aggressively as I could. I made it clear I'd take the fight to our enemies. We're at that point already. Our enemies have arrived and each passing day increases the chance they'll send more to reinforce the others. The vessel our monitoring station detected wasn't another mothership – we suspect it was a battleship. This means they're getting closer to the stage where they can send their entire fleet through if they wish. Each successful transit puts an advanced, hostile warship amongst us. The worst thing of it is, we don't know if their last incursion managed to transmit their intelligence to their home planets. They might know where Atlantis is located, or Sinnar. They could descend upon our worlds at any moment and we'll have little chance to repel them."

"You're saying we're screwed, sir?" asked Duggan.

"No, that is *not* what I'm saying. What I'm telling you is that we're not going to sit on our hands and hope the Dreamers disperse into space and we never see them again. You're going to see what's on the other side of that wormhole and provide us with the knowledge. This time, we'll act first!"

"We've never managed to get anything through the wormhole, sir," Duggan protested, knowing that Teron would have an answer to the objection.

"The reason is partly because we've rarely tried. We threw a couple of probes at the Blackstar a dozen years ago. They vanished, but we don't know if they were destroyed, or simply ended up too far away for their comms signals to return."

"I can't risk the life of my crew on the basis that a couple of probes might have got through!"

"I'm not asking you to." A note of bleak humour crept into Teron's voice. "Believe it or not I have humanity and compassion."

"I know that, sir."

"The gravitational force of the wormhole increases as you get closer to it. Our scientists believe that with sufficient structural strength, a warship can get to a position where activating its fission engines will fire the craft into the wormhole, rather than past it. They further believe that a vessel with sufficient capability will be able to break free from the gravitation pull on the other side in order to make a clean escape."

"If it's so straightforward, why haven't an advanced race such as the Dreamers been able to do it reliably?" asked Duggan.

"Oddly enough it's the fact they are so advanced which makes us believe they've had problems. I read in one of your reports how you thought their ships to be delicately-built, possibly because they have enough control over their technology that they have moved on from the dense wedge-shapes of our ships."

"I remember."

"We've had a short time to examine the wreckage of the Dreamer mothership, such as you left for us. The signs are that it had enormously thick walls – in fact, you got extremely lucky when you lightspeed jumped inside it."

Duggan's mind raced ahead. "You think our fleet warships are solid enough to survive the transit?"

"That's exactly what I'm saying. Of course, they lack sufficient engine power to pull free at the other end. As for the processing power required to time it perfectly, well, we've made big jumps since we got our hands on the Dreamer core, but we aren't there yet."

"Except for the one warship equipped with that core."

"Which you are going to take through the wormhole in order to see what's on the other side."

Without him realising it, the trepidation Duggan had felt only moments ago was replaced by something else – a rush of excitement hit him, washing away the years of accumulated circumspection and making him feel as though anything was possible.

"One moment, sir," he said, muting the comms. He caught McGlashan's dark eyes, witnessed the wonder and fear there. "Well, Commander? Are you ready for one last adventure?"

"A *last* adventure, sir? Don't you think we'll make it back?"

"Whether we do or we don't, it'll be my last."

She caught his meaning and saluted. "Reporting for duty, sir."

"How about you, Frank?"

For the shortest of times it looked as if Chainer wasn't sure, only for Duggan to find the impression was mistaken. "I've got nothing better planned, sir."

"Bill?"

"I think it'll be my last one as well, sir. I wouldn't miss it for the world."

Duggan took the comms off mute. "We'll give it a try, Admiral."

The sound of Teron blowing out a pent-up breath reached them. "I hoped you'd say that."

With the decision made, everything else was details. "What happens when we arrive at the other end of the wormhole, sir?"

"I'm working on mission priorities, Captain Duggan. Suffice to say you'll be required to adapt according to circumstances. We have no idea what you'll find, if anything. The Dreamers could live many weeks distant from their side of the wormhole, or they might have a dozen planets on the doorstep."

"There's no point in us delaying further, sir. I'll set the *Castigate* on a course to rendezvous with the *MHL Gargantua*."

"I've had the coordinates sent to your AI. The *Gargantua* is a couple of hours low lightspeed away from the Blackstar. We didn't want them to stay too close, in case of a bad luck encounter."

Duggan took a deep breath. "Thank you for this opportunity, sir. When we get back I would like to have the promised talk with you."

"You'll have your wish, John."

"We'll go to lightspeed in a few more seconds."

"I'll have ironed out as many of the details as I can by the time you arrive in local space. Goodbye."

"He's gone," said Chainer.

"And so have we," added Breeze. "We're running nicely at Light-J.5. It'll be ten days and twenty-one hours until we reach our destination."

"I put each of you on the spot back there and I apologise," Duggan said. "You have until we arrive to change your minds without recriminations. There'll be no effect on your career or your standing."

"You mean you'd get someone in to replace us?" said McGlashan. "I'm offended."

"It's been nearly a month since we last risked our lives, sir," said Chainer. "I feel as if things have been a little bit quiet. A trip through the Helius Blackstar is just what we need."

"The sooner I'm dead, the sooner my children can benefit from my death in service payments," said Breeze.

Duggan knew when he was facing a concerted effort at insubordination and he gave his crew a glare which would have caused others to quail. His stare failed to have the required effect, so he sat in his seat, doing his best to hide the smile which had crept onto his face.

Sometime later, Chainer returned from one of his many visits to the replicator. He carried a tray with three cheeseburgers and a coffee. The others had long since stopped remarking upon his appetite, and upon the fact that Chainer could seemingly eat an endless quantity of calorific food without gaining any weight at all. The lieutenant did pay occasional visits to the gym, without being an enthusiastic participant.

"I might request a transfer onto one of the monitoring stations when this is over," he said. "I'll bet there are plenty of opportunities on the Juniper as well."

"Had enough of doing what we're doing?" asked Duggan.

"I love it, sir. Sometimes I think to myself that I'll have missed out on a lot of what life has to offer if I do the same thing forever. Assuming I don't get killed in action, I don't want to die old and lonely."

"You've got plenty of time yet," said McGlashan.

"Not so much. Before I know it, I'll be fifty and serving under some young, upstart captain who lacks respect or skill. Whenever I return to base I'll spend the days sitting staring at a wall, wondering if I should retire. Except there'll be no point in retiring because there'll only be more walls to stare at."

Duggan understood Chainer to be a man who needed someone to provide him direction. He was an excellent comms man, but he'd never be more than a lieutenant. Not everyone was cut out to be a leader and Chainer had no desire to be one.

"I'll put a word in for you with Admiral Teron, if you want. You'd do well on the Juniper. There's always something happening."

"Thank you, sir. My mind changes often, so tomorrow I may want something else. This time I don't reckon it'll happen so soon."

"That makes three of us wanting a change," said Breeze. "How's about you, Commander? What's in store for your future?"

"You should apply for a promotion," said Chainer. "You're the best officer I know who isn't in charge of her own warship."

McGlashan didn't have an immediate response, as if the question had caught her off-guard. She could have kept quiet – none of the others would have pressed for a response. "I know what I want," she said. "Once we're done, I'll take a gamble and see what comes from it."

"You can tell us when you're ready," said Breeze.

An eleven-day journey was a comparatively long one. A fleet warship only had certain amenities to keep the occupants entertained, such as a gym and access to television and electronic books. The problem for Duggan was that he didn't enjoy television and wasn't an enthusiastic reader. McGlashan had advised him to give it a try, but he couldn't seem to find anything that interested him. There were times when there could be too much choice.

Consequently, he worked out in the gym, he slept and he paced endlessly around the bridge, driving the others mad with it. What he really wanted, was to spend some time with McGlashan. During their brief meetings in the mess room, they both agreed now was definitely not the time. Their budding romantic involvement could compromise the mission, the crew and each other.

"I hope this works out," McGlashan said one morning. She nibbled at a remarkably accurate reconstruction of a slice of toast, produced by the replicator.

"I hadn't planned to be bounced from mission to mission," he said. "We're at the mercy of events."

"You're excited about this one. I can see it in your eyes."

"I am," he admitted. "Thinking about it makes me feel like the young man I once was. It burns inside me."

"What if the addiction keeps pulling you back? Once this is over, Admiral Teron will call on you again and again."

Duggan shook his head. "I don't think so. I've spoken to him and I think he has other plans. He's a good judge of character and he'll know when the game's up – when my heart's no longer in it."

"We can wait," she said.

He smiled. "I don't know about you, but I've waited long enough."

She smiled in return. "Yeah. One last mission for us."

"Are you happy?" he asked.

"Yes, John, I think I am. Nothing good ever came easily."

He looked at the wall clock. "My break time is up. Frank and Bill will be wondering where I've got to," he said, getting to his feet.

"I've got another couple of hours. I'll put my feet up somewhere."

Duggan returned to the bridge, finding it exactly as he'd left it.

CHAPTER NINE

THE *ES CASTIGATE* arrived at its destination five seconds early, entering a solar system consisting of eleven planets and a vibrant sun. There was a tiny archaeological base on one of the worlds and they sent up a greeting before Chainer had the opportunity to get his bearings.

"They're looking for signs of ancient life, sir. And they ask why it's getting so busy out here."

"Tell them a polite lie," said Duggan. "I need you to find the *MHL Gargantua.*"

"I've got them, sir. They're stationary above the eighth planet. The coordinates are with you."

"I see them. We were told to rendezvous, so let's go and see what awaits us."

Duggan put the *Castigate* on autopilot for the moment and instructed it to make full speed towards the *Gargantua*. The Imposition class vessel was quick on its gravity drive and it sped across the intervening space.

"The *Gargantua* says hello," said Chainer.

"They picked us up quickly. I thought the lifters carried the oldest kit the Space Corps could get away with fitting."

"Not this one, sir. Its comms are only a generation earlier than ours. That likely means it has high-powered sensor arrays to match. There are four Anderlechts close by, eight Gunners and a second Imposition class. A sizeable escort."

"The *Gargantua* itself is surprisingly well-armed, too," said McGlashan. "They'll be no sitting duck if anyone decides to take a shot at them."

"Return the greeting, Lieutenant. We're less than an hour away and I'm expecting to hear from Admiral Teron shortly."

The Admiral was generally punctual. On this occasion, they didn't hear from him immediately and soon the *ES Castigate* was in position a few thousand kilometres away from the heavy lifter. Duggan preferred to keep his spacecraft in constant motion, so he circled around at a medium speed.

"Captain Dramer asks us to slow down, sir. He says we're making him dizzy."

"They're always a bit crazy on the lifters," said McGlashan.

Duggan wasn't without a sense of humour, but he wasn't in the mood to engage with the captain of the *Gargantua*. He kept the *Castigate* in its circle and pondered if he should try and reach Admiral Teron, or take matters into his own hands and ride a shuttle across to the lifter. The decision was made for him.

"The *Gargantua* has launched a shuttle, sir," said Chainer. "It's coming towards us."

"It sounds as if they know more than we do. Ask them what their plans are."

"They're coming to relieve us, sir. There are six officers inbound."

The shuttle didn't take long to reach the *Castigate*. Both vessels were moving at a reasonably fast speed, which seemed no impediment to the docking computer on the transport. With a clunk, it linked to one of the *Castigate*'s two docking irises, which were a recent addition to Space Corps vessels, allowing shuttles to deliver their passengers without the need for a landing bay.

"Our port-side iris has opened," said Breeze. "There are six additional personnel onboard."

"There's no sign of the transport leaving, sir."

"It'll be waiting for us," said Duggan. "I'll check for confirmation before we go anywhere."

The six new arrivals made their way directly to the bridge. Their senior officer introduced herself as Captain Picket and she respectfully awaited Duggan's invitation to enter.

"Good day," said Duggan, extending a hand.

Captain Picket shook his hand and returned the greeting. She was tall and dark-haired, with a commanding presence which made her easily recognizable as a competent officer.

"I've received no orders," said Duggan.

Picket raised an eyebrow, in a well-practised gesture. "I'm told you're under Fleet Admiral Teron's direct instruction, Captain. We've been asked to relieve you, that's all."

"Admiral Teron must be running late with the details," said Duggan.

"Want me to get him on the comms?" asked Chainer.

"Please."

"He's unavailable."

Duggan puffed out his cheeks. "Pass on a message to let him know we've arrived and let him know we're headed to the *Gargantua*."

"Message sent."

Duggan and his crew wished the others good fortune and hurried through the corridors of the warship. It was less cramped than a Gunner or an Anderlecht and the temperature was more even. Nevertheless, they were hot by the time they climbed through the long, circular tunnel which took them to the tiny spacecraft latched outside.

Without delay, Duggan called up the autopilot, intending to program in the return journey.

"It's already set to go back," he said.

"There wasn't anywhere else for it to go."

There was a noticeable shudder, accompanied by a grinding vibration when the shuttle disconnected from the docking iris. Its guidance systems executed a sharp turn and propelled it in the direction of the *Gargantua*. The four of them stared at the sensor feed. It took a lot to inspire awe these days and the heavy lifter managed it.

"I've seen bigger ships," said Chainer.

"Probably only one," McGlashan replied. "Even if the *Sandarvax* is a lot longer, I doubt it has the same volume. That leaves only the Dreamer mothership."

"The *Sandarvax* has greater volume," said Breeze with an unexpected certainty. "Still, the lifter is a wonder right enough."

The transport swished effortlessly into a wide, well-lit opening in the *Gargantua*'s side. There were three other shuttles like it inside, clamped in place and attached to docking irises. Duggan wondered why it had taken so long to come up with such an efficient system. He supposed there were other priorities.

"Out," he said, once the landing manoeuvre was successfully completed. Something caught his eye – an inbound message, diverted from the *Gargantua*'s main comms. "Wait!"

"A message?" asked Chainer.

They knew who it would be from - they'd waited nervously for an update since arriving in this solar system.

"Admiral Teron," said Duggan. He put his earpiece in place and listened. The message was concise and didn't require an elaborate response.

"What's up, sir?" asked Chainer, after Duggan put the earpiece down.

"He's going to speak to us in ten minutes. Would you believe they've got a dozen meeting rooms onboard? We're going to one of them."

They emerged from the shuttle into the crowded interior of the heavy lifter. The cargo bays were further along the ship and this area of the vessel somewhat resembled the Juniper. Groups of people passed by, walking swiftly along the wide, metal-walled corridors and across the open spaces. In terms of design, the *Gargantua* was a world apart from the deserted passages of most fleet spacecraft.

"They must have thousands of people here," said Breeze.

"Look at all these rooms," said Chainer. "They've got researchers, scientists, engineers. Everything you need to support a war."

"Its personnel could live here for years," said McGlashan. "It's less vulnerable than the Juniper, too, if somewhat smaller."

"The Juniper can't fit anything much over a thousand metres in its bays. The *Gargantua* will be a lot more flexible, assuming it can perform repairs as well as we've been told."

"I'm surprised they've sent it so close to danger," said Chainer. "No disrespect to the guys walking around us, but they don't look as if they signed up for frontline duty."

"They'll be hand-picked, Lieutenant. I doubt they had the wool pulled over their eyes."

There was something about the heavy lifter which pleased Duggan. It represented a step forward in the Space Corps' capabilities and he set himself a mental reminder to check if there were any more of these vessels under construction.

They reached the meeting room. There was enough space inside to hold a conference and the four of them sat in the front row, feeling lost amongst the hundred or so seats which remained empty. The walls were clad in a wood-effect material and there was carpet on the floors. It was as though it had been designed to give the impression of being anywhere except on a spacecraft. The room smelled of new-cut cloth and resin.

This time, Admiral Teron didn't keep them waiting. His image appeared abruptly on the largest of the room's four screens, winked out, then reappeared, shimmering slightly until the feed stabilised.

"Good day. It seemed for the best that I address everyone at once, since you're all facing the same dangers."

"Have you finalised the mission objectives, sir?" asked Duggan, impatient to know what was expected.

"I have. Some is for your ears only, much of it I will tell you shortly." Teron caught the look of confusion on Duggan's face. "There are others due."

Duggan *was* puzzled. "Who is coming, sir?"

The sound of the meeting room door caused them to turn. Lieutenant Ortiz stood there, peculiarly abashed at the attention. "Hello, sir," she said in greeting.

Duggan nodded in return. "Good to see you, Lieutenant. I must confess I wasn't expecting to see you here."

"That makes two of us, sir. They put me and a few of the guys on one of those Anderlechts and the next thing I knew I was told to get here. Top priority."

"Do you know who this is?" asked Duggan, directing her attention to Admiral Teron.

Ortiz didn't miss a beat. "Yes, sir, I know who that is." She lifted a hand and waved. Teron raised his eyebrows. He'd been a soldier himself once and few things surprised him these days.

"Take a seat, Lieutenant Ortiz."

Ortiz sat.

"Can we begin?" asked Duggan.

"I'm awaiting one more arrival."

Duggan could tell when the Admiral was playing games. He drummed his fingers impatiently and glowered at the video screen, while Teron pretended he didn't notice.

"Sir?"

The question spurred Teron into life. "Several hours before the *ES Castigate* arrived here, another spaceship visited this solar system, bringing with it an important guest – someone who will play a pivotal role in determining how we face the approaching conflict. The captain of the *Gargantua* was unpleasantly surprised when the Trivanor exited lightspeed less than an hour away from his vessel. Luckily, I had provided advance orders for the Ghast Oblivion to be treated as an ally, not an enemy. The battleship departed a short time before the *Castigate* arrived."

Duggan wasn't stupid and guessed where Teron was going. He could have jumped in and spoken the name, but he knew the Admiral had a streak of the theatrical in him, even in life-or-death situations like this one. The meeting room door opened and the last attendee walked inside, unbowed in spite of his years. Duggan stood at once and gave his acknowledgement.

"Subjos Gol-Tur. It's good to see you."

CHAPTER TEN

IF TERON HAD a liking of the theatrical, the Ghast did not. Gol-Tur strode to the front, where he remained standing, his face towards the screen.

"Have you told them, Malachi Teron?"

"I thought it best to wait for your arrival, Subjos."

"I am here. We should not delay."

Teron pursed his lips. "Let's get on with it, then. Captain Duggan, the scope of your mission isn't something we can perfectly define, so I plan to give you some guidelines."

"Assuming you survive the transit through the wormhole," said Gol-Tur bluntly.

"We will try to equip you for a number of eventualities, specifically ground combat and ship-to-ship engagement with the enemy. Your primary goal is to fill in our many blanks."

"Gather information and return, sir?"

"We're hoping for a little more than that, Captain Duggan. You've already guessed you'll be taking the *ESS Crimson*. By the time you leave, it will have been returned to full operational capability. The stealth modules should allow you to discover what we're facing - or at least give us a general idea, which is more than we have at the moment." He leaned forward. "Here's the important bit. You've heard me use the term *taking the fight to the enemy*. That's exactly what I'm expecting you to do. If you get the chance, kill as many of the bastards as you can."

Duggan had been more or less prepared for the instruction, though he hadn't expected Admiral Teron to deliver the words in such a cold-hearted fashion. There again, the Dreamers hadn't earned the right to be granted mercy. The instruction necessitated the asking of one vital question.

"Does that include using the Planet Breaker, sir?"

"Use it without hesitation. If that isn't clear enough I will spell it out as follows: if you find any of their populated worlds, destroy them at once and let the deaths lie on my conscience."

Duggan wasn't sure the guilt was so easily transferred. Whatever Teron's words, the burden would be carried by more than one. "If it comes to it, I'll do as you order, sir. You're aware the Planet Breaker failed last time, leading me to believe their populated worlds could be protected against attack."

"That in itself is valuable information and assists with the direction of our research."

"I think I can summarise the rest of the conversation. We're to act with caution, but not hold back when I judge it the right time to strike."

"Exactly that. Returning to the situation with the *Crimson*. You'll find it's had a few minor modifications to allow it to carry more troops and ground-based weaponry, as well as a more effective method of delivering said armour."

"It'll be best if we avoid any ground combat, sir."

"I'm aware. Like I said, I want to ensure you're not held back by a lack of options. The changes to the *Crimson* weren't especially difficult to make – there's a huge team on the *Gargantua* who have completed the alterations in double-quick time."

Duggan was familiar enough with the Admiral to know when he was holding something in reserve. "What is it you're not telling us, sir?"

"You'll be wondering why I asked Subjos Gol-Tur to attend this meeting." He left the words hanging in invitation.

Duggan duly obliged. "The thought had occurred."

"This fight is as much ours as it is yours, Captain Duggan," said Gol-Tur. "Now that we are allies, it is right that we face the battle together and that is what we'll do."

"You have a warship ready to make the transit?"

"Not yet. Soon. I have agreed with your Admiral Teron that a contingent of our best troops will accompany you on your warship."

The meeting had been building towards this announcement. Even so, Duggan was a little taken aback that Teron would permit Ghasts onto a fleet warship so soon after the signing of a peace treaty. He wasn't afraid to speak openly about his concerns. "I am not convinced this is wise, sir, though I appreciate the decision has been made."

"It *has* been made, Captain Duggan and this is the right thing to do. Subjos Gol-Tur has given me assurances there will be no subterfuge."

Duggan realised the significance when Teron said the Ghasts could be trusted – the aliens were either very poor liars or so accomplished that even the most suspicious of humans couldn't detect when they were telling mistruths. On the balance of probabilities, Duggan was certain the Ghasts were above-board.

"I command the *Crimson* and the troops," he said, the tone of his voice making it clear he wasn't expecting an argument. "Will this be a problem?"

"Were you on one of our vessels, then yes it would be a problem," said Gol-Tur. The translation module lacked the subtlety to betray the Ghost's precise feelings on the matter. "As it is, my troops will accept your command."

"Without question?"

"Those are the orders I have given them."

"There are no Dax-Nides amongst your troops?" Duggan asked, referring to the captain of the Oblivion class *Kuidenar*, who had defied his orders to withdraw from an attack on Atlantis.

"You are in command because you can deal with problems," said Gol-Tur. "However, I don't expect you to encounter insubordination."

Duggan felt Gol-Tur wasn't telling him everything. He considered a number of additional questions. In the end, he left them unspoken. The Ghost was right – Duggan had to expect problems, particularly if the first joint human-Ghost ground attack ever came to pass. As long as the aliens obeyed his orders, anything else would have to be dealt with as it arose.

"How many are coming?"

"The roster is available on the *Crimson* if you're looking for names and combat records. In terms of numbers, you'll have twenty human troops and a further ten Ghost soldiers," said Teron.

"Red-Gulos leads them," said Gol-Tur. "He is one of our most decorated men."

"I'm sure he'll do his duty," said Duggan, wondering if the concept of duty was something the Ghosts were familiar with. *I'll have to learn quickly,* he thought.

"Is there anything else you need to ask before we end the meeting?" asked Teron.

"Only one thing, sir. When do we leave?"

"Not long. Several hours at the most. I suggest you make yourselves comfortable on the *Crimson*. The interior work is complete and the hull repairs are due to be finished any time now."

Duggan got up to leave with the others.

"Captain Duggan, I need a very brief word with you alone," said Teron.

"Sir?" he asked, when the room was empty.

"I've found some information about your kidnapping incident."

"Someone in Military Asset Management?"

"I thought you might have reached your own conclusion. Yes, it was someone from that organisation – a man of middling seniority."

"What has happened to this man?"

"At first he claimed I had no authority to have him arrested. He soon discovered the fallacy of his beliefs. He later said he was a personal friend of Lieutenant Nichols and that he only wanted to ask you directly what happened to result in the man's death."

"And?"

"I didn't believe him, so I had him given certain drugs to make him remember what he wasn't telling us."

"What did he say."

"Bits and pieces. He was only a participant in what happened, rather than the mastermind."

"The MAM directors spoke to me before, sir. They asked me to answer some questions."

Teron looked perplexed. "Why didn't you tell me before?"

"It didn't seem important enough at the time. They appeared to be children trying to play an adult's game."

"There could be more to it than you think, John. Their department has access to a number of important ears."

"Their department is already an anachronism."

"Maybe not. If we remain at total war, it's possible their influence will increase."

"They are just a single department amongst many which orbit the Space Corps."

Teron laughed. "That they are. I haven't forgotten what's happened, but I can't be everywhere at once. Keep an eye out."

"They can't follow me through the wormhole, sir."

"Indeed not. Perhaps I'll have dealt with the problem before you return. Rest assured I'm treating it as a high priority. They've overstepped the mark and as soon as I have proof, they'll find themselves up the creek without a paddle."

It was a long time since Duggan had heard that saying – Teron was a man with a surprising turn of phrase. "Thank you for the update, sir. I've got more important things to worry about than a vendetta against me. If our meeting is concluded, I'll join the others on the *Crimson*."

"We're done. I won't speak to you again before you leave, so I'll wish you good luck."

"Thank you."

"I don't think you have to worry about the loyalty of the Ghasts you're taking with you. We know they can fight and Gol-Tur has promised these are amongst the best."

"I'm worried they'll want to show off, sir."

"That will go for both sides, won't it?" asked Teron. "You'll need to keep it under control if it looks like jeopardising the mission."

"I'll severely punish anyone who oversteps. Human or Ghast."

"That's the way to play it. Goodbye."

"Goodbye, sir."

Duggan put thoughts of his human enemies to one side and left the room, his stride purposeful. Outside, he realised he had no idea how to reach the *Crimson*, so he spoke to a woman passing by. She directed him to a shuttle capsule, which was part of an ingenious system of horizontal and vertical lifts to take the *Gargantua*'s crew to their destinations as quickly as possible. After a matter of five minutes, during which several other people entered and exited the cylindrical capsule, Duggan stepped out through a door and into one part of the spaceship's colossal cargo bay.

The sight caught him unawares. The cargo bay was brightly lit in stark blue-white, allowing him to see for several thousand metres to the left and right. The shape of the bay echoed that of the ship's exterior, being a flattened cylinder. To a large extent, the internal walls were featureless, apart from the rows alloy cubes which housed the power systems for the gravity clamps. He looked into the heights above and saw rows of huge observation windows which looked across the interior. Pervading everything was a bone-deep vibration, which Duggan recognized as the vessel's incredibly powerful gravity engines, running at little more than an idle.

There were two ships inside – the ES *Rampage* was far to Duggan's left. The air around it was busy with a constantly-moving army of self-propelled repair bots. Their welders sparked and crackled as they sealed the damage to the warship's armour. Some of the bots were at least three hundred metres wide and over two hundred tall. Duggan had never seen anything close to that size, except on a few major ground-based shipyards. These bots were designed specifically to accompany the *Gargantua*.

The *Rampage* had been subjected to an extraordinary level of punishment at the recent conflict above Atlantis and it was a wonder the Space Corps hadn't scrapped it. Duggan thought it testament to the toughness of the Galactic class that the decision had been made to salvage rather than dismantle. Before he looked away, his eyes caught one more detail in the vessel's hull – the tell-tale indentations which indicated they'd decided to install four Shatterer tubes at the same time as they completed the repairs. He was sure the technical problems with the missiles still existed, but it seemed wise to look to the future and get the *Rampage* prepared.

Then, there was the *Crimson*. The warship appeared small in the cavernous interior of the bay. It was clamped in place near to one side wall, with nothing to support it from underneath and there were no repair bots circling around. It looked forgotten in comparison to the organised chaos that surrounded the heavy cruiser. The front boarding ramp was in the down position, the bottom step resting against a retractable platform which protruded from the side wall of the cargo bay.

With the familiar and unshakeable excitement he felt when action beckoned, Duggan set off to see what his future had in store.

CHAPTER ELEVEN

THE PROCESS TO allow the *Crimson*'s departure was swift, all things considered. Most of the repair work was automated, so it didn't take long to clear the bay of human personnel. There had been a team of four technicians on the *Crimson*, performing some task or other which they didn't seem keen to discuss. Once the bay was clear of the living, the vast external doors slid aside. There was nothing ponderous about them and they vanished into gaps between the layers of the *MHL Gargantua*'s hull.

Clearance to leave was granted immediately and Duggan activated the auto-pilot, since he had no desire to be party to an accidental collision at the start of such a vital mission. The *Crimson* fell away into space and Duggan took the control bars once they were a few hundred kilometres clear. The metal felt cool in his palms as if they were part of his flesh, rather than something separate.

"Do you know where we're going, Lieutenant?" he asked.

"Yes, sir," said Breeze.

"Get us to the Blackstar at full speed."

"The AI is calculating the path. It'll take us one hour and fifty minutes to arrive."

"Get us in as close as you can. There's no need for us to wait around – I want to be through the wormhole as quickly as possible."

The *Crimson* flashed away across space, carrying its cargo of weapons, troops and armour. Duggan recalled the time when they'd first discovered the ship and how its life support had been insufficient to completely sustain the crew on the surge to light-speed. Now there was scarcely more than a slight bump, easily missed if you didn't know what you were looking for.

"Lieutenant Ortiz, please report."

"It's interesting down here, sir."

"Anything you can't handle?"

"Nothing so far. These Ghasts are big, but they don't say much."

"Can they understand you and do they respond when you speak to them?"

"They've got language modules on their chests. I've checked out a few of our space suits and they have the modules ready to go. I believe they're standard fit these days. The Ghasts have their own kit, sir."

Duggan was curious to know what the aliens had brought with them. He'd seen much of their weaponry in the past, though he was still interested in how it looked close-up. There wasn't much time until they reached the Blackstar, so he put the matter to one side – he was sure Ortiz would make it her personal mission to learn the important details.

"Keep on top of it, Lieutenant. We'll be at the wormhole soon."

"I'll tell the guys to expect a bumpy ride."

"If we're lucky."

"I understand, sir. See you on the other side."

The minutes passed quickly and for once Duggan would have preferred it otherwise. He had time to skim through his mission briefing documents, finding nothing new or unexpected in spite of Teron's hints to the contrary. There were also checks to perform with Lieutenant Breeze, in order for them to be certain they were familiar with the exact routine required to traverse the wormhole.

"The AI will do most of the work," said Breeze. "It's been programmed with a whole new set of instructions to make it happen."

"Instructions which are clearly labelled with the word *experimental*, I see," said Duggan.

"Everything's untested until you give it a go, sir," said Breeze in a matter-of-fact voice.

"Anyone want a coffee?" interrupted Chainer. "I can't travel an infinite distance without a shot of caffeine."

"I've tasted the stuff you manage to extract from the replicator," said Breeze, looking up from his console. "I'll give it a miss."

"Let's get on with this," said Duggan impatiently. "We need to get close enough to the wormhole without being destroyed and then activate a lightspeed sequence. In *theory* our journey should take an infinitesimally short time and we're relying on this pre-programmed sequence to pull us clear at the other side, before we get crushed."

"That sums it up nicely. We activate the fission drives and the AI keeps them on the brink of firing, until we activate this new set of codes. Once the sequence is activated, we can't easily disable it. When it begins, we're going through whether we like it or not."

"In case the life support can't sustain us and we pass out," said Duggan.

"Or worse. There are some remarkably clever people who have devoted their lives to solving this theoretical stuff, sir. Ultimately, there's only so much testing you can do in a lab before you need volunteers to give it go."

"Suckers, you mean," said Chainer, coming back with a cup of something which possessed the consistency of tar.

"Lieutenant," warned Duggan. "We're not playing games here."

Chainer took the hint and sat down without saying anything further. Duggan and Breeze talked for a time, while McGlashan listened in. There was a chance she might end up in charge of the ship if something went wrong.

Eventually, Duggan rose from his stooped position and stretched the muscles of his back to ease them. "I don't know if it'll work, but I'm ready to give it a try."

"Not long until we arrive, sir. Five minutes."

"Let's get ready, ladies and gentlemen. We have to assume the area surrounding the Blackstar may contain hostiles. I want a thorough scan of local space and we'll activate the stealth modules as soon as we're able."

"We won't be able to use them, sir. They have a cooldown before and after lightspeed use."

Duggan kicked himself for not realising. The *Crimson* couldn't go to lightspeed immediately after the stealth modules were switched off, which would delay their launch into the wormhole. "Forget about the stealth and keep your fingers crossed we don't run into something we can't handle."

"Sir."

"Commander McGlashan? Get ready to fire everything we've got at the first sign of trouble."

The crew knew when it was time to concentrate and they went through their tests and checks to ensure everything was ready to go.

"Exiting lightspeed, sir," said Breeze.

The *Crimson* entered local space, half a million kilometres from the Helius Blackstar - a journey of approximately four minutes on the gravity drives until they were close enough to launch. It was not going to be straightforward.

"There's a nearby fission signature," said Breeze.

"Coming or going?" asked Duggan with alarm. He set the gravity drives to maximum output and aimed directly for the wormhole.

"Going. Something big made a jump a few seconds before we arrived."

"Lieutenant Chainer, make the Juniper aware as soon as you're able."

"Yes, sir. There's zero sign of hostiles in our vicinity. Switching to the fars to see what's there."

Duggan brought the forward sensor feed onto the bulkhead screen. The Helius Blackstar showed as an area of absolute darkness, visible only because it blocked out the stars behind it. The AI overlaid a speckling of red dots, to show the wormhole's outer reaches and the centre where its gravity became ever more powerful. The dots spiralled slowly inwards.

"I think there's something out there," said Chainer.

"Think or know, Lieutenant? We can't make decisions based on guesswork."

"Sorry, sir. When you've done this long enough, you begin to get a feeling for it."

Duggan had worked with Chainer long enough to be concerned at the words. He was already on edge and now he experienced the clenched feeling in his stomach which he got when something was beyond his control. "Come on," he muttered.

"We can begin the launch sequence for the wormhole anywhere between fifty and a hundred thousand kilometres out from the centre," said Breeze. "At the extremes of range, our hull will definitely survive the gravitational crush, but the chances of a successful launch into the wormhole have been calculated at no more than five percent. At fifty thousand kilometres, we're looking at the contradictory combination of certain success and certain death."

"The closer the better, as long as we judge it right." said Duggan.

"They've left it to your judgement to decide when to go, sir," said Breeze. "There must be too many 'what-ifs' for them to give a firm recommendation."

"Crap!" said Chainer.

It wasn't a word Duggan wanted to hear. "What is it?"

"I've got something big on the fars, sir. I have no idea what it is – it's smaller than the mothership and bigger than the Dreamer battleship. It's heading towards us at more than two thousand klicks per second."

Duggan looked at the updated tactical screen and saw the other vessel. It was far to starboard and moving on a course that would bring it close to the *Crimson*. "Does it know we're here or is this bad luck?"

"It won't *precisely* intercept us, sir. It'll be close enough to make no difference. For the avoidance of doubt, they *will* know we're here from this range."

"Damnit, why now?"

"There's a second vessel out there as well, sir. This one's coming from the other side. It's a lot smaller, if that helps – another new type."

A second dot appeared on the tactical – this one only a little further away than the first. Duggan gritted his teeth as he stared at the display.

"Tell the Juniper how crowded it is here, Lieutenant. Priority message."

"Our primary comms are down, sir. Switching to the backups."

"They must be modifying their existing fleet in order to get them through the wormhole," McGlashan guessed. "Increasing their density or changing the shape so they can withstand the stresses."

"We're two minutes away," said Breeze.

"Prepare the fission drives for the launch sequence," said Duggan, his voice even.

"Warm-up is underway."

"The enemy warship has launched a wave of fifty missiles – impact in forty seconds. Past data suggests it won't be long until they can use their particle beams. Once they start hitting us with those, we might lose enough of our engines that we can't make the jump."

"We're caught between them," said Duggan. He evaluated the situation – if they maintained their existing course, there would be a period during which both enemy spacecraft would be able to attack the *Crimson*. The timings weren't easy to work out in his head and he tried to figure out if the Dreamer missiles would be quick enough to reach them if he kept the *Crimson* on its existing trajectory towards the wormhole.

"Sir, if we turn to intercept the smaller craft and make a quick kill, we'll buy ourselves some time," said McGlashan. "The larger vessel is only a little quicker than we are. It won't close the gap before we can activate our launch into the wormhole."

"It'll have plenty of time to launch a thousand missiles at us, Commander."

"We have no good choice, sir."

"No, we don't," he replied. "Outnumbered and outgunned in a fight we don't want. Get ready on the countermeasures as soon as you're able. I don't want anything else fired – we'll conserve our ammunition for what lies ahead."

"Yes, sir."

"The launch sequence is ready to activate whenever you want, sir," Breeze advised. "We're too far out for the time being."

"Acknowledged."

The situation wasn't good and Duggan knew that whatever choice he made it might still result in failure. They needed to get as close to the Blackstar as they could manage, without pushing the *Crimson* to the point of destruction and without allowing the enemy enough time to shoot them down with missiles. It wasn't time to dwell on the chance of failure and he made his decision.

"We're maintaining our existing course," he said. He had one eye on the tactical screen and saw how close the inbound missiles were.

"Countermeasures away."

"Launch more."

The shock drones scattered away from the *Crimson*, sparkling with the light of their own power cells. The enemy missiles detonated against them, exploding in pure white. One, lone missile remained on its course and its guidance system sent it colliding with the *Crimson*'s starboard armour. There was a thunderous, reverberating clunk.

"It failed to detonate," said McGlashan, with a look of shock. "There's a second wave incoming – this time it's a hundred."

"It's like they're picking us off at their leisure," said Chainer. "Disrespectful bastards."

"Of course!" Duggan exclaimed. "They have no idea what we're going to do. They must think they have us trapped!"

"The smaller ship's firing. Fifty more to add to the pile."

Duggan checked the distance counter – they were still one hundred and fifty thousand kilometres from the wormhole. The larger ship fired a third salvo of one hundred.

"We could make this," he said.

"I don't think so," said McGlashan. "Those missiles are faster than a Shatterer."

Duggan saw that she was correct and that he'd miscalculated. There was hardly anything in it – no more than a second or two, but the wave of a hundred missiles would reach them at eighty thousand kilometres away from the wormhole.

The tactical display filled with targets, shown as a variety of angry reds depending on their priority. The distance counter raced down towards one hundred thousand kilometres.

"The hull is showing signs of stress, sir," said Breeze.

The early indications of it appeared with an upward flickering on several of the hull gauges. It began slowly and then at a rapidly-increasing rate. Then, the forces on the hull rose so rapidly that the *Crimson* went close to its design tolerances within the space of moments. An automated siren began.

"Shut that off!" Duggan shouted.

The siren continued and was joined by the emergency lights. Their rich blood-red light burned in sympathy with Duggan's growing anger.

Time and distance counted down. Far from being hurried, Duggan found himself able to make decisions almost at his leisure. "We're going faster," he said, the words coming as soon as his mind registered the fact. "Nineteen-fifty klicks per second."

"A hundred thousand klicks from the wormhole," said Breeze.

"Get ready to activate the launch sequence on my word."

The *Crimson*'s speed increased again as it raced towards the wormhole ahead. *Two thousand three hundred klicks per second,* he thought. *I hope the lab guys know what they're doing else we'll never escape at the other end.*

There was a creaking, groaning sound, coming from all about. To his horror, Duggan realised it was the *Crimson* being crushed by the immense weight of gravity. The spaceship was little more than a lump of solid ultra-dense metal, so he knew the pressure was unimaginable. *We might just escape the missiles at this speed, if we don't break up first.*

The impression of time slowed down further and Duggan wondered if it was a result of their proximity to the wormhole, or nothing more than an illusion created by his own fevered thoughts.

The *Crimson* shook and rumbled. A harsh, abrasive scraping noise intruded upon the bridge, drowning out the siren.

"Sir? Should I activate?" The words came from Lieutenant Breeze, spoken as if in slow-motion.

The warship's status displays spoke of nothing but the crew's imminent death. The inbound missiles were nearly upon them, their Gallenium propulsion and warheads strong enough to resist the pressure. Shock drones appeared on the tactical, their lives measured in moments as the wormhole's gravity crushed them in its irresistible fist. Duggan experienced surprise when he saw how close they were to the Blackstar. *Sixty thousand klicks.*

He opened his mouth and spoke the words. "Activate launch sequence."

The *Crimson* disappeared.

CHAPTER TWELVE

DUGGAN OPENED HIS EYES. He had no idea how long they'd been closed. Had he simply blinked, or had he been unconscious for an eternity? His limbs and mind felt weighed down by a powerful memory of dislocation. One part of his brain reminded him that early lightspeed travellers had reported symptoms similar to what he felt now. *Am I alive?*

With a growl, Duggan took his head in his hands, trying to shake off the fugue. He slowly became aware of his surroundings – the siren and emergency light had mercifully shut off and he saw with relief that the others of the crew were rousing themselves.

"What?" Chainer muttered, his mouth incapable of uttering anything more significant.

"We've got to get moving," said Duggan, the words sounding like they came from a great distance.

Breeze made a noise, somewhere between a groan and a grunt. He lifted a hand and stared at it in fascination, as though he'd never seen it before.

"Come on!" Duggan urged. He tried to marshal his thoughts

and looked at the screens around him. For a moment, he couldn't make sense of the information and panic rose within him. Then, his mind settled and the swirling disarray snapped into sharp focus. They'd come through the wormhole – somehow, they'd managed what his primal instinct told him was impossible. The time would come for a full status check. For the moment, they needed to move.

Duggan recalled the Dreamer ships on the other side of the wormhole, as though it was years ago. Even blurred by the warping effects of the transit, the memory was enough to remind him of the great dangers they faced. Without sparing time to decide on the best heading, he powered the *Crimson* away at its fastest speed.

"Frank, I need you!" he called loudly.

"Yes. Yes, sir," Chainer stammered. He thumped the palm of one hand against his forehead and straightened his back.

"Tell me what's out there."

"I can help on the sensors, sir," said McGlashan.

"Stay where you are, Commander!"

"Commencing scan," Chainer mumbled. He cleared his throat. "Commencing scan!" he repeated, louder and clearer.

Duggan breathed a sigh of relief to see Chainer's recovery. "Lieutenant Breeze, I need status updates."

"It'll take me a moment, sir."

"Not too long." Duggan paused to see if Chainer would give him immediate news. There was nothing forthcoming, so he opened an internal channel to the troops' quarters. "Lieutenant Ortiz, please report."

"Ortiz answered immediately and Duggan had to suppress a smile at the chirpiness in her voice, as well as at the details she provided.

"Everything is perfect, sir. A few of the guys have forgotten which day of the week it is, but there's a calendar hanging on the mess room wall for when they want a reminder."

Ortiz would have mentioned injuries before saying anything so flippant, but Duggan couldn't stop himself asking. "Anyone hurt?"

"No, sir. Don't you know we're the best the Space Corps has to offer? It'll take more than the impossible to slow us down."

"What about our friends from the Ghast navy?"

"Those boys look just fine as well, sir. I spoke to Red-Gulos and he assured me they hadn't even realised we'd gone through."

Duggan laughed. "Brave words from our new allies, Lieutenant."

"They look tough, sir."

"I'm sure they are. Very well, wait for further updates."

"Acknowledged."

The brief conversation gave the others time to rally. Chainer was the first to speak and he provided a brief update of what he'd found so far.

"The good news is, there are no signs of the enemy in our vicinity," he said. "That's where the good news ends. The first piece of bad news is that while we were incapable of action, the *Crimson*'s sensors picked up another enemy spacecraft doing a lightspeed jump towards the Blackstar from a place near to where we arrived. We got lucky, sir – really lucky. If we'd been a few seconds earlier, we'd have got here and been an easy kill for them."

"It happens," said Duggan, unwilling to think about what might have been. "Where's the wormhole?"

"For want of a more technical term, it's behind us, sir. A good distance behind us."

"How the hell did that happen?" he asked, when he saw just how far away the Helius Blackstar was. "I thought we were relying on the gravity drives to pull us away. We should be much closer to it."

"I'll give it some thought," said Breeze. "When I've finished with the other items on my critical list."

Duggan turned his attention to Chainer again. "What else?"

"I've checked and double-checked our location against all known stars. In summary, I have absolutely no idea where we are. On top of that, we're on the backup comms. They work well at medium distances, even if they travel at a fraction the speed of a modern comms system. Out here? I have no idea how long they'll take to get to one of the Confederation's monitoring stations. What's even worse is I can't actually send a message since I have too little data on where to aim the transmitters."

"In other words, we're lost," said McGlashan.

"No more than we expected, Commander."

"Stealth modules are ready," said Breeze.

"Thank you, Lieutenant," Duggan replied. "Activate them at once."

From the corner of his eye, Duggan saw the available power for the gravity drives plummet to fifty percent – it was a price well-worth paying for the reassurance offered by the stealth cloak.

Chainer continued. "I've still got the fars and super-fars scanning. I don't need their reports to tell you what's close by. Look." With that, he pointed at the bulkhead screen and Duggan saw a computer-generated map of the local solar system.

"A big sun, eight orbiting worlds and a dozen or so moons," said McGlashan. "So far, so normal."

"Not quite," said Chainer. "There's something on the fourth planet."

"Any ideas what it is yet?"

"Sorry, sir. I'm using too many processing cycles analysing everything else. I can tell you that whatever's on the surface, it's made of metal and it's fairly large. Do you want me to prioritise the object?"

"No, keep on as you are. You've given me enough to go on," said Duggan. He made a snap decision and altered course towards the fourth planet. "I'm very interested to learn what's down there."

"It's close enough to the wormhole to be significant," McGlashan answered. "We should count ourselves lucky."

Duggan understood what she meant. They could have emerged from the wormhole into a place with nothing, many hours lightspeed from anywhere. They'd have been reduced to circling around near to the Blackstar in stealth, waiting to see what happened by. Or perhaps a Dreamer warship could have returned from Confederation space and led them to something significant at sub-light speed. Both possibilities would have been fraught with danger and uncertainty. At least this confirmed sighting of an object on the nearby planet gave them an instant purpose.

The target planet was close to fifteen million kilometres away – a journey of about two hours. Duggan could have ordered a short lightspeed jump towards it, in order to save a little time. In the circumstances, slow and steady was much the preferable choice, especially given the incomplete status updates.

Eventually, Breeze was able to provide the necessary details.

"The hull took a beating, but it's intact. They built these things well," he said fondly. "If the pressure doesn't break it outright, we can assume it's effectively undamaged."

"That's promising for the return trip," said Duggan.

Breeze went on. "The logs confirm we travelled for exactly zero amount of time, sir. In reality, we have no way of knowing what the AI counted. Maybe we've come across half of the universe instantaneously or perhaps we travelled for a thousand years and when we get home everyone we know will be long dead."

"Admiral Teron didn't tell us that might happen!" said Chainer in alarm.

"I doubt he knew," said Breeze. "Anyway, I'm just guessing, Frank. Don't take it so seriously."

"Go on," said Duggan.

"I'm not entirely certain how we made it so far from the Blackstar. The audits show a few things I've not seen before. There's a sustained utilisation jump on the Dreamer core from the moment we activated the launch sequence until the time we arrived here. In addition, the fission drives show an unusual reading – as if we've performed a double jump."

"I didn't think that was possible," said Duggan, frowning.

"Until today, I'd have agreed with you. Look here, though – the AI was close to burning out during the process."

"Did they fit overdrive hardware to give it a boost? They must have learned a lot about the Dreamer core to have patched that in."

"Maybe that's what they did. The Space Corps doesn't take risks with its warships, Captain. We can make our hardware run a lot faster than it does – it simply increases the failure rate. Drastically increases it."

"It sounds like they've done some trickery to bounce us from one lightspeed jump to another without any need for ramp-up."

Breeze held out his hands to show he wasn't certain. "That would be as good a guess as any. We don't need to know how they've managed it, as long as it works. We're only a few seconds away from the wormhole if you assume we travelled at high lightspeed once we came through."

"Will we be able to make the return journey? That's the important question."

"I wouldn't like to do any more transits than necessary, put it that way."

"One more is all we need," said Duggan, nevertheless worried by what his conversation with Breeze had raised. Another concerning thought came to him. "Lieutenant Chainer – what are the chances those Dreamer warships we escaped have transmitted details of our presence to one of their home bases?"

"I wouldn't like to say. Confederation space could be as unknown to them as their space is to us. If we assume they have enough idea of where to point their comms, you could be looking at days, weeks, months or years for messages to travel, depending on their technology."

"Not hours?"

"Definitely not hours. If you put your foot on my neck hard enough, I would venture a guess that their messages have a delay of several weeks - probably months."

"That's far," said Duggan.

"Yes, sir. We're talking about distances that make the whole of Confederation space look like a bird dropping on the New Earth Capital Shipyard main landing pad."

"Damn."

"Yup. It's no wonder the Dreamers have thrown their efforts at getting through the wormhole, instead of trying to fly everywhere using only their engines."

Duggan returned to his seat to mull things over. The *Crimson* and its passengers had survived. Against the odds, the ancient hull of the warship had succeeded in accomplishing the near-impossible on the first try. It had carried them deep into uncharted, hostile enemy territory on a mission with few goals and no boundaries. As long as they remained here, they had a chance to give the enemy a bloody nose – or they might encounter an overwhelming force that would destroy them. He stood again.

"We made it, folks. We really made it."

McGlashan was the first to smile. "That we did. Now all we have to do is show these bastards that we won't lay down while they try to murder us."

"We've jumped the biggest hurdle," said Chainer. "We've got to make it count."

"With the greatest risks come the greatest rewards," added Breeze.

"I didn't know if we'd succeed," admitted Duggan. "Since we did, it's our duty to get the best out of this opportunity."

"Starting with what's on that planet ahead," said McGlashan.

"Exactly. Let's get to it."

The excitement returned, filling Duggan's muscles with strength. Around him, the others felt it too, eyes glittering with the acceptance of danger and a determination to win, no matter what came.

CHAPTER THIRTEEN

THEY REACHED the fourth planet without encountering anything hostile. Duggan was cautious and kept the *Crimson* at a distance, also keeping low to the horizon in case they were detected and had to escape quickly. Chainer gave out new details as he uncovered them.

"The planet has a diameter of fifteen thousand kilometres, so it's similar in size to Pioneer. There's lots of ice – mostly made up from water with traces of methanol. You can see the streaks of white even from this distance. Other than the cold it's quite hospitable with no sign of storms. If you're interested, our logging software has given it the name Frades-2."

"That's pronounced fray-dees, Frank," said Breeze. "Presumably the software decided to name it after the physicist Exa Frades."

"Whatever," said Chainer. "The installation is right on the equator and is about sixteen square klicks in size – a near-perfect square. There are lots of shapes which I imagine to be buildings the enemy have left planted on the ice."

Duggan looked at the grainy, wavering image Chainer had

summoned. There was no doubt in his mind that *installation* was the correct word for it – the enemy had committed a lot of resources to its construction.

"These cuboids at each corner are big," Chainer continued. "Half a klick at the base and a couple of thousand metres tall."

"They look like towers," Duggan mused.

"This pyramid in the middle is bigger than the others we've seen – it's two klicks long at the base and proportionally taller. If it's a power source, it could hold a whole load more of that obsidian than the smaller ones the Dreamers left around Confederation space."

"What about these other features I can see on the ground?" asked Duggan.

Chainer held out his hands in a *who knows?* gesture. "Some of them could be air defences, sir. There're too many different shapes and sizes for them to be all defence emplacements."

"Any sign of life?"

"There's no way to tell from here. I'll need you to fly overhead at thirty or forty thousand klicks to be sure. The angle is no good from where we are."

"What about power readings? Is there anything we can learn from them, Lieutenant Breeze?"

Breeze raised his head, with an expression that suggested he'd been waiting for the question. "The base is running on idle at the moment, sir, which makes it difficult to guess at what they can do."

"But you've prepared a guess for me anyway, haven't you?"

Breeze grinned. "Yes, sir. If we compare the at-idle output levels from the other pyramids we've come across to the at-idle output from this one and assume they scale up in the same way, we're looking at something a lot more powerful on the ground here. Several orders of magnitude greater, if you want me to continue the guessing game."

"Just from the central pyramid?"

"No, sir. Those towers have their own signature, so they're generating too."

"Is there an active energy shield?"

"Negative. I'd say they're probably not expecting an attack, but if those really *are* air defences, then they've clearly considered the risks."

Duggan rubbed his chin in thought. "The proximity to the wormhole has me wondering," he said.

"It's exactly the sort of thing we've come to investigate, sir," said McGlashan.

"Or destroy," added Breeze.

"What're the options?" asked Duggan, looking for input.

"We should hold off using the Planet Breaker," said Breeze. "Those towers will easily have enough juice to absorb such an attack, plus it'll alert them to our presence."

"What about a high-altitude attack?" asked Chainer.

Duggan couldn't deny he was tempted. "I need more information on what we're facing. They may be able to shoot down our missiles – nukes or conventional."

"This place is important to them, sir," said Breeze. "That suggests to me we should destroy it."

"That brings us back to square one," said McGlashan. "We'll be in Dreamer space, with no way to find our way onto the next target."

"If we blow up one of their bases, they'll definitely come," said Breeze.

"I'm not certain I want the attention."

Duggan waved them to silence while he considered it further. The scope of the mission called for a combination of intel-gathering and surprise assaults where circumstances demanded. If they destroyed the base, it would bring other warships to the area. Duggan had no intention of hanging around to slug it out with a flotilla of battleships. He made his decision.

"We'll destroy this place and move on."

Chainer promptly unmade the decision.

"Sir, I'm detecting a tight-beam transmission going either to or from the installation. The receptor is one of the buildings external to the central pyramid."

"Can you read what it says?"

"Not a hope, sir. I got lucky even noticing it was there. I don't know if they are receiving, sending or if it's two-way traffic."

"Where's the other end of the signal?"

"I can't tell you that either, sir."

"I thought you could do anything with comms, Lieutenant?"

"That's a highly-focused beam, sir. If you get us to a position directly overhead, I'll be able to tell you approximately where it's going to or coming from. If the destination is close by, we might be able to pinpoint the location, but the further away we are from the other end, the less the chance I'll have a meaningful shot at finding it."

"This alters my recommendation, sir," said Breeze. "We should do everything we can to find the sender or receiver."

Duggan agreed – this was an opportunity to get deeper into enemy territory. They might find nothing more than a comms station - or it could be vastly more significant. "It could be one of their home planets or something else we need to see," he said, finishing his thought out loud.

"I can't realistically say I'll be able to give you a precise destination, even if you fly close to the signal, sir. Our databanks have no information about this area of space in order to assist with the prediction. That means I'd be left checking the super-fars to see if I can spot a likely-looking planet somewhere out there."

"I thought we could do this stuff easily?" asked Duggan in irritation.

"I'm afraid not, sir."

"How do we find out where the signal is going, then?"

"You'll have to send someone down there. If we could set up one of our emergency beacons within a few feet of the transmitter or receiver, it could send out a parallel transmission that traces the exact path of the enemy signal. I'd be able to follow that, since our own beacon will happily tell us where it terminates. As long as it doesn't go too far."

Duggan furrowed his brow. "You've done things like this before, Lieutenant, without us having to commit to a surface venture."

"It's different when the ship's AI has an extensive map and coordinate list of the space around, sir," Chainer insisted. "It makes it easy to tally a signal with its destination. Out here, we don't even have coordinates. I'll have to set the wormhole as a zero coordinate and use it to build a map of everything we see. That'll give the emergency beacon something to tie into and then..."

"Fine, Lieutenant," said Duggan, not wanting to hear the full explanation. "Can you reassure me that the enemy won't detect the signal from our beacon at the same time as they detect their own?"

"There should be enough divergence that they don't see our signal. It's not guaranteed."

"It's a risk we'll have to take," said Duggan.

"Speaking of risks, it could be swarming with enemy troops on the ground," said McGlashan. "We should attempt a reconnaissance run overhead. The stealth modules have proven reliable up until now."

An apparently straightforward choice had suddenly become more complex than Duggan wanted. It would be easiest to simply attempt the installation's destruction by firing missiles at it from a high orbit. There might be an extensive shield of countermeasures, in which case they'd need to rethink, but at least it was fairly low-risk. Now he was contemplating the deployment of his troops, with little in the way of advance knowledge about what they might expect. *This is what we're here for,* he told himself.

"Take your seats," he said. "We're going for a closer look. Lieutenant Chainer, I want to get this over with as quickly as possible."

"Come across them at thirty thousand klicks, not too fast and I'll get what you need, sir."

"Please do, Lieutenant. If they see us, there's little chance we'll be able to surprise them on the ground."

Five minutes later and it was done. With the scan complete, Duggan flew the *Crimson* a quarter of the planet's circumference away from the base and kept it hovering a few kilometres above the surface.

"Those are not ground-to-air missile batteries, sir," said Chainer, pointing at the recorded image. From above, they looked like featureless, grey-metal squares, hardly visible against the ice-covered surface. "There are thirty-two of them across the site and I have no idea what they are – maybe they're additional backup generators or something."

"They're really not short of power," said Breeze. "Whatever those are, they aren't generators."

"Should we be worried about them?" asked Duggan.

"Only because we don't know what they are, sir."

"Could these other buildings hold surface-to-air launchers?" he asked, indicating a number of similar buildings towards the centre."

"I don't know, sir. I'd say not, but they may be disguised."

The lack of clarity wasn't reassuring. "Was there any other movement?"

"I didn't find any," said Chainer. "There are quite a number of smaller buildings and I can't help but feel they're about the right size for people – aliens – to live in or do whatever it is that Dreamers do in places like this. Frades-2 isn't the sort of place you'd willingly go outside for a breath of fresh air, so I'm not surprised there's a lack of obvious activity."

"It's not very well-defended, given the size of it," said McGlashan. "Assuming they have nothing hidden."

"Which tells me that our enemy are confident of their strength in this area of space, Commander."

"They're cocky bastards, in other words," said Chainer.

Duggan ignored the interruption. "I think we're deep inside their territory, where they don't expect to be attacked."

"They've been throwing ships at that wormhole for decades," said Breeze. "They must consider themselves so superior that they can't envisage another race coming through from the other side."

"If they can't do it, then no one else can," said McGlashan. "It's things like this which give you a measure of your opponent. Not that there's much useful we can do with the information."

Duggan made a decision. "I'm going to send the troops to take a look."

Chainer raised his hand, something he didn't normally bother to do when he had something to say. "I think I'll have to go with them, sir."

"We have comms experts in the squad, Lieutenant."

"There are known comms and then there are unknown comms. I'd like to see what kit our enemy have got. In addition, the emergency beacon might need a bit of tweaking to ensure it's set up right."

"I understand. Very well, I'll send you along with the others." He opened a channel to Lieutenant Ortiz. "I need you to prepare for a full deployment," he said. "We're going on foot and leaving the armour behind."

Ortiz sounded as ready to go as ever. "I'll have them ready in fifteen minutes, sir. You'll have to land if we're leaving the tanks behind."

"Your keenness is admirable, Lieutenant, but we'll need a briefing in the mess room first – get there at once. You'll be deployed soon after."

"Are you taking control of this mission, sir?"

"For once, I'm going to sit it out, Lieutenant. I need to stay with the ship."

"Right you are, sir," she said, her voice betraying nothing of her feelings on the subject.

With that, Duggan ended the connection.

"Commander McGlashan, Lieutenant Breeze. You stay here in case something shows up. Lieutenant Chainer, you're coming with me for the briefing."

The two of them made haste to the mess room, with Duggan little aware that one part of his plan would soon be thrown into disarray.

CHAPTER FOURTEEN

"WHAT DO you mean you won't obey Lieutenant Ortiz?" shouted Duggan, filled with anger.

Red-Gulos didn't flinch. The Ghast was seven and a half feet tall and powerfully built. He had thick black hair and the look of a brawler, though his eyes and speech marked him out as highly intelligent. "We were told to follow Captain John Duggan's orders," he rasped through his interpreter. "There was no ambiguity."

"I am ordering you to obey Lieutenant Ortiz!" Duggan roared.

"Subjos Gol-Tur will need to amend our orders," said the Ghast. "This is how our command is structured."

Duggan had come across a similar example of Ghast intransigence before, when Nil-Far had been told to follow the orders of another warship captain during the attack on Atlantis. He hadn't thought he'd encounter it here and it could easily jeopardise what he wanted to accomplish.

"Only Gol-Tur can change your orders?" he asked.

"Yes."

"We can't get a message to your command until we return through the wormhole and I am not about to try it. We're here and we're staying." He clenched and unclenched his fists. "This does not show you in a good light, Red-Gulos. It's a very poor beginning to our alliance."

"I cannot change the instructions I received, Captain Duggan."

Duggan paced back and forth. The briefing had gone well up until this point. The twenty human soldiers were steely and filled with fire – their experience and competence shone like a light. The Ghasts stood apart from the humans, though there was no obvious tension between the two parties. The aliens appeared the equal of their human counterparts in terms of willingness and competence. The whole room had sat attentively while Duggan talked and pointed out the best approaches to their target on one of the large display screens. There'd been a few questions, incisive and helpful. Then this had happened.

"You'll remain on the ship," said Duggan at last.

A few of the Ghasts stirred at the words. "We are here to fight," said Red-Gulos. "We will be shamed if you send these others and leave us behind."

"It is usual to split a fighting force," said Duggan, watching the Ghast closely.

"You are correct. However, we have been told we represent our people against an adversary we'd hoped was forever lost. It will shame us if humans fight our battle without us."

Duggan began to understand Red-Gulos' depth of feeling on the subject and knew he had to handle things carefully. The obvious solution would be to send the Ghasts as a separate force, but that would bring problems of its own if there was no overall commander on the ground. If the *Crimson* was out of comms sight for whatever reason, the two ground squads could end up in a disagreement about how to deal with something unexpected.

Thirty-one pairs of eyes stared at Duggan, waiting for him to agree to the only way around the problem. He found his mouth speaking the words, even before his mind could fully explore if there was a better option.

"I'll lead the force," he said. "We'll land in one hour. Get suited up and be ready in the forward airlock."

There was a chorus of acknowledgements and Duggan left the troops in order to break the news to those he'd left on the bridge.

"That'll leave only two of us to look after the ship," said McGlashan, the accusing look in her eyes a result of more than just the additional responsibility.

"It's not what I wanted," Duggan replied. Even just few weeks ago, he wouldn't have been able to make such a statement without lying to himself and McGlashan.

She met his gaze for a long moment and then nodded slightly. "Come back safely, sir."

"What about me?" asked Chainer.

"You too, Frank."

Duggan spent a few minutes conferring with McGlashan on what he wanted. "Stay at a distance – the longer you remain overhead, the greater the chance they'll realise there's a spaceship close by. It'll alert them and we also don't want them taking shots at the *Crimson*. If we need to abort, get anyone alive away from the surface and then do whatever you have to in order to destroy this place," he said. "If we run into enemy forces on the ground and are defeated, there is no one in the Space Corps who will criticise your decision to return through the wormhole."

"There'll be no criticism, but there'll be plenty of disappointment," she said.

"That there will," Duggan admitted. "Do what you feel is right, Commander."

"You know we'll stay."

"Yes, I know."

"Don't die," she whispered.

"I'll do my best. You do the same."

The hour was running out, so Duggan and Chainer dashed to one of the lockers closest to the front boarding ramp. They fought their way into their spacesuits in the confines of a tiny alcove. Duggan snapped out a gauss rifle for each of them and fastened a bandolier of cylindrical plasma grenades across his chest.

"Want some grenades?" he asked Chainer.

"No, sir. I'm taking a beacon."

Duggan reached into the locker and pulled out a backpack containing portable comms equipment. "Byers and Durham are carrying these. It weighs about twenty-five pounds – are you sure you want one?"

Chainer took the pack and grunted as he pushed his arms through the straps. "I've carried one before, sir."

"What I'm trying to say politely is that I don't want you to slow us down."

"I know exactly what you're saying. I'll keep up."

"Good," said Duggan. "Grab your helmet and let's go see what these Ghasts are wearing for the occasion. We've got less than ten minutes until Commander McGlashan sets us down."

"There's not been much chance to check our inventory, has there?" said Chainer, breathing heavily as he followed. "Mech suits might be a bit unwieldy where we're going."

Right on schedule, McGlashan set the *Crimson* onto the ground, a few kilometres away from the perimeter of the base. Duggan and Chainer were running late and they reached the forward airlock five minutes after the agreed time. There were a few witty observations on the virtues of good timekeeping from the troops and Duggan acknowledged them ruefully.

"Sorry we're late, folks," he said, knowing his tardiness could have presented a genuine risk to the mission.

"No problem, sir," responded Ortiz politely, though he knew she was only trying to make him feel better.

The airlock was compact - a few square metres filled to over-flowing with human soldiers, each fully suited and with their helmets ready to fix in place. To the front, the Ghasts loomed large over the others. Duggan could see enough to tell they weren't dressed in their full mech suits, though he couldn't iden-tify exactly what they wore. They had dull metal encasing their heads and shoulders, giving the impression they were ancient gladiators. The rest was hidden from sight.

With no time to delay, Duggan put his suit helmet in place, ignoring the disconcerting feeling as it tightened about his neck. The others followed his lead, until everyone was ready to face the sub-zero temperatures outside the airlock.

He created an open comms channel for the human soldiers. There were ten other receptors close by and he brought those into the channel as well, pleased to note that the tech labs had been working hard on the interfaces between the human and Ghast technologies. There was no need to confirm with each man or woman that they could hear him. Instead, he spoke to the ship's bridge.

"We were late, Commander. We're lowering the ramp. Get away as soon as we're clear."

"Yes, sir."

It was a tight squeeze to get everyone into the airlock. The alternative was to go through two cycles of opening and closing, which was something Duggan was keen to avoid. With some pushing and shoving, they managed it and the ramp dropped away with a clunk of gears.

"Everybody off!" shouted Duggan.

Moments later, they were clear and standing in the dim light of Frades-2's dusk, the sky above visible through the cloaked outline of the spaceship. The boarding ramp rose until it joined seamlessly with the rest of the spaceship's hull. McGlashan didn't wait until they'd made any distance and she lifted off at once, the landing gear creaking as the thick legs were relieved from the unimaginable stresses of the *Crimson's* weight. There was scant turbulence on the ground – the planet had little in the way of air for the spaceship's passage to disturb.

After a short time, the *Crimson* was high above them in the dark sky. Duggan watched for a moment longer, trying in vain to catch sight of the vessel using his spacesuit sensor. Then, the craft was gone, leaving only a pattern of deep, rectangular indentations in the surface to mark the place it had landed. Its cargo of former passengers was left behind, waiting in a low shallow-walled valley out of sight from their intended destination.

Duggan stared around him. The terrain was bleak and inhospitable by most standards, though it was nothing worse than many other places he'd been. Now he was standing on it, Duggan saw how dirty the ice was. There was nothing clean and pure about it. This ice was riven through with grit and surface dust. It crunched beneath his feet and provided a surprising amount of grip.

Duggan turned left and right, ensuring the suit's direction-finder was properly calibrated with those of the squad. When his face was pointed towards the enemy emplacement, he spent a few seconds studying the lay of the land ahead. They'd landed six kilometres from the target. The terrain was rougher than he wanted, though this had been the most favourable place to begin. Once they emerged from the valley, there was a series of gullies, wending across rocky ground and leading to a final slope which would take them to the emplacement. The troops would be visible for a time, but there'd been no satisfactory alternative.

He took a few paces, passing through the men and women who clustered around him. One of the Ghasts – Rastol – was before him and Duggan got his first glimpse of what he wore. The aliens had evidently put some work in to modify the clumsy mech suits which Duggan remembered from his last encounter, and Rastol wore an evolution of the old kit.

The Ghast's helmet was a metal alloy trapezoid at the front, with a clear visor to the face inside. To the back, the helmet became more intricate and multi-faceted, giving an overall shape for which there was no precise word. Wide, angular plates of metal covered Rastol's shoulders, with several joints to allow him to move freely. His torso, arms and legs were covered in a heavy grey polymer, which closely resembled a human spacesuit, though it appeared to be less flexible. The Ghast's hands were clad in metal gauntlets which grasped the thick barrel of a repeater, and he wore heavy grey boots of an unknown material on his feet. All-in-all, the alien was a bizarre sight, though one which was filled with great menace. The suit must have weighed over a hundred pounds and Duggan was glad he wasn't wearing it himself.

"I've divided us into four squads of eight," he said, getting on with business. "Four *mixed* squads of eight. You know what we've got to do. Stick together until we get close. Let's move out."

Duggan set off and the others fell in behind, staying in their assigned squads. The slope stretched upwards for a few hundred metres. It was more difficult to climb than it appeared from below. The sides were treacherous with loose stones and gravel, held in place by the ice until an unwary foot pressed down upon it too hard. There was little risk of serious injury, but plenty of opportunity to snap an ankle. Duggan looked upwards into the never-ending sky. Even in Confederation space, there were too many stars to memorise their patterns. Here on Frades-2, the scattering of white dots was as different as anywhere else, but Duggan had never felt further from home.

CHAPTER FIFTEEN

AT THE TOP of the rise, the terrain flattened somewhat, yet it remained challenging to walk. One or two of the soldiers slipped, cursing onto the ice. Only their pride was hurt, though eventually something more severe would result from such accidents.

The *Crimson*'s scans of the surface had highlighted a series of channels through the rock, possibly resulting from the movement of ice. The squad picked their way across to the closest one. It was deeper and wider than Duggan had expected and he had to scramble down a short, steep slope until he was within. The channel was v-shaped and it wended onwards, not affording him a view more than a couple of hundred metres ahead. It was darker here and his sensor feed took on edges of intensified greens and the sharpness of the focus was replaced by grainy edges.

At the bottom, he carefully made his way another fifty metres and turned to watch the others join him in the gully. One figure came up to him, stepping carefully around the patches of ice.

"I don't like this," said Lieutenant Ortiz, through a private channel.

Duggan took her input seriously. "You think there's danger?"

"Not from the enemy, sir," she said firmly. "It's going to take us half the night to get along here." She kicked at the ground, knocking a hole through a nearby covering of ice which had looked solid at first glance. Duggan saw that the ice concealed a narrow, deep hole, which could easily have broken the leg of anyone who stepped into it.

"I've seen this shit before," Ortiz continued. "We could end up with four broken bones and half a dozen sprains before we get to where we're going. Corporal Weiss is good, but she can't fix injuries like that without getting back to the ship."

"You think we're better off climbing out of this channel?" he asked, indicating upwards with his hand.

"No, sir. If there's anything in those corner towers, they'll be able to pick us off easily when we advance. We need to remain hidden for as long as possible and that means we need to stay here. I just don't like it."

Duggan passed on the warning to the others. If this had been a rookie group, he'd have had real concerns after his conversation with Ortiz. As it was, he put the fears from his mind. If this team really was the best from its respective navies, they should be able to manage.

It took three hours careful march until the channel tapered off, forcing them towards the surface. The four towers were clearly visible from here, even without using magnification. Before leaving the protection of the gully walls Duggan spent some time with Ortiz and Red-Gulos, watching for anything that might indicate lookout posts at the top of the two-kilometre structures.

"They're featureless as far as I can tell," said Ortiz.

"That's what I gathered from the *Crimson*'s sensors when we flew overhead," said Chainer. "Sometimes you can miss things on a fast reconnaissance flight."

"What do you think?" Duggan asked, speaking directly to Red-Gulos. He didn't know if the Ghast's suit carried a more effective sensor than the ones in the Space Corps suits.

"It's clear," was all he said.

"In that case, we can go," said Duggan.

He pulled himself out of the gully and rolled smoothly to his feet. Instinct made him remain in a crouch to keep his profile low. The area around him contained good cover – there were large, loose stones, along with dips and crevices in the ground. Ultimately, it made little difference – if there were sophisticated early warning systems on the towers, there was scant chance they could arrive without being spotted. There was no indication the base was fortified and Duggan kept his hopes pinned on that.

The squad crossed a few hundred metres of ice-crusted stone. They were laden with weapons and encumbered by their space-suits, yet they managed to keep the noise to a minimum. Duggan heard the occasional contact of metal on metal and there were a few scuffs and scrapes as the troops fought to keep their footing. The Ghasts were unusually silent – Duggan had seen their protective clothing and worried they would sound like a hundred tin cans rattling when they walked. The aliens proved themselves better than expected and made no more noise than the others.

The ground levelled off, reaching a long summit that could almost be called a ridge. The towers and central pyramid reached into the night sky, their outlines so dark they could hardly be seen against the background by the naked eye. Only the glistening of distant ice provided a counterpart to the unending greys of unlit alloy.

Duggan lay flat on the ground and watched for a time, using the helmet sensor to look for anything which might be a threat.

"Two klicks to the perimeter," said Ortiz.

"No sign of movement," muttered Duggan.

"They are in there," said Red-Gulos. "This place is too big to be unguarded."

"I agree," said Ortiz.

"The target building is nine hundred metres past the perimeter," said Duggan. "We're going to get in and out as quickly as we can. As soon as our beacon has calibrated successfully with the enemy signal, the *Crimson* can use the data to locate the source transmitter. We won't need the emergency beacon to remain active for long."

He studied the place where the transmission was coming from. It was a long, rectangular building made from the same alloys as every other structure here. From a human perspective, it was four or five storeys in height. The squad needed to pass numerous other structures to reach this one – they varied in shape and size, none of them possessing any beauty or appeal.

"These were made off-world and dropped here," Duggan said, feeling compelled to speak the obvious.

"They didn't bother to fortify," said Ortiz. "There's not even a wall."

Duggan didn't need to warn against complacency - Ortiz was anything but lax. "We need to find better cover to get closer," he said. "The *Crimson's* scans showed we'll need to run the last part to the perimeter, but I'd prefer to stay under cover until then."

The spacesuit computer contained a topographical map of the area, downloaded from the *Crimson's* databanks. Duggan checked it to see what their options where. He'd plotted a route before they landed, but once on the surface, the terrain wasn't quite how it appeared from the fast scan they'd done.

"Over there," said Red-Gulos. "There is a channel which leads to the end of the downward slope."

"I think that's our best option," said Ortiz.

That was enough for Duggan. "Let's move. Single file," he said.

With his rifle held firmly in one hand, Duggan advanced

down the bank. He struggled for grip on the gritty, icy surface and had to put out his other hand to steady himself. The air was crystal clear and his suit told him it was touching minus two hundred degrees Fahrenheit. He suddenly felt exposed and he fought the urge to hurry.

No enemy gauss projectiles struck him and he reached the channel without injury, whereupon he clambered inside. A line of his soldiers followed, one or two of them swearing loudly into the open channel when they stumbled or slipped.

"Quiet in the channel!" barked Ortiz. "If you're not critically wounded, keep your mouths shut!"

The Ghasts made no sound. They found the terrain similarly challenging, yet when they lost their footing, they didn't speak of it and simply continued without complaint. *Different, not better,* Duggan reminded himself.

It took another forty minutes until they reached the end of this second channel. Vaughan was limping after twisting his knee between two rocks. Corporal Weiss gave him a shot of something in addition to whatever medication Vaughan took from his space-suit. Duggan checked the man was able to continue.

"It'll hurt like hell when all this crap wears off, sir," the soldier said. "Until then, you could stick a knife in me and I wouldn't know about it."

"Fine," said Duggan. "Shout out if you can't keep up."

"I'll keep up, sir."

Duggan left it at that. He'd already taken the measure of the squad and could tell there'd be no false bravado. These were men and women who'd seen it before and who would rather die than be remembered as the one who put their fellows in danger.

He conferred briefly with his officers.

"That's a five hundred metre run across open ground to the closest building," he said. "There's cover close to where the channel ends. Squad Four will stay here and provide sniper support. The other three squads will run for the perimeter and wait until Squad Four joins us."

"Will Squad Four be more effective if we leave them here while we do the business?" asked Ortiz. "We might need the cover."

"No," said Red-Gulos, crouched a few feet away. "Once we are amongst the buildings, snipers will become ineffective."

"I agree," said Duggan. "There are two main paths to our target. Squads One and Two will go to the left of this structure, Three and Four will go to the right. We'll move quickly and quietly. Shoot without asking questions and if the shit hits the fan, I'll make the decision on whether or not we withdraw. The *Crimson* can destroy this place from above if necessary. We don't need to take unnecessary risks. Is that understood?"

"We'll not throw our lives away, Captain Duggan," said the Ghast. "Not unless you order it."

"I look after my troops, Red-Gulos," Duggan replied, wondering if Ghast officers commonly gave orders for suicidal attacks. He'd seen the aliens act recklessly on many occasions and assumed it was part of their nature. Perhaps it was time to reconsider what he thought he knew.

The approach went smoothly at first. As silently as ghosts, Squad Four established positions that overlooked the lower buildings of the base – there wasn't much of a height advantage, but there was some. When Duggan gave the signal, the remaining three squads crept out from the gully. They kept fifty metres apart and dashed as quickly as they were able down the gentle slope towards their destination. The towers and central pyramid appeared brooding and threatening from such a close range. Duggan was accustomed to the enormity of what could be contrived by living hands, but there were still occasions when he was left in wonderment.

While he ran at the head of Squad One, Duggan studied the

closest buildings, trying to determine their purpose. They were tiny in comparison to the main power-generating structures, though many were the equivalent of three storeys tall or more. Mostly, they were featureless and cuboid. A few were cylindrical and others had corrugations on their outer surfaces. Whatever their purpose, they'd been placed in a haphazard manner, as if their position mattered not at all.

At three hundred metres, the suit detected a humming sound, which it relayed accurately to Duggan's ears. He identified the sound at once – it was similar to the gravity engines of a space ship, though he couldn't tell if the noise came from the main structures or from the smaller buildings.

The final two hundred metres was a treacherous scramble across dirty ice. Someone near Duggan fell over with a grunt, almost tripping up another soldier on the way. The trooper got up and followed without visible sign of injury. The space suits were tough and durable, but Duggan had seen them crack open under hard impacts before. It still put him on edge when he heard the sound of a suit helmet knocking against stone or metal – a breach meant certain death for the occupant.

At one hundred metres, Duggan was breathing hard. It wasn't so much the outright speed of his run, as it was the effort required to move fast while not sliding or falling. The buildings seemed to beckon him invitingly. He noted with satisfaction that there was no ice in the wide passages between them and the ground had been scoured flat by machinery of some sort.

Then, he heard the words. "Something's happening, Squad One - on the side of the building to your left."

Ahead, a square of bright light suddenly appeared in the wall of the closest building. It was unmistakeably a doorway, large enough to permit the exit of a creature in excess of seven feet tall. A shadow appeared within the doorway, then something stepped out into the dark of the night.

CHAPTER SIXTEEN

THE UNSUSPECTING CREATURE was met by a hail of gauss fire. Metal slugs fizzed from the barrel of Duggan's gun as he fired three shots in rapid succession. He was too late – the snipers in Squad Four had already put half a dozen rounds into it before he could pull the trigger. The alien toppled headlong to the ground, making a crunching noise when it impacted with the unyielding rock.

The ice underfoot was gone and Duggan broke into a sprint, his feet pounding against the pocked stone.

"Squad Two hold position!" he shouted into the comms.

Forty metres ahead, the body lay fallen across the threshold and the light from the interior continued to spill outside. Duggan reached the dead alien, the others of Squad One close behind. They fell into a circle, their rifles aimed outwards. There were two Ghasts whom Duggan had learned were called Rastol and Braler. They stood upright, the barrels of their repeaters aimed into the doorway.

"Help me get him out!" said Duggan, pulling at the body. It

was clad in a matte grey, flexible metal. Duggan could feel the material was incredibly thin and lightweight, though it hadn't been proof against a volley of gauss slugs. The enemy's spherical helmet had additionally been struck by three or four rounds, making a mess of whatever had been inside.

Stanton grabbed the creature's other arm and between them they hauled it out of the doorway, leaving a thick smear of frozen blood behind. Duggan had time to look into the aperture and saw nothing but the inside of an airlock, the same as he'd seen countless times in spacecraft and on various outposts throughout Confederation Space. As soon as the body was clear, an alloy door slid across, sealing the building once more.

"Rastol, Braler, pull this body out of sight," Duggan said, setting it down. "Get it around the corner towards the perimeter."

Without speaking a word, they moved to comply. They had holsters strapped to their backs into which they tucked their repeaters, taking care they didn't tangle the ammunition feed tubes. Once they had their hands free they pulled the dead Dreamer rapidly away, dragging it out of sight around the building which faced the perimeter.

"If you're going to abort, now is the time, sir," said Ortiz.

There was no other movement and nothing to indicate anyone else on the base had been roused.

"We'll stick to the plan, Lieutenant. Bring up Squad Four. Once they're here, we'll split and make our way to the target."

"Yes, sir!" she said, the relief evident in her voice. Ortiz didn't like to back away once the fighting had started.

Squads One, Two and Three waited anxiously as the final group broke cover and came towards the perimeter. Duggan fidgeted, tapping the barrel of his gun with his fingers. He spoke to the other squad leaders – Red-Gulos, Lieutenant Ortiz and another Ghost known simply as Gax. They understood what was expected and none of them showed outward concern at the unexpected encounter with the enemy.

"This base is big," said Duggan. "If we poke too hard, we could get out of our depths in no time."

Squad Four joined the others. Duggan immediately ordered all four groups onwards, deeper into the installation. He spoke to his own squad directly.

"Keep your movement sensors on. We're overlooked, so don't fall into the trap of watching your feet."

He strode away, keeping close to the left-hand wall of the nearby structure. Squad Two kept pace, twenty-five metres away next to the adjacent building. There was plenty of room, but it seemed best to travel independently. The last thing Duggan wanted was a friendly fire incident.

They reached the end of the wall and Duggan peered around. His breathing sounded loud in his ears – the imminence of battle had always heightened his senses. Whenever the fighting stopped, he told himself it was something he didn't crave. *The only person I ever lie to is me,* a treacherous voice in his head told him.

There was an open space to the left, which led to a wide gap between two more square buildings. Squad Two was moving out to the right, their rifles aimed in all directions. One person in each squad carried a shoulder-fired plasma launcher in case things got really tough and Duggan noticed the soldier in Squad Two had the weapon in place and ready to fire.

"Rasmussen, take heed," he said to his own squad's launcher man. "We have no idea what's coming."

"Yes, sir."

They sprinted across the space – eighty metres of hard running to find a wall they could put their backs to. Still there was no sign of the enemy and Duggan was sure this base had only a comparatively small number of personnel. On the other hand, sixteen square kilometres was enough to house a few hundred of the aliens, even if they were dispersed throughout the place.

"Door," grunted Rastol, thumping his elbow backwards onto the surface behind him. The contact made a solid thud which was in no way suggestive of there being a door. However, when Duggan looked, he noticed a fine seam in the alloy that did indeed indicate there was a way inside.

"We'd best move," said Duggan.

He led Squad One onwards, deeper into the base. The walls loomed above them to either side. The structures weren't crowded, but they somehow felt close. Above everything were the towers and the main pyramid. At times they were all visible, at others, they were obscured by these low buildings. The buzzing in the air which Duggan had noticed earlier became more prominent to the point that it set his teeth on edge.

He brought the others to a halt at the corner of one particularly high building. There was an open area beyond and there were at least two hundred metres to cross in order to reach the comparative safety of the passage opposite.

"That noise is pissing me off," muttered Byers while he waited.

"Your helmet can tune it out," said Cabrera.

"Yeah, I don't like to think I'm missing something."

"We've got action," said Ortiz on the open channel. The whine of gauss coils was audible in the background, their disturbance of the near-vacuum detected by her helmet sensor and converted into familiar sounds.

"Lieutenant, please report," said Duggan.

"Three of the enemy down, sir. No casualties of our own and no sign we were heard."

"We're running out of time until we find someone who shoots back or raises the alarm," said Duggan. "Move fast."

The words hadn't left his mouth when he saw a flash of movement, followed by the fizz of a rifle. "Got the bastard," said Camacho.

"There's more," said Braler, leaning past Duggan to look around the corner. "Six."

"Trust us to arrive in the middle of party time," said Rasmussen.

"Have they seen us?" asked Duggan.

"No," said Braler. "They show no indication they are aware of our presence."

Duggan had a look. The movement sensors on his suit helmet highlighted the enemy with an outline of orange. Alongside the greens of the image intensification and whites of the heat detection, it was a sickly combination of colours, which performed an excellent job of pinpointing to the suit's occupant things they might want to shoot.

The enemy were heading away from Duggan's squad and he was content to wait until they were out of sight. His suit estimated the largest to be over seven and a half feet tall, with the shortest at seven feet. He didn't know what he should call them – they were Dreamers, Ghasts and Estral. *Stay focused!* he thought angrily, realising his mind had drifted onto unimportant matters.

"We are under attack," said Red-Gulos. "Estimate seven Estral soldiers."

A muted roar accompanied the Ghast's voice – it was his repeater, firing with the muzzle silencer turned on. It reduced the accuracy and velocity of the projectiles at the same time as it cut down on the noise.

According to his spacesuit's positional overlay of the area, Lieutenant Ortiz was closest. "Squad Three, move to assist," said Duggan.

"Yes, sir. Moving to assist," she said, her voice business-like and crisp.

"The six enemy we've sighted are coming to investigate the noise," said Braler.

Without waiting for orders, the Ghost took a large step sideways, the muzzle of his repeater level and the feed tube tucked under his arm. The gun shook as it launched hundreds of rounds from the alloy ammunition pack Braler wore on his back. There was no light, only the sound of perfectly-machined metal striking perfectly-machined metal as the weapon spewed out a cone of death into the coming enemy. Seconds later, the cacophony stopped and Braler ducked into the protection of the wall again.

"Pathetic," he spat.

"Dead?" asked Duggan.

"Yes."

"Next time, you wait. Do you understand?"

"I understand," said the Ghost.

"Good. I say when you shoot," said Duggan. He put the incident aside for now – it was a minor transgression, but he didn't know if it was indicative of the Ghasts' thirst to fight anything, or specifically this particular enemy. He was brought crashing back to the present.

"Enemy down," said Ortiz. "We lost Fuentes."

"Understood," said Duggan. "Any movement?"

"Not yet, sir."

"They'll be coming. Let's get to the target."

In terms of maintaining surprise, the game was up. They were far into the base now and Duggan was determined to finish what they'd come to do. He got his head down and launched himself at the space between him and the next structure. According to his HUD, the target building was less than four hundred metres away, though there was no way to get a visual on it until they were right there. While he ran, Duggan spoke briefly to the *Crimson*.

"*ESS Crimson*, this is Duggan. We've met resistance. We are proceeding to the target."

"This is Commander McGlashan. Need support?"

"Negative, Commander. I am not able to guarantee there are no air defences. Stay out of sight until you hear otherwise."

"Understood. I'll await further orders."

There was a flickering hint of orange to the left. Duggan fired off a snap shot, sure he'd missed by a good two metres. Someone else in the squad aimed better and the orange shape fell into clear view. Duggan fired again and the movement stopped.

They entered the scant protection of a wide corridor between two structures. Duggan would have preferred to take stock of the situation and catch his breath. He had plenty of stamina, but his aim was better when his heart wasn't pounding. Someone fired a shot and he spun around to see Camacho lower his rifle.

"Camacho gets another one," the soldier said.

"You need to stop talking about yourself in the third person, man," said Stanton.

"Camacho only does it when he's in the zone," joked Camacho.

"Quiet!" warned Duggan. "Squads Two, Three, Four, please report."

"We're approaching the target," said Red-Gulos. "No casualties."

"We're sticking with Squad Two," said Ortiz.

"Nothing to report," said Gax. "No enemy sighted."

"We've poked the nest," said Duggan. "There'll be more."

Squads Two and Three reached the target building ahead of the rest. Duggan moved at a fast pace which nevertheless still allowed his own squad to react to the unexpected. There was something about his time within this installation that gave him an insight into the life of a mouse travelling around a maze. Everything was so totally alien, he wondered if he'd been knocked unconscious and left to dream about an endless succession of walls, filled with an endless series of enemies for him to fight. The voice of Lieutenant Ortiz came through his comms.

"No sign of a way in, sir," she said.

"Any doors?" asked Duggan.

"Two that we know of, sir. Not a handle or a doorbell to be found."

"Get Reilly and Bonner on it," he said. These two were in charge of the explosives.

"They're already looking."

"What about the enemy?"

"They've gone into hiding."

"The calm before the storm," said Duggan. "I see you."

Duggan's squad came within sight of the target building. It was taller than he imagined it would be and perhaps three hundred metres long, with a brushed appearance to the exterior. Several other structures were close by, making this area fairly tight, with narrow alleys leading off. Squads Two and Three had arranged themselves defensively. They lay flat on the ground, or hid behind the walls of the other buildings nearby. The Ghasts were easily identified by their suits and their outright size. Duggan was pleased to see they'd fitted in well and the aliens had mixed with the humans, rather than keeping close to their own.

"Reilly, Bonner? We need to get in and fast."

"Understood."

"Got inbound to the east," said Chan. "I'd estimate fifteen or twenty. They've got hardware with them." The soldier's voice varied not one bit with the pressure of the situation. He could have been reporting how many potatoes he'd found on his meal tray for all the excitement he betrayed.

"How long and what hardware? Plasma or coil?"

"Coil, sir and they'll be here in thirty seconds. There's me, Barron and Kidd to hold them. We need someone with a tube."

"Rasmussen, get over there," ordered Duggan. "Squad Four, where the hell are you?"

"Coming your way," said Gax. "One minute. There's movement to the north-west. Big numbers and organised."

An inner voice told Duggan it was about to get tough.

CHAPTER SEVENTEEN

THE COMBAT BEGAN. It started slowly, with the coil whine of sporadic rifle fire. Repeater fire joined – the harsh edge and clanking roar telling Duggan that the Ghasts no longer had their weapons silenced. More sightings of the enemy came in from the west and the east. The base personnel were on full alert and looking for the intruders.

"Get us through that door, or we're going to be overrun," said Duggan.

Reilly and Bonner continued to examine the metal, occasionally knocking at it with gloved fists. They had packs of explosives on the ground nearby, though showed no inclination to remove the contents.

"Do you want it to remain pressurised inside, sir?" asked Bonner, dead calm.

"I don't give a shit, soldier. We need to get inside however it happens."

Reilly gave the strange little jumping motion with her upper torso that indicated a shrug. "Get one of the plasma guys to shoot it. The walls here aren't thick."

"Berg, shoot this damned wall as soon as we get clear," said Duggan.

"Aye, sir. You'd best run."

Duggan didn't hang around. "Keep clear of the door," he yelled, charging towards a wall opposite.

Thirty metres away, the suited figure of Berg raised a plasma tube, positioning it on her shoulder like it was a natural extension of her body. The tube bleeped softly and its high-pitched whine cut through the metallic clattering of the other weaponry. She fired and the tube spat out its projectile. A split second later, the darkness was dispersed by a brief flash of plasma fire. Duggan's suit registered an abrupt change in temperature. When he turned, there was a smouldering, ragged gap in the metal. The edges burned in fading whites and reds, causing the alloy to sag and drip. The suit registered a soft whooshing sound and informed Duggan there was a low-speed wind, which he knew was the internal atmosphere of the building rushing out.

"Watch out for anyone inside!" he shouted.

The vignette ended and the brutality of combat filled Duggan's senses. His troops were pinned down, but had so far managed to keep the enemy at bay. The arrangement of the buildings allowed the Estral three approaches and they darted in and out of view, firing their rifles. Across the way, Duggan saw Rasmussen pre-charge his plasma tube and then fire it along a passage to the east. Orange movement was lost in a wash of white flame.

Then, something ripped through the fire – something which didn't care what was in its path. Large bore, high-velocity slugs tore into the wall of the transmission building, leaving a series of indentations for fifty metres or more.

"Coil gun!" shouted Chan.

"Hendrix, assist Rasmussen," instructed Red-Gulos.

"We need to get inside!" said Duggan.

"It's not good for falling back, sir," said Ortiz.

Duggan could see she was right. His troops were in good positions, from which they could keep the enemy at bay. If they moved, they would be exposed to gunfire, or weaken the position of the others.

"Hold!" he said. He opened up a separate channel to the *Crimson*. "Commander McGlashan, this is Duggan. We need support. Get here now."

She answered at once, as though she'd been waiting to hear his voice. "Two minutes until we're overhead. We'll have to come in low and use the Bulwarks, unless you want to risk the Lambdas. Any more sign of anti-air defences?"

"Negative. Don't take it for granted, though. Hold off the Lambdas."

"Yes, sir."

Duggan ended the conversation and shouted through the open channel to the troops. "Keep your heads down, we've got air support incoming. It's not going to be pretty."

"I'm shot," exclaimed Stanton.

"On my way," said Corporal Weiss.

"Aw crap, save your legs," said Stanton.

With that, the man was gone, his suit reporting a loss of vital signs to the network. Duggan caught a glimpse of the body, or what remained of it. The wonder was how the man had lived long enough to say anything, let alone speak as calmly as he had.

The chaos went on unabated, this man's life washed away in the storm of metal. Duggan looked to the skies, before berating himself for thinking he'd be able to see their salvation even with assistance from the helmet sensor. He pressed his rifle to his shoulder and pulled the trigger until his finger ached, aiming along the passage to the east. The enemy were becoming bolder and he saw the ominous shape of another large-bore gauss gun. A plasma round shrieked towards it, exploding with a thump and scattering a dozen shapes away from the blast. When the flames receded, the gauss gun remained, vibrating with the recoil as it fired.

"It's looking busy down there," said McGlashan.

"Tell me something I don't know," Duggan replied.

He armed one of his plasma grenades and threw it into the alley, trying to hit the coil gun. Another man nearby did the same and the grenades detonated simultaneously. The coil gun was tipped onto its side, though it continued to fire into the wall of an adjacent building.

Duggan sensed something overhead. To his surprise, McGlashan had brought the *Crimson* in so low he felt as if he could touch it. The spaceship remained cloaked, but a positional feed from its AI told him it was there. It hung in the air level with the corner towers, like an ancient god come to bring wrath upon the enemies of its worshippers. The sound of Bulwark fire rose above everything, a cacophonous rumble of slugs colliding with the ground and the alloy buildings. The projectiles left white lines in the air, enough to show that McGlashan had opened fire with all four underside cannons. The traces danced through the darkness and whatever they touched was ripped to pieces, shattered and ruined. Duggan looked around him and saw a nearby structure torn into molten fragments. Shards of rock clattered and pinged, before rattling down to the earth. Duggan crouched as low as he could and waited for the tempest to end.

"Shit," said a voice across the open channel, the word almost drowned out by the noise. Laughter followed the voice, high-pitched and with the hysterical edge of a man lost to battle.

The Bulwark fire stopped. Duggan checked the *Crimson*'s position and saw it was moving. A grumbling of stressed gravity engines shook the ground and the spaceship raced off, vanishing within moments, its hull already burning hot as it disappeared across the horizon.

"Got an inbound enemy vessel sir. I'm drawing them away," said McGlashan, breathless with excitement. "You've got about twenty seconds before the troops on the base realise we've gone."

There was no time to ask further questions. "Fall back! Get inside the building!" said Duggan.

The soldiers didn't need to be asked twice. With well-oiled precision, they came away from their positions and dashed for the opening in the wall of the communications building. Some remained to provide cover, throwing grenades and firing their rifles indiscriminately into the passages between the surrounding buildings. Once the first groups of soldiers were inside, Berg and Hendrix remained outside to launch plasma rockets at whatever they thought might be a threat. The remainder of the squad made it safely inside and Duggan climbed through the opening after them.

He took stock of their situation. The plasma launcher strike against the wall of the target building had opened a hole in the outer wall and also through the side wall of the inner airlock. This provided access to the building's interior and Duggan ducked through the opening to where the others waited. If there was any oxygen still to escape, it hardly registered as a breeze through the hole.

There was a large room beyond, lit in pale blue – it had long walls, a high ceiling and was more than big enough to accommodate the four squads with space left over. A few pieces of curved metal furniture were scattered randomly about, and there was a fixed console in the far corner. Everything was bare, unpainted metal, including the floor. In addition, there were a couple of doorways. One was sealed by a door, whilst the second had closed halfway and been stopped by the body of one of the former occupants.

"It's dead, sir," said Ortiz. "Suffocated when we burned our way through the wall."

Duggan had seen the effect a vacuum had on his friends and enemies alike – swollen tissues, hands raised to the throat and a look of terror on the faces of the victims. He didn't need to see it again.

"Squads Two and Four hold this entrance," he said. "Watch out for explosives. We don't know how many ways in there are, so watch your backs. Squad Three, you're coming with me. We need to fix the beacon in place and then get out of here." With a shock, Duggan realised he'd forgotten all about Chainer since they'd landed. "Lieutenant Chainer, where are you?"

"I'm here, sir," said Chainer.

"Ready to see how our enemy work their comms?"

"Yes, sir."

"Let's move. Quickly, people!"

With that, Duggan jogged the ten metres to the half-open doorway. He looked through cautiously and saw another room, similarly-sized and with an array of screens in the wall. There were rolling lists of text, too small for him to make out from where he was standing.

"Two more dead," he said. "Killed because this door was jammed open."

It appeared as though the breach in the outer wall had activated the emergency lock-down on the internal doors. The three exits from this second room were all sealed. Just then, he heard the sound of gunfire, reminding him of the urgency to act without delay.

"Braler, Rastol. These are your long-lost cousins. See if you can figure out how to open their doors," he said.

"These are not our cousins," said Rastol, heading over the room towards one of the doors.

Duggan ignored the rebuke. "Lieutenant Chainer, where do we need to be?"

"Top floor is usually a good guess, sir. Even if their main receptor and transmitter is underground, there's likely to be a conduit which carries the signal to the roof."

"I thought you might say that," he said.

A faint hiss made him look in time to see the far door slide open. There was no outrush of air and he wondered if much of the building had depressurized before they could lock it down. In the Space Corps, with its emphasis on safety, it seemed absurd that such a thing could happen. He remembered his suspicion about the Ghasts' lax approach to such matters and guessed they still had much in common with the Dreamers.

"Clear," said Braler.

"We need stairs," said Duggan. "Or a lift."

The two squads went through the doorway into another room, near-identical to the previous one and with more sealed doors. Duggan was struck by how similar it was to many of the working areas in a Space Corps building. Whatever the function of a place, the occupants still needed to sit and they still needed screens to work at.

"Which way?" asked Ortiz. She kept her rifle pointed outwards and its barrel didn't waver.

There were more sounds of gunfire from outside and something else clattered against the building, sending reverberations through the walls.

"They've got another coil tube," muttered Camacho. Ground troops had a healthy respect for the stopping power of these guns.

"Rastol, show us how to open these doors," Duggan commanded, walking to the closest. He signalled the others to stay to the sides so they wouldn't present a target to anything which might be waiting in the room beyond.

There was a square indentation in the metal wall, shallow

enough that it was easy to miss. Rastol reached out an alloy-clad hand and dragged the tips of his middle three fingers diagonally across. "Like this," he said.

The door opened and Duggan heard something ping away from the metal nearby. He crouched to the side of the door, but not before he'd seen the movement of several shapes the next room. Gauss rifles discharged and Duggan heard one of the enemy crash into something heavy.

There was a further exchange of fire. Duggan and his squad weren't exposed and they unleashed a volley of slugs though the opening. Two more of the enemy died and the gunfire ceased.

"Camacho gets another."

"I got that one," said Byers.

"Shut up unless you want to hear me say *Ortiz shoots two stupid bastards*," snarled Ortiz. "I need some damned discipline!"

"Sorry Lieutenant."

"These aren't organised," said Duggan, taking a look into the room. There were three dead bodies, wearing the same suits as he'd seen on the others outside.

"It's a comms building, sir," said Chainer. "You'd find the same sort of people at the Tillos base. They're not likely to be trained for this."

"I'm not in the mood to feel sorry for them."

They entered the room, scanning the far corners for anyone who might be hiding. It was quiet and Duggan's helmet sensor registered no movement, only the rapidly-dissipating heat from the aliens they'd just killed.

"We are under great pressure," said Red-Gulos on the squad leader channel.

"Keep them back," Duggan replied, trying to decide which exit to take.

"We'll have to retreat into the building soon."

With every passing moment, the situation become steadily

more perilous for Duggan and his troops. Even if they managed to install the emergency beacon, they were still confronted with the knowledge that the *Crimson* was gone and an enemy warship was somewhere above.

Pushing the worries from his mind, Duggan got on with business.

CHAPTER EIGHTEEN

"THIS ONE IS A LIFT," said Braler.

The Ghost stood adjacent to a doorway that looked like all the others – two metres wide and three tall.

"Open it," said Duggan.

Braler made a different gesture to the one required to open the other doors. "This is something we have in common with our former brothers," he said. "Our doors open in the same way."

The words concealed a thousand feelings and centuries of unspoken history. Duggan didn't respond and waited for the lift door to open. The others of his squad were positioned around the room, several with their rifles aimed at the descending lift. It took a few moments to arrive and as he stood, shifting his weight impatiently from foot to foot, Duggan caught sight of one of the display screens mounted into a wall next to him. He had to do a double-take when he realised some of the words were familiar. Then it came to him – the Dreamers and Ghasts shared a language. There may have been several hundred years of divergence, but the language modules in his suit computer knew enough of the Ghast script to be able to offer him a rough interpretation. *Haxun-TN to Control Room B,* he read. *It's the same shit in a different language.*

The thought was comforting – the realisation that the enemy had motives he could understand. He might not know why they were so hostile to other races, but the fact they were trying to exterminate humanity was something he could look at and respond to appropriately.

Had the lift pinged when it arrived, Duggan would have struggled to cope with the peculiarity of it all. However, the lift made no sound and the door opened. It was empty inside and there was room for only one of the two squads within.

"Squad One and Lieutenant Chainer get in," he said.

There was a panel on the right-hand wall of the lift. "Where to?" asked Rastol.

"Top floor."

The Ghost poked a finger at the top area of the panel. The door closed and there was the sensation of movement. The feeling of being within the enemy lift intensified the strangeness of the situation. Duggan had fought for years, but it was usually on inhospitable terrain. Occasionally he'd fought the Ghosts in mining outposts or research stations. On the Frades-2 base, he felt like he was involved in the first truly urban combat since he'd joined the Corps. The enemy weren't civilians, but they weren't exactly combat-ready.

"This is crazy," said Rasmussen, leaning against his plasma launcher.

"There's still zero atmosphere," said Camacho. "I thought they'd have got the top floors locked down."

"Be grateful they haven't," Duggan replied.

"Some of that Bulwark fire must have punctured the walls."

"Sucks for whoever wasn't in a suit."

"It doesn't suck for us, Cabrera. That's the only thing I care about," said Byers without emotion.

The lift stopped moving. "Ready?" asked Rastol.

"Open it," said Duggan, crouching with the others.

The Ghost pressed the panel and the door opened. The space beyond was in darkness, with no sound or movement. "Out, quick," said Duggan, exiting the lift and pressing himself to the right-hand side of the aperture. He could hear the discharge of weapons from the area outside the comms building and when his sensor adjusted to the darkness, he could make out a series of jagged holes through the ceiling and into the floor. The punctures in the alloy were about two metres across and their edges were still cooling.

"Looks like you were right about the Bulwarks, Camacho," said Duggan. He had no idea if McGlashan had fired at the building accidentally or by design. Either way, it had likely saved numerous lives amongst the *Crimson*'s contingent of soldiers. "Lieutenant Ortiz, please reinforce the other squads on the ground floor. It looks like we can handle what's up here."

"Roger."

"This way," said Chainer, keeping his voice to an unnecessary whisper.

Duggan gave a mental shrug at the man's certainty and headed to a closed door in the far wall. The room was more than thirty metres across and he passed several holes, marvelling at the destructive ability of the Bulwark cannons when put to this unintended use. He peered into one of the two-metre holes through the floor – it went all the way to the bottom, cutting through the building at an angle.

Chainer's pace increased, as if he were desperate to see what technology the aliens possessed, or perhaps he simply wanted to be out of this place as soon as possible. He reached the door first.

"Can I open it?" he asked.

"Go ahead," said Duggan, keeping himself flat against the wall on the opposite side of the door.

Chainer copied the gesture he'd seen the Ghasts make and the door opened. There was a smaller room beyond – little more than three metres square. There was a single exit door – this one unmistakeably designed to repel casual attempts to get through. It was thickly banded with alloy and there was no panel to either side.

"Bingo," said Chainer.

Duggan took one look at the door and got on the comms. "Reilly get up here," he said.

"Reilly's dead," said Red-Gulos.

"Send Bonner."

"On my way, sir," Bonner replied.

"Rasmussen, leave your launcher. Go back and help her find her way."

"Sir," he said. He propped the plasma tube against the wall. It slipped to one side and Rasmussen was only just quick enough to catch it. "Sorry," he said. "It wouldn't have gone off."

While they waited, Duggan took a look at the door. He thumped it with his fist – it could have been a metre thick for all he knew. "Any ideas how to get this open without explosives?" he asked, directing the question at the two Ghasts.

"This would be internally controlled on one of our bases," said Braler.

"Let's wait for Bonner to get here."

It didn't take long. Bonner would have been easy to spot even without the HUD within the spacesuit helmets, since she carried the distinctive pack which any soldier would know contained explosives.

"It's getting hot back there," she said.

"I know," Duggan replied. "Get this open and do it fast."

Bonner stepped past and into the small room. She repeated the procedure of hitting the door. Duggan was half-expecting a long show and he was pleased to find the soldier didn't keep them waiting.

"Get back to the far wall near the lift and hide behind something," she said. "And so you know, anyone beyond this blast door is going to be incinerated."

"I only care about the comms kit," said Duggan.

"It should be okay, but I'm not offering any guarantees. If you want quick, those are the compromises."

"Do it," said Duggan. "Make sure you don't fall through any of these holes when you're finished." He waved the others away and hurried out of the small room as Bonner began removing grey bundles from her pack.

"There's room over here," said Cabrera, waving from the far corner.

Duggan changed direction and skirted around one of the holes in the floor. There was a wide console fixed to the floor, five feet high and with a chair before it. Two of the four screens were still operational and they displayed a list of status reports relating to something else on the base.

"Keep your heads down," said Bonner.

There was the sound of footsteps, rapidly coming closer. A few seconds later, there was a crackling, spitting noise, which Duggan recognized as a limpet charge burning a hole into the alloy. This allowed a larger, secondary charge to rip open the door.

"Here goes."

The secondary charge went off with a sharp crash, followed by a loud hissing that went on for a further ten seconds. Even though Duggan was a good distance away, the surrounding temperature climbed several degrees and the room was bathed in brilliant light for a moment. Then, the light faded to a sullen, distant glow.

"Done," said Bonner.

"Don't rush in!" called Duggan. "Check for hostiles!"

He put his head over the top of the console. The explosives were smokeless but they generated an enormous amount of heat and light. His sensor took a time to adjust to the contrast. There was burning metal through the doorway, which made it difficult to determine if the enemy hid within.

"Anything alive will have been burned to a cinder," said Bonner, rising to her feet and advancing towards the doorway. "Come on."

Without warning, Bonner spun around in a grotesque parody of a ballerina's pirouette. She fell to the ground behind another of the metal tables, out of Duggan's sight.

"Wait, I said!" he bellowed.

"There's something in there," said Byers.

A gauss rifle whined. "Camacho shoots an alien in the face."

"Stay the hell down!" said Duggan. "Bonner, where are you hit?"

"In the shoulder. It looks bad, but the suit's sealed it up nicely. Sorry, sir."

Slugs pinged off the wall nearby.

"You didn't get shit, Camacho," said Byers.

"Three more hostiles," called Cabrera. "*At least* three more."

"I can get a plasma shot straight into there, sir," said Rasmussen.

"Hold!" said Chainer. "No more explosives!"

"Do as the lieutenant asks," Duggan ordered.

The situation became a stalemate. The enemy were holed up in the room beyond, having taken cover behind some of the equipment which was installed in there. As the outer door cooled and hardened, the Estral became easier to see – their orange outlines appearing and then vanishing as they ducked in and out of cover. Duggan guessed them to have coil guns or something similar and was relieved they didn't start throwing explosives. At the first sign of an enemy grenade, he'd be forced to order Rasmussen to use the plasma launcher to take them out, and that might well do enough damage to cut off the transmission they'd come to trace.

As the seconds passed, the messages over the open comms gave away the increasingly desperate situation of the troops below. They were being pushed and pushed hard, and it was doubtful they'd be capable of holding off the enemy for much longer.

A figure rose to its feet in the corner closest to the enemy. It was Rastol, having made his way across the room, keeping the angle too tight for the enemy to get a shot at him. On the other side, Braler climbed upright. Without hesitation, they ducked into the ante-room, Rastol first. The Ghast fired his repeater as soon as he turned the corner. The weapon produced no muzzle flash, but the noise was thunderous. He went down under a hail of enemy fire, only for Braler to take his place, pouring hundreds of rounds into the room ahead of him. The repeater stopped and a temporary quiet descended.

"It is clear," said Braler.

Duggan broke cover and ran the length of the room. Rastol was dead, his body chewed up by a dozen slugs. Braler was hurt – he'd taken a shot in the arm and there was blood. The Ghast acted as if nothing was wrong.

"Make your transmission," the alien said.

Duggan pushed past into what was unmistakeably a comms and control room. There were screens covering one wall, many of them damaged by ricochets from the repeaters. Two consoles were off to the side – big, complex affairs similar to the sort found on a warship or in a military base. There was damage to the equipment – a combination of heat and impact. To the left, a wide, grey cylinder reached from floor to ceiling. It had no markings – it didn't need them for Duggan to know what it was.

"Lieutenant Chainer, get in here. Bring Byers with you. She needs to see this as well."

Chainer arrived, lugging his pack, with Byers close behind and carrying her own.

"Is this what you wanted?" asked Duggan?

"This'll do nicely, sir."

"Get on and do it, then."

Chainer practically jumped across to one of the seats and sat himself in front of a panel, his foot resting carelessly on the dead body of one of the enemy. Duggan was feeling the pressure and he took himself out of the room, pacing about as he waited.

CHAPTER NINETEEN

"I THINK I can use this stuff, sir," said Chainer after a short time. "My old mother always said if you can read Ghast, you can read anything. The Dreamer kit clearly has the same origins."

"We're in trouble here, Lieutenant."

"I'll let you worry about that, sir. I won't need long."

In the minute or two since Chainer had sat himself in front of the enemy comms, the squads below had been forced into an orderly withdrawal deeper into the building. Duggan was concerned in case they became separated, so he was relieved when Lieutenant Ortiz entered the room, bringing several other soldiers with her.

"We're facing the proper troops now," she said. "They're disciplined and show good order, which wouldn't normally be a problem except that there're so damned many of them." She gave a command and those with her ran away to help fortify this part of the building. "Why haven't they turned the really heavy stuff on us?" she asked.

"It's their base, Lieutenant. Why would they do that? It's the only thing keeping us alive with that warship of theirs flying overhead."

Duggan had a growing certainty that this base was of profound importance to the enemy. *What's important to them is vital to us,* he thought, remembering the adage from his training classes.

A sound reached him through the many holes in the roof of the building. At first he thought it might be thunder, before his brain dismissed the idea. The noise built and he felt a vibration in the walls and the floor. It continued, increasing rapidly until Duggan feared the enemy had brought a new weapon into the attack. A shockwave struck the building from the east. The outer wall creaked and buckled, before splitting with a rending shriek. Wind rushed in, buffeting the soldiers inside. They dropped to the floor in alarm.

"What the hell?" shouted Cabrera.

"Stay down!"

The building was huge and made from hard alloys, but it had been damaged by the Bulwark rounds. It flexed and groaned while the floor crumpled, leaving rows of irregular creases from one side to the other. Duggan's HUD flashed up an emergency warning.

"Gamma rays," he said. "The *Crimson* must have dropped a nuke somewhere!"

The shockwave subsided, leaving half of the outside wall torn open. Duggan waved the troops deeper into the room so they wouldn't present a target to the enemy troops on the ground outside.

"Commander McGlashan, please report," he said, doing his best to keep the alarm from his voice. He got no response and he swore, wondering if the radiation was interfering with his signal or if something had happened to the spaceship.

As he looked outside into the sky, something struck one of the corner towers a third of the way up from the ground. A huge plasma detonation shook the structure, the blast spreading for several hundred metres. The light faded and the tower remained standing, blackened in places and burning in others. There followed a series of further blasts in rapid succession, each new detonation adding to the ballooning cloud of plasma. Half of the tower vanished behind the roiling fury.

For a brief moment, it seemed as though the combat nearby had ceased, allowing everyone in the room time to stare in awe at this display. The plasma burned out, leaving the tower leaning at an angle and canted inwards towards the centre of the base. It was a wonder it remained upright, given the huge craters clustered across its side.

"It's going to fall," said Camacho.

It happened slowly at first, as if the tower was reluctant to submit to the relentless stresses it was under. The tilt increased and there was a grotesque screech of tortured alloy.

"Shit it's coming our way," said Chan.

He was right – whatever bad luck dogged them this day, it pushed its invisible hand against the tower, sending it inexorably towards the comms building.

"Stand up and face it," said Ortiz.

Duggan attempted an estimate based on the tower's height and the distance from their location, to see if they would survive. He gave up at once – it would take too long and ultimately, he was either going to live or die with no say in the matter.

With increasing speed, the tower fell. It crashed into the ground, flattening everything beneath. The impact was far beyond anything the rock could support and the earth shook again. A couple of the soldiers staggered and grabbed for something to steady themselves, still unable to wrench their eyes away. The tower bounced a few metres into the air and slid along a few more, before coming to rest fifty metres from the split in the wall of the comms building.

"I'm lost for words, man," said Barron. "In all my years..."

At that point, Chainer came from the inner room. "All done," he said, affecting nonchalance. "What was all that commotion?" One of the soldiers pointed and Chainer looked over. "I see," he said.

A series of reports came across the open channel in quick succession from the troops guarding the lift and a nearby stairwell.

"What're the orders, sir?" asked Ortiz. "The enemy are gathering and we need to get out of this radiation."

"One moment, Lieutenant. I'm trying to reach the *Crimson*." Duggan tried once more to get through. "Nothing!" he said.

"There're too many emissions for the suit comms, sir," said Chainer. "They've got some big signal amplifiers through here. Come on, I can get you a piggyback."

Duggan followed into the other room. Chainer sat down and pressed at the console like he'd been using it since birth. "If I've said it once, I've said it a thousand times. Everything has a best way. Wherever you go in the universe, certain things will need to be done in certain ways."

"Indeed," said Duggan, not really listening. "Will it take long?"

"It's done, sir."

"*ESS Crimson*, this is Duggan, please respond."

"Captain?" It was McGlashan and she sounded relieved.

"Lieutenant Chainer has sorted out the beacon. Can you see it?"

"Yes, sir. The AI's analysing the feed. I'm sure Frank's done what we needed."

"The problem is we're stuck in the enemy's comms building

with an entire base worth of troops wanting to say hello. We need assistance."

"I'm still dancing with the enemy warship, sir. Since they know you're there, I figured it couldn't hurt to send a couple of high explosives into the vicinity. I'm a few minutes away now."

"Can you drop some armour at our location?"

"That's something I can manage. I won't be able to stick around for long."

"Think you can put it on the roof?"

"I can leave it wherever you want it, sir."

"Aim carefully – if it lands in on the ground instead it's game over for us. And Commander? Make sure on your next flyover you do the maximum possible damage to this facility."

"Will do, sir."

"Good luck."

With McGlashan gone, he spoke his orders into the open channel. "We need to get to the roof. Things are really going to get interesting in the next few minutes."

Whilst he'd been distracted with other matters, the enemy had penetrated deep into the comms building. Duggan's squads held them at two stairwells on the top floor, where they engaged in a deadly game involving grenades and small-arms fire. It was the sort of situation which could take a long time to play out, or one in which the balance might suddenly shift. If nothing changed, there was only going to be one losing side.

"There's no way up," said Ortiz. "You'd think these alien bastards would have put in a ladder or something."

The sounds of gunfire came through her helmet speaker and Duggan assumed she was getting herself into trouble somewhere close by. "We don't need a ladder, Lieutenant. There are a series of perfectly good holes in the ceiling."

"Whatever you say, sir."

"Braler, Glinter, break off and get here," said Duggan. "I need some muscle."

Before the Ghasts arrived, Duggan, Chainer and Byers hauled whatever loose furniture they could find into position beneath one of the holes above. The ceiling was high and Duggan hoped he'd not been too cocky in asking for the armoured vehicle to be dropped on the roof.

Braler entered the room, the barrel of his repeater glowing red.

"We're going out there," said Duggan, indicating the ceiling. "Help us uproot a couple of these consoles."

"There's no time. I can lift our soldiers high enough for them to get through."

"That means leaving you behind. I won't allow that to happen."

The Ghast grinned, showing the first signs of humour Duggan could recall from him. "There'll be no one left."

"You've been shot."

"It's of no consequence. I'll see the medic when we've returned to the warship."

That was what Duggan needed to hear and he gave an order. "Lieutenant Ortiz, Red-Gulos, Gax, please organize a withdrawal into this room. As quickly as possible."

In pairs, the troops came through the doorway. Braler put his repeater to one side and boosted the men and women up towards the ceiling, lifting them easily. The soldiers were strong and fit, so it was no great hardship for them to drag themselves out through one of the holes and onto the roof.

"Watch the edges," said Barron, the first one up.

"Lay flat," warned Duggan. "I'd like to avoid notice for as long as possible."

"Roger."

The next one due up was Glinter – he was a Ghast from Red-

Gulos' squad. Duggan was concerned the extra weight would cause problems. He need not have worried – with a grunt of effort, Braler lifted his comrade high enough that he could grip the edge. With a swing, the Ghast got one of his booted feet onto the rim and then it was a simple matter for willing hands to drag him through. One by one, the rest of the soldiers reached the top.

"The last guys will need to move fast," said Ortiz. "I don't know how much longer the enemy are going to be fooled."

There were still six inside, plus Duggan and Braler – it was going to be a tough move to pull off without being overrun.

"Berg have you got any ammunition?" asked Duggan.

"One left in the tube, sir and zero grenades."

"Everyone fall back. Berg, you watch the door. Burn anything that moves."

With a clatter, the remainder reached the room. Braler had perfected the routine and he practically threw the first two human soldiers through the hole. Red-Gulos was a tougher proposition, but there were enough people above to pull him through in seconds.

Berg's plasma launcher bleeped and its final round whooshed out. The explosion was low and muted as the plasma engulfed the lift doorway.

"That's my last round," she said.

"Up!" Duggan ordered.

Berg didn't need a formal invitation. She dropped the launcher and was soon away onto the roof. Duggan came and then Ortiz. At last, there was only Braler.

"Come on," said Duggan, leaning across so he could look into the room below.

Red-Gulos and Link-Tor lay flat on the roof, their hands stretched out for Braler to grab, whilst others sat on their legs to stop them sliding into the hole. Braler jumped with his arms outstretched and got hold of Link-Tor's wrist. The Ghast swung in the air and then Red-Gulos lunged forward, grabbing his other arm.

Some of the troops lay near to one of the other holes, which gave a better vantage into the area below. Duggan heard them fire their rifles and he gritted his teeth.

After a brief struggle, Braler's head appeared and Duggan added his own strength to the effort, closing his eyes against the wounds he expected to see on the Ghast's body.

"Got him!" exclaimed Ortiz in triumph.

Duggan dared to open his eyes and found Braler in front of him, alive and with no additional injuries.

"ESS *Crimson*, this is Duggan. What's your position?"

"You'd best get down, sir. The fires of heaven are coming."

"Down! Now!" he shouted.

A few seconds later, he found that McGlashan had not exaggerated her warning.

CHAPTER TWENTY

"TWENTY-FOUR CLUSTERS OF TWELVE LAMBDAS, four underside Bulwarks," Duggan repeated to himself as he lay flat.

The eruption of plasma told him at once that McGlashan had used everything available. Night became the shortest of days and the installation was engulfed. It started as a wave at the far side of the base – a wall of white flame which advanced at incredible speed, destroying everything it touched. Like an ancient miracle the wall parted around the comms building, leaving it completely untouched. When it passed, the wall became complete once more as it raced onwards. The corner towers and the central pyramid suffered greatly in the barrage, each taking a dozen or more direct hits.

In the centre, the squad huddled, waiting for the cataclysm to end. When it died away, shards of stone began to fall, thrown up by the Bulwark fire which had raked unseen through the explosions. Duggan felt something catch him in the shoulder and he grimaced with pain. He stood, feeling suddenly, stupidly, invincible.

The base was ruined, taken from what it had been and reduced to molten alloy amongst craters of magma. Two of the towers remained upright, though they looked as if they might fall at any moment. The final tower had fallen away from the base, while the central pyramid had taken on a new, indefinable shape.

Something else caught his eye – a shape dropping through the air above at great speed. He knew what it was. "Stay down!" he said.

A few hundred metres above, the tank's gravity engines braked sharply, arresting the vehicle's fall. Some of the soldiers scrambled away, though most knew there was no need to try. The landing was perfect and the tank dropped dead-centre on the roof, where it remained in a stationary hover a metre above the alloy surface.

There were a few soldiers underneath. They rolled out, completely unharmed, having seen enough deployments of armour in the past to know the tank would have plenty room for them as long as they lay flat.

"In we go, ladies and gentlemen!" Duggan said. "What are you waiting for?"

This was one of the Space Corps' mid-sized tanks which they'd evidently managed to squeeze into the *Crimson*'s adapted cargo bay. The vehicle had thick armour and a powerful gravity engine to complement its large-bore gun and twin plasma launchers.

Duggan got himself inside, along with the others. It was as cramped as he'd feared, with room for only twelve in adequate comfort. His suit informed him there were twenty-eight inside - they'd lost four in the fighting.

"Who's driving this thing?" he asked, prioritising the living over the dead.

"That'll be me, sir," said Kidd.

"Have you got a direction?"

"Yes, sir. The *Crimson*'s programmed one in for us."

"Good – follow it at once."

"Already on it."

The tank moved off, remaining horizontal as it plunged down the side of the building. It couldn't climb vertically, but it could drop safely. Duggan experienced the sensation of a rapidly-plummeting lift. The gravity engines hummed and they were on their way.

"I need a casualty report confirmation," he said. "I've got Stanton, Reilly, Rastol and Fuentes."

"That tallies with mine, sir," said Ortiz.

"We'll honour them when we're safe."

They were definitely not in a secure position. Duggan patched into the tank's sensor feeds, trying to ignore the jostling which resulted from being crammed into a space meant to hold far fewer people.

The view outside was entirely different to the one he'd experienced on the way in. The sensors showed metal structures melted into bizarre, nightmarish shapes, with varying gaps between them. The tank forged on through the devastation. Here and there, debris blocked their path and Kidd was required to pilot them away in a different direction, through passages and alleys. Whatever remained of the enemy, they'd lost their organisation and they ducked away from the oncoming tank.

At one point, the tank sustained a barrage of high-velocity impacts against its left-hand side. The noise echoed within the confines of the interior chamber as if the hull had been struck by a hundred giant hammers. A few of the squad laughed without fear – they'd seen it before and were still here to tell the tale. The tank's main gun thundered its retort, firing a dozen rounds at whatever the targeting computer had detected.

"Hostiles eliminated," said Kidd.

A sudden, worrying thought came to Duggan. As soon as

they crossed the perimeter of the base, the enemy warship would have a far easier job of picking them up. Even the tank's tough outer plating wouldn't stand up to more than a single orbital missile strike.

He connected to the tank's comms modules, which were far superior to those on the spacesuit. *"ESS Crimson*, this is Duggan. Where are you?"

The comms crackled and fizzed. He repeated the message and still there was no response.

"Sir we're coming to open ground," said Kidd.

"Maintain course."

He trusted McGlashan's skill and judgement and knew she'd do everything in her power to get them off the surface. There were times when skill and judgement weren't enough – the *Crimson* was undermanned and she'd have a hard job taking out an enemy warship with just her and Breeze on the bridge.

"We've crossed the perimeter," said Kidd.

The forward sensor showed kilometres of rough, undulating terrain. Ice covered everything and where the rocks jutted high above their surroundings, clumps of frozen grey hung precariously over the ground below. It didn't matter how much they tried to stay hidden – if the enemy warship was looking hard enough, it would find them. The soldiers weren't ignorant of the risks.

"We won't know about it when it comes," said Rasmussen.

That was how combat went – if you died it would usually happen at once, your body incinerated in a flash of high explosives. If you managed to survive, there were medical facilities to patch up almost any injury. They'd fix you up and send you off to roll the dice again.

The minutes ticked by. Duggan tried several times to contact the *Crimson* without success. He felt helpless, stuck in the middle of the tank's passenger bay and with no room for him to reach the cockpit. Kidd knew her stuff and Duggan told himself he should enjoy the ride.

"We sure kicked the crap out of those bastards," said Cabrera on the open channel.

"Commander McGlashan kicked the crap out of them," someone else corrected her.

"Camacho did his share."

"It's going to take them a while to get their base fixed up."

"Once they stop running."

The conversation washed away Duggan's fears and reminded him of years gone by – the times before he'd been an officer on a warship. Concealed by the opacity of his visor, he closed his eyes and let the memories come flooding back. He reflected that his life had been easier then, but he knew he wouldn't go back if someone offered him the chance to become a young man again.

"Our destination is dead ahead, sir," said Kidd, her crisp tones returning him to the present.

"How far?"

"A couple of klicks. We'll be there in less than five minutes."

"Any sign of pursuit?"

"Nothing, sir. We left them in a mess."

"I still can't get through to the *Crimson*. Have you seen anything on the scans?" he asked. It was a long-shot. The tank was designed to work on the surface and wasn't equipped to locate something forty thousand kilometres above.

"Not a whisper. It's cloaked, isn't it?"

"It's not the *Crimson* I was interested in."

They reached the coordinates which were programmed into the tank's guidance system. It halted, awaiting further instructions.

"Put the tank on auto and bring the remote-control packs," said Duggan. "We're getting off."

It only took moments until they were outside, sighing with

relief to have space to move their arms and legs. Duggan looked around – there was nothing remarkable about the place, with the same rocks and ice as there was everywhere else on the planet. The base was visible from here and he saw that another of the towers had fallen over. The air above the installation was hot and the outlines of cooling metal sketched a madman's pattern on his heat sensors. He tried the *Crimson* again and still there was nothing.

"Dig in," he said. "I want positions four hundred metres to the north of the tank. I'm not expecting the enemy to have rallied so quickly, but I want us to be ready."

The squad scattered. There were plenty of places to crouch amongst the rocks, or lie prone in the many cracks along the ground. The tank was a sitting duck for an orbiting warship and Duggan could only hope the Dreamers would be careless and overlook the smaller troops. Four hundred metres was enough for the suits to withstand the heat from a direct hit on the tank, yet close enough that they could return to it quickly if necessary.

They waited ten minutes until someone announced the bad news.

"I think there's movement coming from the base, sir," said Chan. He'd climbed halfway up the side of a high rock, which gave him good view back the way they'd come.

"What sort of movement?"

"Soldiers, sir. And some kind of armoured vehicle – it's bigger than what we've got with us."

"Where the hell did they get that?" asked one of the other men. "There's nothing left of their base."

"The pyramid," Duggan guessed. "It wasn't completely destroyed. McLeod - see if the tank will get a lock on that vehicle."

"Trying, sir. The targeting computer isn't reading it too well."

"Their spaceships do the same thing. Try aiming manually and knock it out for us."

The tank was in clear sight. Its turret rotated jerkily to the right and back as McLeod corrected his aim. The muzzle thumped four times in quick succession, sending depleted uranium slugs at the approaching enemy. The angle wasn't good and McLeod reported four misses.

"I can't even get the plasma launchers to fire," he muttered. "No, wait. I've got a lock."

It was too late. Without warning, the hull of the tank was ruptured by a fusillade of incoming projectiles. The vehicle was built to take punishment and its turret fired in return. One of the plasma launchers was smashed away and the second failed to fire. A second and third volley knocked the tank a few metres across the ground. Then, it crashed to the ground.

"All major systems offline," said McLeod. "We got two or three hits but they're still coming. I reckon we'd need a Colossus tank for this engagement."

Duggan's faint hope that the enemy might think they were victorious after the destruction of the tank was short-lived.

"They're moving," said Chan. "Less than two minutes and we'll be facing a tank and sixty troops."

"If only we had a dozen Camachos," said Cabrera sarcastically.

"You two should get a room," said Berg.

The response was not polite and Ortiz stepped in to keep the troops focused.

"Come on, Lucy. Where the hell are you?" Duggan muttered to himself. The comms were empty and he felt like he might as well shout his message into space for all the response he got.

The enemy vehicle came into sight, a few hundred metres away. It was low-slung, with angles at the front and back, giving it an unusual shape. There were short bars protruding from it in numerous places, their purpose unknown. There was no mistaking the gun – a long, narrow barrel pointed from the front of its turret. The pilot evidently wished to engage as soon as possible and he'd left the following troops a distance behind.

It fired before Duggan realised what had happened. Chunks of ice and stone blew away from a position close by, sending the pieces thousands of metres away. *It's going to chew us up,* he thought.

There was turbulence in the air as something ripped through the thin atmosphere. Duggan felt the suction of its passing - it dragged at his body and tried to pull him from his hiding place. A shuddering thump shook the ground, dislodging rocks and chunks of ice for hundreds of metres around. When he looked to where the enemy tank had been, there was nothing recognizable left of it. The vehicle had been crushed into a state where it was only centimetres thick.

The comms erupted in a chorus of questions. Duggan had already seen the signs of an imperfectly-hidden shape that was a little over a kilometre in length. He stared until he saw the place where the boarding ramp was descending.

"It's the *Crimson!*" he shouted. "Hold your positions!"

The last thing he wanted was for someone to rush headlong towards the safety of the interior and get shot halfway there. Two of the rear Bulwarks opened up, shredding ice, stone and the approaching enemy troops.

"That's the last of them," said McGlashan. "Sir, you need to get onboard and fast. We don't have long."

Feeling an immeasurable relief, Duggan gave the order to make for the ship. As soon as the last of them had climbed into the forward airlock, he closed the ramp. The gravity engines howled under full thrust and the *Crimson* vanished into the sky.

CHAPTER TWENTY-ONE

DUGGAN REACHED THE BRIDGE, with Chainer a few paces behind. McGlashan and Breeze saluted and he responded with one of his own.

"A timely arrival, Commander," he said.

"We're not clear yet, sir. The enemy warship has pursued us doggedly."

"What are we facing?"

"I'm not sure, sir. It's a big vessel – not like the battleship we fought, but a lot bigger than we are. It's another kind of heavy cruiser."

"Where is it now?"

"I don't know exactly – somewhere behind us. It knows we're here, even if it can't target us directly. We lured it away past the moon of the sixth planet. Once we were out of its sight we dropped the cloak, which allowed us to lightspeed hop towards the rendezvous point. Then we came to pick you up."

"I am especially glad you did," said Chainer, taking his usual seat. He studied his screens. "I've detected the enemy vessel. They're heading in fast towards the surface of Frades-2."

"Are they coming towards us?"

"No, sir. We might have lost them. By which I mean Commander McGlashan and Lieutenant Breeze might have lost them."

"Excellent – we'll keep on our current trajectory until we've had time to take stock."

He checked their course - the *Crimson* was pointed into space and towards nothing in particular. McGlashan had chosen a heading to put them as far from the planet as possible.

"The beacon we installed has shut down. They found it quicker than I expected, given the circumstances," said Chainer. "It's no problem – our AI has plenty of data to allow it to track where the signal was aimed."

"Is it somewhere near?" asked Duggan.

"I can't tell you, sir. I'll need time on the super-fars to build up a map of what's over in that direction."

"Do you think the enemy knows what we've done?" asked Breeze. "We had the element of surprise, but that's gone."

"Properly gone," said Chainer, clearly still buzzing from taking part in the raid on the base. "They'll probably guess, given time. It depends what happened to the beacon – if a soldier found and destroyed it without realising what it was, they may take a while to put the pieces together."

"More likely we'll find our next destination on high alert," said Breeze.

"Maybe," said Chainer. "We've already accomplished enough."

"Not enough," Duggan corrected him. "I want more, Lieutenant. I want to know what the purpose of that base was and I want to know more about the forces they have close to the Blackstar."

"I wasn't suggesting we leave, sir. Simply that our mission

won't be an abject failure if we have to return to Confederation Space."

"That's fine. I didn't think you'd run out of appetite for the fight."

"We did pick up one or two clues about the base while you were away, sir," said Breeze. "I believe the pyramid was one of their usual power sources and the corner towers were designed to act as amplifiers."

"Why would they do that?" asked Duggan. "I thought the pyramids could generate practically unlimited energy."

"I don't have an answer for you."

"The proximity to the wormhole must be suggestive of its function," mused Duggan, coming back to his thoughts from prior to the surface assault.

"They'll not be doing much with it for the foreseeable future," said Chainer with satisfaction.

"Keep up with your scans, Lieutenant. I need to know where we're going."

"Sorry, sir. Will do."

Duggan opened a channel to Ortiz. "How are things going down there?"

"We've got four walking wounded, including Braler, sir. Flesh wounds according to Corporal Weiss. She thinks they'll be ready for combat soon."

"Meet me in the mess room in ten minutes and bring the troops. I know you'll all be hungry, so I'll talk while you eat."

"Sounds good."

Duggan was one of the first to arrive. The others came in small groups, invariably stopping at the replicators before they took their seats. It wasn't long until Duggan was able to address them - only ten minutes after he'd left the bridge.

"Fleet Admiral Teron said he'd given me the best for this mission and he was right. We faced overwhelming odds tonight and we came out on top." He met the eyes of Red-Gulos. "Subjos Gol-Tur told me the same about his men and again, he was right. We lost some good people, so I can't call this a success. However, we got what we wanted – the *Crimson*'s AI and comms man are working on our next destination. Once we arrive, there's a chance we'll have to do the same thing again."

"Welcome to the Space Corps," said Cabrera fondly.

"The enemy's base is destroyed. We still don't know what its purpose was, but we can be sure they'll not be using it again. We're here to gather intel and to cause maximum disruption, and you can be sure that by the time we return home, we'll have accomplished both a hundred times better than our superiors could have hoped." He smiled "And Admiral Teron is not an easy man to please."

There were a few dutiful chuckles before Duggan continued.

"Before I let you get on with your well-deserved meals, I need to make you aware of some field promotions I am making, in order to establish a clearer chain of command. Two of our friends from the Ghast navy will now be known as Sergeant Red-Gulos and Corporal Gax. You will afford them all the respect due to their rank and you will acknowledge their orders appropriately."

The announcement didn't even produce mutters, let alone open discontent. They'd once been enemies and now they were not. Above everything else, they were soldiers and they would look out for each other.

Duggan said his last words for this meeting. "We'll hold a ceremony for our dead once we hit lightspeed."

He left the mess room and returned to the bridge. Although he was hungry, he didn't want to spend the time it would take him to eat, especially since he was keen to hear if Chainer had discovered anything of interest. There was news waiting for him.

"The signal goes here," said Chainer, clearly pleased with himself. "The divergence between our signal and theirs is just beginning to become significant given the distance we're talking about, however, it's not so significant that I can't tell you with confidence what our heading will be."

"I'm all ears, Lieutenant."

"There's a solar system a day and a half's lightspeed travel away from us. In fact, there's a cluster of solar systems. The signal ends there."

"Have you been able to find anything more specific?" asked Duggan. "It would be good to know what we're getting into."

"Sorry, we're too far out, sir. I can only recommend we exit lightspeed a long way distant and do the rest on the gravity drives."

"That's what we'll do." Duggan returned to his seat. "We'll make the jump as soon as we're at a safe distance from Frades-2."

"There's nothing hostile on the scans, sir."

"We should have ample time to get away," added Breeze.

"Let's do it. Disengage the stealth modules and prepare for the jump. I'd prefer you to err on the side of caution when it comes to our re-entry into local space, Lieutenant."

"Stealth deactivated. I'll bring the fission drives up to speed as soon as I'm able and I'll aim for four hours out."

"That should be fine."

They made their escape to lightspeed without incident and Duggan sighed noisily as soon as they made the transition.

"What is it?" asked McGlashan.

Duggan laughed. "For once, I'd prefer a longer journey time than we have."

"It got pretty hectic back there."

"You did exceptionally well, Commander," he said. "I haven't had the chance to say it yet."

"Lieutenant Breeze played an equal part, sir."

"I don't doubt it," Duggan said with a smile. "I'll make sure the right people hear about what the two of you achieved."

"If I need to do it again, can I put in a request for an additional pair of hands, sir?" she said. "They can graft them underneath the ones I've already got."

"You did well enough with the two you've got."

"While we're on, can I put in a request for a single, additional hand, sir?" asked Chainer.

Duggan shook his head, wondering what nonsense was about to spill from the man's mouth. "Why is that, Lieutenant?"

"So I can hold my coffee while I work, sir. I need to keep putting the cup down when I'm using the super-fars."

"You do talk some crap, Frank," said Breeze.

"That he does," agreed Duggan. "However, he also performed well today, so I'll forgive him."

The AI-generated rota favoured Duggan and he didn't have to wait long for an opportunity to take a break. His stomach rumbled and he could tell he'd burned a lot of calories over the last few hours.

The mess room was still busy, though some of the troops had dispersed to do whatever it was they wanted to do. Duggan caught sight of Braler – showing no sign of his injury - in one corner and was pleased to see the Ghast talking to Barron and McCarty. The better they communicated, the better they'd perform in pinch situations.

Ortiz was there, sitting alone at a table, her eyes lost in a distant stare. She was well-liked, but there was a fine line between command and friendship, which cut her off from some of the talk. Duggan knew what she was feeling since he'd been there himself. When she'd been a sergeant, the gap was smaller. Now he'd promoted her to lieutenant, the troops would be much more aware of the difference between them. He sat opposite with a tray of his usual steak and was pleased when she smiled at him.

"What's that?" he asked.

"Chicken salad."

He peered at it. "Not a bad impression of one, either."

"The replicators get better every year."

Duggan wasn't fond of small talk. "The Ghasts did well," he said. "If a bit eager."

"I didn't expect anything else, sir. Their methods are similar to ours. Those repeaters are good at close range."

"Expect an extensive debriefing when we return," he said. "There are many in the Space Corps who want to know about the capabilities of our new allies."

"Are they hoping for failure?"

"Maybe some people are. The war lasted for many years and it'll take time before there's anything like acceptance."

"I can understand. Out here in enemy territory there's no choice other than to work together."

Duggan took a deep breath. "Any regrets about promotion, Lieutenant?"

"There are some things I miss," she said. "I don't think I have regrets. I'm good at what I do, sir – it means I get to keep these poor bastards alive a bit longer than they might otherwise manage without me."

"You've got your work cut out – we're a long way from home."

"This is home now sir," she said, indicating the walls around her.

"What about the ring you carry?"

"I'll always have it with me. I can't let the memories slow me down – I've got others to look after."

"That you have," said Duggan.

He finished his meal and returned to the bridge, an hour before his break was over. There was something about his conversation with Ortiz which left him saddened. Everyone needed a future, but she appeared ready to forsake her own. He didn't know how to help, nor even if he should try. He shook the thoughts away and brought his attention to the matters at hand.

A few hours later, he conducted a short ceremony to remember the dead from the recent mission. It put him in a foul mood for the rest of the journey and he spoke few words to the others. Eventually, Breeze announced the imminence of their arrival.

CHAPTER TWENTY-TWO

"WHOA!" was the first word Chainer spoke when the *Crimson* switched onto its gravity drives. "What the hell is going on here?"

Duggan could tell he was going to hear something important in the very near future. "Activate stealth as soon as available," he instructed. "Weapons on full alert."

"Yes, sir," Breeze and McGlashan replied at once.

"What have you found, Lieutenant Chainer?" Duggan asked, resisting the urge to leave his seat. His eyes roved across his console, seeking reassurance there was nothing immediately threatening in the vicinity.

"This place...I've never seen the like before," said Chainer. "It's like the comms capital of the universe or something."

"Speak plainly, man," Duggan snapped.

"There are signals everywhere, sir. Coming here, or leaving to places an infinity away. Our backup comms is struggling to make sense of them and I'm sure we're only seeing a fraction of what's out there."

"Stealth modules online," said Breeze.

Reassured they were safe for the moment, Duggan rose and

stood next to Chainer, wrinkling his nose at the steaming cup of too-strong coffee nearby.

"This is incredible, sir. Look at the traffic – it makes the New Earth comms hub look like two tin cans tied together with a piece of string."

"The signals are coming from that planet there?"

"Definitely. I've had a little peek, but we'll need to be closer before I can make much sense of it."

"Give me a view of this solar system on the main screen," said Duggan, looking at Breeze.

"Here you are, sir. Another one to add to our incomplete chart of the great Dreamer Empire."

"An old, red sun with five planets, a few moons and not much else worth mentioning," said Duggan. "Any sign of breathable atmospheres? Are these planets populated?"

"I would venture a negative to both of those questions," said Chainer, not looking away from his screens.

"You're not certain?"

"You'll know as soon as I know. Here, check this out, sir."

New detail appeared on the bulkhead screen. The graphic of the third planet became highlighted in yellow, and countless thin orange lines stretched away from its surface until they disappeared from the edges of the display.

"Each one of these lines is a comms signal," said Chainer. "They could be inbound or outbound and each one could potentially carry zettabytes of data."

"There are thousands of them," said McGlashan.

"And like I said, these are only the ones we can see. I'd expect any military signals to be much tighter and harder to detect."

"You mean this planet might house the main comms network for the enemy's military forces?" asked Duggan.

"No, sir, definitely not. You'll notice that as the planet orbits the sun, some of the signals stop – deliberately stopped, I would say. They haven't yet discovered a way to transmit directly through an entire sun, so when the planet is in the wrong place, the poor bastards at the far side of the sun won't get their telephone calls."

"Are you saying it's part of a network?"

"I believe so. There might be six, ten, hell another *hundred* of these hubs across enemy space."

"Can you get an estimate of how many others, based on which signals switch off and on?" asked Duggan.

"I thought you might ask that, sir. The answer is yes, but it's going to burn the AI for a long time, plus we'll need to be close enough to watch them and discover the switching pattern."

"I don't need a precise answer, Lieutenant. Get me something, even if there's a wide margin of error."

"I'll get started, sir." Chainer shook his head. "I can't believe I'm seeing this. This is in an entirely different league to anything in the Confederation. These Dreamers have either been around a whole lot longer than us or they work a lot faster and harder."

"This is the enemy we face," said Duggan. "They brought the war to us and we have to fight back, regardless of their apparent superiority. I'll bring us closer."

Duggan took his seat and turned the *Crimson* towards the hub planet.

"If they've gone to the trouble of installing this comms equipment here, it makes me think we've arrived somewhere in the middle of their territory, rather than on the outskirts," said Breeze. "It's best to keep your comms network central."

"That's a good thought," said Duggan. "It increases the chance their defences are weak."

"Thinking long term, it also means we can drop into the middle of their space, while the Helius Blackstar only takes them to the edges of ours," said McGlashan. "This might be the first significant advantage we have over them."

"I've had another thought," said Chainer. "Try not to fly through any of the transmission beams if you can avoid it. It's unlikely to alert them, but you don't know what alarms might be raised if there's a temporary interruption in the signal."

Duggan felt Chainer was over-thinking it in his excitement. Nevertheless, he acknowledged the advice though he didn't have to take significant steps to alter his behaviour. There were many signals, but there was a lot of space for them to go through, ensuring there was little chance he'd accidentally pilot them into the middle of one.

The closer they came, the better the picture Chainer was able to paint. "The entire planet is studded with transmitters," he said. "There are smaller ones every two hundred klicks and larger ones every thousand klicks, give or take."

"How is it strung together?" asked Breeze. "They can't function independently of each other, surely?"

"I'm trying to figure it out," Chainer admitted. He waved to Duggan for attention. "Sir, I've sent you details of a new heading – there's something I need to see."

Duggan nodded and altered their course. Whatever Chainer was interested in, it was on the far side of the hub planet and coming towards them with the planet's spin.

Chainer practically jumped from his seat "There!" he shouted. "They've got a main comms facility that's hooking the smaller transmitters together."

"I see it," said Breeze. "By which I mean I can read the power spikes on the surface. This is big."

"You might want to stop the ship while we have a think, sir," said Chainer. "I wouldn't like to approach without giving due consideration to the possibilities."

Duggan brought the warship to a halt and tapped into the sensor feed Chainer was studying. "That's a huge installation," he said.

"Seventy square klicks," said Chainer. "We've got bigger military bases, but I'm sure this is nothing other than comms we're looking at on this planet."

"Astorn," said Breeze. "I just had the AI generate a name for us."

From this distance, the image was grainy and it wavered on the screen. Duggan didn't need a clear view to reach a swift conclusion. "This is going to be a tough nut to crack."

"I think it's beyond our capabilities," said Breeze. "Or to be more precise, I think we'll be taking an enormous risk if we take a head-on approach."

"There is a total of sixteen mid-sized power generators," said Chainer. "Those are the square buildings you can see in two clusters of eight. Each is approximately a third the volume of a single one of those pyramids they kept dropping around Confederation space. There are three larger buildings, which I imagine house the central control and monitoring, as well as several dozen transmitters."

"These low buildings could be anything," said Breeze. "We don't know our enemy well enough to be certain."

"They house troops," said Duggan with confidence. "They're too similar to the buildings on the Frades-2 installation."

"In that case, they have thousands stationed there," said McGlashan.

None of this was what concerned Duggan the most. He did a mental count of another type of building in the base. "Approximately fifty structures that bear an unmistakeable resemblance to surface missile launchers."

"Not small ones," said Chainer. "They've likely got good range and speed."

"Plus this," finished Duggan, running his finger along a four-kilometre shape off to one side of the installation.

"A heavy cruiser," said McGlashan.

"All hidden away beneath an energy shield," added Breeze.

"What are our options?" asked Duggan.

"Move on or Planet Breaker," said Breeze without hesitation.

"Planet Breaker," said McGlashan. "If we can knock this hub out, we'll have given them a good kick the balls."

"Lieutenant Chainer, what do you think?"

Chainer scratched at his stubble, as if he wanted to say something without being quite sure what it was. "It seems a shame to blow it up without coming away with something first."

"What do you mean?" asked Duggan, his curiosity rising.

"Just think of the information flowing through that place, sir. Not only details of their lives and their civilisation, but locations and maps. Each of those signals has a destination and if we could find out where, we could build a picture of their space and their planets. The war has only started, yet think what we could do if we knew exactly where they lived."

Chainer's growing enthusiasm rubbed off on Duggan. "How do we get that information, Lieutenant? Their base may as well be impregnable. The signals will be heavily encrypted. How can we pull this off?"

"I don't know, sir." His face brightened. "I can think of a way to attempt a partial victory."

"In the circumstances, a partial victory would be an excellent result."

Chainer became animated, as he often did when talking about comms technology. "If we ignore the main base and instead focus on some of these other transmitters covering the surface, we may be able to steal the information which flows through them. I mean specifically these larger ones which appear every thousand klicks. They're likely to feed the data into a number of the smaller transmitters. If we could tap into that data and then escape, we can trawl through it at our leisure."

"Are these secondary and tertiary transmitters likely to be garrisoned?" asked McGlashan.

"I should imagine so," said Chainer. "I very much doubt they'll be unoccupied."

"How do we steal the data?" mused Duggan. "Would I be correct in thinking we'll need something with a high storage capacity?"

"We usually rely on the suits for that sort of thing," said McGlashan.

"We'll need something with a much greater capacity than a spacesuit," said Chainer. "Assuming you want to steal more than a nanosecond's worth of data."

"The ship's core," said Duggan quietly.

"We can't pick up the AI like it was a briefcase, sir," said Breeze. "It's behind several hundred tonnes of bulkhead and requires tools and equipment to reach."

"I'm not talking about the Space Corps computer," said Duggan. "I mean the Dreamer core."

"We can reach that?" asked Breeze incredulously.

Duggan stamped on the floor with his feet for effect. "It's about two metres below us. I have authority to eject it from where it's housed."

"Couldn't we simply land and then run a cable or something?" asked McGlashan. "Instead of removing our only method of getting through the wormhole? I mean, what if it gets damaged?"

"A cable won't work," said Chainer. "We still use cabled interfaces in some of the Space Corps kit, but we're unlikely to be able to plug in to the enemy's comms units as easily as that, even assuming we had several hundred metres of appropriate cable. It'll be far quicker and easier to stick the core a metre or two away from their data source and suck it up wirelessly."

"Is this definitely feasible?" asked Duggan. "If we took the

Dreamer core away from the ship and placed it close enough to their comms unit, we could make a copy of their data?"

"Oh it's certainly feasible, sir. Of course, it's the details where the problems usually arise. On the plus side, an interception at source will probably allow us to circumvent their encryption. A signal is usually encrypted right as it leaves the transmitter. If we're lucky, we could find ourselves with lots of raw intel, ready to be combed through."

That made Duggan's mind up. "The potential benefits outweigh the undoubted risks," he said. "We'll try a small-scale assault on the furthest transmitter from the main installation. In, out and away."

"Sounds easy," said McGlashan drily.

"We should ban the e-word from the bridge," said Chainer. "Something's up on the base. That heavy cruiser looks as if it's preparing to lift off."

"Warships come and go," said Duggan. "Could it be routine?"

"I don't think so," said Breeze. "Those missile batteries are powering up as well. It's happening across the entire installation."

"Yep and I can see a significant increase in ground activity," added Chainer. "I think they've finally learned about our arrival."

Duggan cursed loudly. He'd mentally decided that the opportunity to steal the enemy's comms data was too significant to pass up. It was a dangerous plan with the enemy on low alert. Now it had become much harder to succeed.

CHAPTER TWENTY-THREE

"THE HEAVY CRUISER'S UP in the air, though it remains stationary," said Chainer.

"What are the chances of them detecting us from here?" asked Duggan.

"Low. I wouldn't want to sit waiting forever, especially if they're actively scanning for us. They know we have stealth capabilities."

"I'm going to put Astorn between us and the enemy warship," said Duggan.

"Once the cruiser is out of sight, we'll have no idea where it is," Chainer reminded him.

"We're in no rush, are we?" asked McGlashan. "If we took ourselves away for a couple of weeks, they might stand down."

"We don't know if they'll remain on high alert until they've found us," said Duggan. "Furthermore, they could send dozens of their warships through the Blackstar while we're waiting for them to settle. There are plenty of reasons for us to act with best speed."

"I'm obliged to point out that we still have the option to abort, sir," she said.

"I understand your obligations, Commander, and I haven't yet dismissed the possibility of a withdrawal. Firstly, we're going to have a closer look at one of these secondary transmitters. The time we spend here may also give us an idea of whether the enemy are on a general alert or if they have specific reason to think we're in the vicinity."

It took thirty minutes to come around the planet in a wide arc. During that time, Duggan advised Lieutenant Ortiz that she should prepare the troops for a possible deployment.

"Some of them were expecting a breather, sir," she joked.

"I thought these soldiers were so good they no longer require oxygen to function."

"Only some of them, sir. They aim better with air in their lungs."

"This will be a quick visit, Lieutenant. If it happens I'll need to come along. We'll be bringing the ship's core with us and it's not something I want to let out of my sight."

"We'll be ready to go in fifteen minutes, sir."

"Prepare and then hold for further instructions."

"Roger that."

When Ortiz was gone, Duggan became aware of Chainer clearing his throat loudly. "What is it, Lieutenant?"

"I'll need to come along as well, sir. You may require my expertise if the enemy hardware is unfamiliar."

"He's getting the taste for it," joked Breeze.

"Next thing we know, he'll be screaming like a madman and charging the enemy with his bare hands," said McGlashan.

"You guys kill me," Chainer replied, trying unsuccessfully to look hurt.

"You're coming, Lieutenant," said Duggan. "Don't get suited up until I've decided what we're doing."

He brought the *Crimson* to a standstill, high above the furthest secondary transmitter from the main base. The sensor feed showed the target to be a squat, flat building, a few metres tall and eighty metres to each side. There was an intricate array of antennae on the roof and they beamed out a non-stop flow of data.

Duggan rubbed his chin while he studied it. "How much of it's likely to be underground?" he asked.

"Some, possibly. I don't know," Chainer replied.

Duggan checked out the surrounding terrain. There was little other than yellow-tinged stone for a hundred kilometres in every direction. It was flat and cold, with hardly any atmosphere. Chainer told him these conditions were what made Astorn a favourable planet to set up a major comms hub.

"Only one door into each building," Duggan said. "And a series of small transport vessels in constant low orbit to shuttle passengers between the transmitters. We land, blow the door, kill anyone inside who resists, steal the data and then leave."

"Sir, if you're so undecided, we should hold off," said McGlashan. "I'm sure Lieutenant Chainer will have no problem following one of these non-military broadcasts to their destination."

"No problem at all," confirmed Chainer.

Duggan stopped his pacing. "The trouble I have is when I ask myself what will lie at the end of a non-military broadcast."

"It could be anything," said McGlashan. She paused. "You don't want to find one of their populated worlds, do you?"

He met her gaze. "You're aware of our orders. We've been told to use the Planet Breaker without hesitation. I'm a military man – we're each of us part of the Space Corps. If you give me the choice between destroying a civilian target or a military one, you know which I'm going to choose. So, to answer your question, I am very much hoping we don't find a planet with twenty billion enemy civilians living on it. While there are military targets, I'm going to concentrate our efforts on them."

"In that case, what are we waiting for?" she asked.

Her words spurred him into action. He returned to his console and issued a series of commands to eject the central AI core. There were several layers of security which took so long to clear he asked himself if it would be possible to extract the ship's core in any situation that approached an emergency.

"It may be a little late to ask, but will the stealth hold when the core is gone?" asked Chainer.

"It'll hold," said Breeze. "Anything which requires a huge amount of grunt will struggle, by which I mean targeting, tracking, countermeasures, long-range sensors and lightspeed. Most things on the *Crimson* rely on the Dreamer core's computational output. In addition to that, the disruptors and the Planet Breaker won't work either. In other words, we count on it for our operational capabilities."

"Here we are," said Duggan, looking downwards at the floor.

A concealed hatch at his feet slid aside. There was a space beneath in which he could see two metal handles. He gripped them – they were uncomfortably warm - and pulled hard. The core was heavy and he had to put his back into it. With a hiss it slid clear, allowing Duggan a view down the green-lit shaft which had, until moments ago, housed the ship's AI.

"That's it?" asked Chainer, looking at the featureless, pale-blue cube. "That can't be more than twenty centimetres to a side."

"I assure you it's exceptionally heavy," grunted Duggan. He lowered it onto his chair. "I reckon it weighs a hundred and fifty pounds."

"I've seen one of our cores before and it was plenty bigger than that," said Chainer. "I know we're lagging when it comes to speed, but I didn't think the Dreamers could miniaturise it so much better than we can."

"That's not the whole thing," said Breeze. "That's the bit that does the thinking. It'll also hold a few critical memory arrays and a power cell. The main data arrays are far larger and so is the main power supply. It's a shame they're locked inside the ship, else we could probably use a separate memory module rather than risk the core itself."

"You're going to have a job carrying it to the forward ramp, sir," said Chainer.

Duggan shook his head. "*We* are going to have a job. Think yourself lucky I haven't ordered you to carry it by yourself."

"Are you going at once?" asked McGlashan.

"There's no reason to wait," Duggan replied. "Once we're ready in the forward airlock, you're going to take us down for a fast landing. You'll wait for us to return unless you judge it critical that you take off. We won't have long until they come."

McGlashan didn't need much guidance and she was ready to take command at once. Duggan and Chainer picked up the ship's core between them, taking one handle each. It was so small that their knuckles were pressed tightly together. They left the bridge slowly and Duggan soon found himself wishing the passages through the spaceship were significantly wider than they were.

As they walked, Duggan did his best to brief Ortiz over the internal comms.

"We've got a target," he said. "Lieutenant Breeze should have sent details through to your suit computers. There's not much to study."

"It looks outwardly straightforward, sir. One door into a compact building. There's little chance of significant resistance if we do our job properly."

"That's right. Once inside, we need to locate the main comms feed so that we can make a copy of it for the Space Corps to analyse later."

Ortiz was a consummate professional and she rarely asked unnecessary questions while on duty. However, in this instance, it came to Duggan's attention that she was becoming increasingly intrigued as the informal briefing progressed. Eventually, she cracked.

"Sir, what's that noise I can hear?"

"That is the sound of a disgruntled man complaining. The ship's core is extremely heavy and Lieutenant Chainer is doing his level best to grumble about the weight every single step of the way. Are you laughing, Lieutenant Ortiz?"

"Absolutely not, sir," she said. "Will you be long?"

"That depends on whether or not I decide to stop and strangle Lieutenant Chainer."

There was more laughter and Duggan found it uplifting to discover that Ortiz still had a sense of humour beneath her hardened exterior.

"I'm sure you'll do the right thing, sir," she said.

Twenty minutes later, the ship's entire contingent of troops was gathered in the forward airlock. Braler had the ship's core in a pack which he carried on his shoulders. The Ghast appeared unaffected by the additional weight and showed no sign of the injury he'd sustained on Frades-2.

Ortiz had organized squads and created an open channel for them, so it only remained for Duggan to go over the last remaining details.

"It's absolutely vital we succeed here," he said. "Our previous mission on Frades-2 is what has given us this opportunity. This is our first real shot at getting proper intel and it could be something which gives us an edge on our enemy for years to come. They're more advanced than we are and their warships are better than ours. Everything we've seen tells us they are considerably more numerous than Ghasts and humans combined. They hold all the high cards except one – they don't know the location of our home worlds. Today, we have a chance to draw the best card from the pack and add it to our own hand."

A few of the soldiers gave an enthusiastic response to that and Duggan continued. "Time is of the essence if we are to succeed. Once the enemy know we're here, they're going to send their heavy cruiser to find us. We're relying on our ability to finish quickly before they learn what we're up to. Do your best."

The talking was over. Duggan let McGlashan know they were ready to proceed as planned.

"I'll set us down fast, sir. The ramp will disengage in twenty seconds. The weather outside is clear and the air is a comfortable minus two hundred and forty degrees."

Duggan smiled and gave a shake of his head. He wondered if everyone on the ship had suddenly been afflicted by the madness of good humour, or if the disease was limited to Ortiz and McGlashan.

The *Crimson* came down hard. The life support system cushioned the blow, though Duggan could tell from the groaning of the landing gear that McGlashan had dropped them onto the ground at speed. Then, the airlock warning light flashed red and the ramp fell away to the ground.

"Move!" shouted Duggan.

In a rush, the troops spilled out of the spaceship and onto the ground outside.

CHAPTER TWENTY-FOUR

MCGLASHAN HAD DONE a good job of bringing them close to the transmitter. When Duggan reached the bottom of the ramp, he saw the target building ahead of him, not much more than two hundred metres away. He ran with the others, past the front two landing legs which were deeply embedded into the soft rock, until he emerged from beneath the cloaked spaceship. Above him, the sun was a tiny light in the sky, illuminating the flat ground faintly and providing no warmth whatsoever. The target building was four metres tall, though the bristling antenna reached for many metres more. They threw a series of bizarre, ever-changing shadows onto the ground before the structure.

There were no windows, but the doorway was easy enough to locate, surrounded as it was by an extruded frame. Bonner was the primary explosives expert following the death of Reilly and she was first to the door.

"Stand to the sides," she commanded, fixing a series of pale blue objects around the frame. "The door will fall inwards."

The troops complied, spreading themselves along the wall to the left and right. The speed with which Bonner acted made

Duggan wonder if the fist banging was entirely for show. Certainly, she didn't waste time on this occasion.

Bonner gave them a short countdown. "Three, two, one..."

The plasma charges crackled and sparked angrily, casting cold blue light onto the ground. A dull explosion followed and plasma splattered onto the rock, where it danced and frothed.

"That's it, we're done," Bonner said. "I misjudged it a fraction - someone give the door a kick."

Duggan was one of the closest and also the quickest to react. He took five paces and spun to face the door. The metal glowed brightly at the edges and there were holes clean through in several places. To Duggan's eyes, it still looked more than adequately fixed in place. Nevertheless, he raised one leg and kicked the door firmly with the sole of his foot, as close to the frame as he dared. The door sagged inwardly under the force of his blow, the softened alloy tearing softly.

A figure joined him – it was Red-Gulos. The Ghast thundered a second kick at the door, knocking it back further and creating a wide opening.

"One more," grunted Duggan, striking out with his foot for a second time.

The door was ripped untidily from its frame, only remaining attached at the lower corner. There was plenty of room to get over the top easily enough and Duggan went inside first, jumping past the door and into the airlock. His suit bleeped to warn about the heat from the metal, but he was able to get far enough inside that it wouldn't cause problems.

The airlock was four metres to a side and lit in blue. Duggan saw the activation panel for the inner door and stepped towards it. He stood next to it, making sure he wouldn't be visible when the second door opened. Without pausing, he swiped his fingers across, mimicking the gesture the Ghasts had shown him. This was the crucial moment – if they needed to blow the inner door, they'd lose at least a minute's worth of their surprise. To Duggan's relief, the door slid open and the pressurised atmosphere inside began to escape. It made a droning whistle as it swept through the airlock.

At the outer door, two of the troops looked carefully around the corner and into the building itself. They fired several rounds from their rifles and then stopped. "Hostiles! Take care!" shouted Ortiz.

Duggan put his own head around and saw a large, open area within. There was a long console in front of the side wall, its surface alight with glowing buttons and with chairs set before it. On the wall in front of the console, there was a screen that might have been as long as fifteen metres and nearly three high. There were several figures slumped in the chairs and there were signs of blood.

Movement caught Duggan's eye and he saw one of the enemy thrashing in the corner. It wore only a grey uniform, which gave no protection against the near-vacuum and it clutched at its face, gurgling quietly. Duggan closed his eyes for the briefest of moments and then he shot the creature with a single round from his weapon. It stopped moving and lay still.

"Clear!" he shouted. "Squad One move inside."

Squad One comprised Duggan, Chainer and six others. They came inside, guns pointing ahead, eyes watchful for movement. There were four dead aliens in total – they looked exactly like the Ghasts, even down to their uniforms which were an identical shade of grey. They were clearly dead, caught unawares by the speed of the attack. There were a couple of hand-held devices on the floor, which looked suspiciously like gauss pistols and Duggan knew he'd been right to order his troops to shoot on sight.

"Lieutenant Chainer, is this what we're looking for?" he asked.

"No, sir. We need the main transmission array panel. These are the secondary interfaces."

"Fine, fine," said Duggan, looking about. "Where will it be?"

There was a single exit door in the opposite wall and a raised square in the floor which looked like a hatch, though it had no access panel.

Chainer stammered for a moment as he did he best to figure out the most likely place to search. "These stations are probably linked by underground cables. There are times you can't beat a physical connection."

"You think it's beneath us?"

"It's the first place I'd look."

"Braler, can you get this hatch open?" asked Duggan. While he waited for the Ghost to come across, Duggan told Ortiz to get Squad Two inside and check out the closed door in the far wall.

"This is opened from within," said Braler. "There might be an override accessible from the equipment in this room."

"Can you identify it? We need to see what's underneath." Duggan was acutely aware of the passing seconds and knew if there was anyone alive, they could have already sent a distress signal to the main base on the planet.

"Given time I might find what you ask," said the Ghost.

Time was something they lacked. "Rasmussen, Bonner. I need these doors open *now*. What're the options?"

"I can open either," said Bonner. "There'll be collateral damage to whatever is behind."

"This plasma tube will get that far door open, sir," said Rasmussen. "I'm not sure it'll burn through the hatch, since the rocket will come in at an angle."

"Everyone out!" said Duggan. "Bonner, get the hatch open. Rasmussen, shoot that far door as soon as Bonner's charges go off."

This was the problem with time-constrained raids on enemy

facilities, especially when there was no way to know what was ahead – it could rapidly descend into chaos.

The soldiers ran out through the airlock and clustered to either side of the doorway. Bonner came last, while Rasmussen stayed in the airlock.

"All set," said Bonner, her voice and breathing elevated.

"Blow it," ordered Duggan.

The second set of charges went off with a thud. Moments later, Duggan heard the bleeping of Rasmussen's plasma launcher and then a second, more distant whump.

"Check for hostiles," said Duggan.

"Looks clear," said Ortiz.

"Squad One, back inside. Cover us!"

The plasma fires hadn't fully burned out when Duggan and his squad entered the room again – there was a fading white glow on the floor for a metre around the hatch and the far door was gone, leaving only a ragged hole. The coldness of Astorn no longer held sway here and the temperature peaked at close to three hundred degrees, before it began to cool rapidly.

"Squad Two get through that far door!" barked Duggan. "If you see anything with buttons and a screen, tell me about it."

He stepped as close to the hatch as he dared and peered into the shaft which Bonner's explosives had exposed. The spacesuits could take extremes of hot and cold, but the metal floor near the edge was pushing the boundaries of what it could handle. Duggan's feet became uncomfortably warm and he hopped from foot to foot. It was still too hot for him to get close enough to see straight down.

"Is everything okay, sir?" asked McGlashan. There was nervousness in her voice.

"Too many doors," he said. "We're staying to complete the mission."

"Understood."

There was the sound of gunfire from the far doorway. The members of Squad Two remained in cover and fired coolly into the room beyond. Squad One were shielded from return fire by the angles of the walls, though Duggan could make out something flashing in the other room.

"No explosives!" said Chainer over the open channel, his voice full of command.

"We've got at least five hostiles within," said Ortiz. "They're fully suited and armed."

"Any sign of explosives?" Duggan asked.

"Not yet, sir."

Duggan ignored the burning in his feet – he guessed they'd blister soon – and he stepped to the edge of the shaft. It was wide – since it was designed to be used by something Ghast-sized, and there was a metal ladder in the wall. The ruined hatch hung within, attached by a piece of heat-stretched metal. Heat came off it in waves, though it was already much less fierce than a few seconds before. There was a room at the bottom, a good thirty metres away and lit with the same blue light as the upper area. There was no sign of movement.

Now that he'd committed to it, Duggan was desperate for the mission to succeed. Since the determination was his own, he chose not to risk one of his soldiers. "Cover me," he said calmly to his squad.

Duggan put his rifle across his shoulders and jumped into the shaft. He grabbed the top rung, arresting his fall. His feet found purchase and he climbed down. The gaps between the rungs were larger than on a human-made ladder and it was a struggle to get into a rhythm. He was effectively blind, since there was no easy way to look at the floor below and he concentrated on the smooth grey wall before him. On the plus side, the heat soon receded and the alarms on his spacesuit HUD changed from red to amber.

"Nearly there, sir," said Cabrera.

Duggan came to the end of the ladder. The floor was laid with fine grating instead of being smooth and it vibrated slightly when he put his foot on it. He turned his head and saw that he was in a smaller square room, a few metres to each side and with an intricate, octagonal console in the centre. Then, he sensed movement and his suit registered a sound. He raised an arm and something struck him, producing a sickly crunch. Pain sparked from the injury, causing him to yell out.

He already had his back to the wall, so the best Duggan could do was pitch himself sideways in anticipation of a second blow. He heard the muted crack of a thin-atmosphere contact between two pieces of metal. Now he got a sight of his opponent – there was a Dreamer in the room with him, close to eight feet tall, clothed in a grey spacesuit and with a rounded helmet covering its head. Duggan's own visor was opaque, but his enemy's was not. There were grey eyes behind a clear screen and its mouth was fixed in a snarl. The alien held a length of metal bar and Duggan would have laughed at the mundanity of the weapon had he not been in such danger.

"Help," he said into the comms, realising he'd moved away from the base of the shaft and brought his opponent with him. There was no way the troops above would be able to get a clean shot.

The Dreamer swung again, missing by a whisker. Duggan noted it was unarmed apart from the bar. It didn't appear to need anything more – it was already far taller and broader than Duggan and would have been a difficult opponent when unarmed.

Duggan feinted one way and then attempted to run around the central console, which he felt sure was the equipment they'd come looking for. The metal bar hit him again, this time on his suit helmet. There was a sharp crack – heard within the helmet rather than without and his HUD immediately listed several critical warnings.

Instead of turning to face his opponent, Duggan darted forward, seeking to put the central console between the two of them. The pain from his arm threatened to overwhelm him and when he instructed the suit to inject a painkiller, he was dismayed to find it too badly damaged to comply.

As he ran, Duggan tried to drag his gauss rifle around from where he'd slung it across his shoulders. His damaged arm hurt too much, so he struggled to free the rifle with the other. With a twist of his body, he got the rifle free and turned, just as another blow landed on his spacesuit helmet. His HUD went blank except for the two words no soldier ever wished to see. *BREACH WARNING!* it said.

Duggan toppled back, firing his rifle wildly with one arm. The shape of his enemy towered above him and he fired again. It toppled over, landing heavily on his legs and chest, making him shout with the agony of his wounded arm. He kicked out, trying to roll the dead Dreamer away. It felt like it weighed three hundred pounds in its suit and he couldn't budge it in his weakened state.

While Duggan fought against the leaden weight on top of him, his suit tried to repressurize, making a violent hissing as it did so. He felt the oxygen race past his face as it was sucked out through the crack somewhere at the back of his head. There was a kit in a pack at his belt – it contained a fast-hardening polymer designed specifically to seal damaged spacesuits. He dropped his rifle and scrabbled at the kit's fastenings, trying to get them free with his one functioning hand. In his head, he knew it was no good – even if he managed to open the pack up, there was no way he'd be able to see where the breach in order to apply the fluid.

The suit's emergency burst of oxygen ended and Duggan

knew the vacuum would kill him. He expelled the air from his body to prevent it from swelling and rupturing his lungs. His hand continued to pull at the repair kit, even as he became aware of the bone-numbing chill entering the helmet from outside. He could feel his scalp tighten in the area where it pressed against the crack. He got the repair kit free and lifted it up. Everything seemed distant now and his arms felt heavy. Mercifully, the pain in his arm faded and seconds later, Duggan's vision went with it.

CHAPTER TWENTY-FIVE

VOICES REACHED HIM. The words were unfamiliar and they may as well have been spoken from half a galaxy away for all the sense Duggan's scrambled mind could make of them. He opened one eye and saw lines of red text across his HUD. *At least it's working again,* he thought. Something nudged him and the pain of his arm came roaring back, jerking him into wakefulness.

"You'll have to move, sir." It was Lieutenant Ortiz, crouched nearby.

Duggan gritted his teeth. "Understood," he said.

"Weiss? Where the hell are you?" Ortiz shouted, a dangerous edge to her voice that she rarely permitted anyone to hear.

With a grimace, Duggan pressed his undamaged hand onto the floor and pushed. Ortiz helped and then Duggan felt a much larger hand beneath his shoulder blades. He was hauled to his feet like a wooden puppet handled by an unsympathetic puppet master.

"We need to go," said Braler.

Duggan's vision finally cleared and he looked around the room – he was in the place he'd fallen, but his dead opponent had been thrown unceremoniously into the corner. The body was riddled with holes from Duggan's gauss rifle and its spilled blood was rimed with ice.

Lieutenant Chainer was at the octagonal console. The pack containing the Dreamer core was propped against it and Chainer's hands jumped from place to place, his fingers pressing rapidly here and there.

Someone came down the ladder at speed, the impact of their landing causing the grating to rattle. It was Corporal Weiss, arriving at the double, her medical pack of wonders held by a strap in the crook of one elbow. Without offering a greeting, she plugged a wire from her pack into the interface port on Duggan's suit.

"One broken arm, a minor concussion, tissue damage from short-term exposure to vacuum. Furthermore, you'll have a crippling case of the bends if you get out of that suit too quickly. Uncomfortable, but nothing fatal. I'm giving you a shot of battlefield adrenaline and some targeted painkillers."

"No adrenaline," said Duggan.

"Too late. Sorry," she replied.

"There's no time for tough guy stuff, sir," said Ortiz. "You need to climb that ladder again."

"Reprimand accepted," said Duggan.

The drugs didn't take long to work. His heart thumped in his chest, like it had been hit with ten thousand volts – Weiss had given him a big dose. The targeted pain relief kicked in moments later, fooling his brain into thinking his arm was in perfect working order.

"What's our situation?" he asked, amazed at the sudden clarity in his voice.

"I'm just this second done, sir," said Chainer. "I'll tell you the good news later, but the bad news is the ship's core fell halfway down the shaft. It *appears* to be working, though it's certainly taken a knock."

"Save it Lieutenant," said Duggan. "Let's get out of here first. Everyone up that shaft and onto the *Crimson*. I'll come last."

His soldiers were brave, but they were also practical. There was no way they could provide any significant assistance to a man climbing a thirty-metre shaft. Braler might have had the strength if he wasn't carrying the core. There were no other Ghasts in the room, since Ortiz had ordered them back to the ship.

The room's occupants climbed eagerly, soon leaving Duggan alone at the base of the ladder. When Ortiz had climbed far enough ahead, Duggan gripped the first rung. His brain felt sharp, though when he gave his broken arm a tentative shake, he could feel the pain hidden deep inside.

With no option, he climbed. The pain remained distant – it was with him constantly, yet it never became so intense that it was unmanageable. The worst part of the climb was the feeling of his shattered bones scraping together each time he pulled himself a rung higher. No matter how hard he tensed his muscles to keep things in place, the bones scratched and grated.

In order to distract himself, Duggan studied the damage read-outs on his spacesuit HUD. Several of its major functions had failed entirely and many others showed amber warnings. Halfway up, its life support unit failed.

"My life support unit's gone," said Duggan.

"You should have sufficient heat and oxygen to reach the ship, sir," said Ortiz. "It's a good job Weiss pumped all that shit into you, since the decompression sickness won't be too comfortable."

"I'd best stop talking and move, eh?" he said.

"There are spare helmets in the forward airlock, sir. Keep going."

Duggan didn't slow. The thirty-metre climb felt like a thousand metres, but he reached the top. Ortiz was there to see if he needed assistance. He waved her onwards and ran behind, out through the transmission station's outer airlock and towards the nearby spaceship. The temperature in his suit was falling and by the time he reached the bottom of the boarding ramp, he was shivering with the cold.

The next voice to reach him was McGlashan's. "You need to move, sir. The heavy cruiser's above us."

Duggan swore and sprinted up the ramp, the battlefield adrenaline giving a huge short-term boost to his strength and stamina. He reached the top and saw the other soldiers inside.

"Close the ramp!" he ordered.

"Close-range missile launch detected. They're falling in a grid pattern," said McGlashan, before the ramp had even begun to move.

Duggan heard the familiar clunking noise of the ramp's mechanical gears and he saw it rising to seal the hull. It was going to be too slow to prevent anyone in the airlock being incinerated if a missile landed close enough and McGlashan couldn't open the inner airlock without jumping through a series of time-consuming overrides.

"I'm going to make an unsealed take-off," she said across the open channel. "You'd better hold onto your hats."

The *Crimson* lifted away from the ground, moving steadily to avoid crushing the soldiers with the acceleration. The life support didn't function well if there was a breach in the hull or if someone was stupid enough to attempt take-off with the boarding ramps in the down position. Duggan's body felt heavy and his arm throbbed under the effects of the monumental thrust from the spaceship's gravity drive. Through the rapidly-closing gap in the hull, he saw the building below recede as they climbed away from it.

"Too late," McGlashan said.

The enemy missiles detonated, covering a huge area of the ground in a carpet of expanding plasma. Heat and flames roared up, pursuing the *Crimson* as it climbed. The upper edge of the bombardment licked at the boarding ramp and fire whooshed into the airlock for a fraction of a second, before the spaceship soared out of reach.

One of the soldiers laughed. "Commander McGlashan knows how to cut it fine," he said.

"That she does," said Duggan, for want of a better reply.

The ramp thumped into place and the inner airlock showed a green light to indicate the occupants could leave. Duggan pushed his way through to the front, frantically trying to get out so that he could reach the bridge. Someone grabbed his shoulder and he saw it was Lieutenant Ortiz. She offered him a suit helmet. "Best wear this until Weiss gives you the all-clear from the decompression sickness," she said.

Duggan broke the seal on his existing helmet and dropped it to the floor. "Thanks," he said with a nod, taking the replacement. He dropped it over his head and it tightened around his neck.

Some of the troops had taken advantage of the distraction to head through the airlock. Ortiz bellowed at the others to halt in order that Duggan and Chainer could get through.

"Braler, follow us," said Duggan. "Bring the core with you."

The three of them made haste, with Duggan desperate to influence the engagement with the enemy warship. The Ghast didn't know the way and he struggled to keep up.

"This pack is heavier than I let on," he said, giving another indication that the alien species had a sense of humour. "And these passages are too narrow."

They reached the bridge. Braler waited at the entrance until Duggan beckoned him in. It might have once been a significant moment to invite a Ghast onto the bridge of a Space Corps warship. In the circumstances, Duggan didn't give it a second thought.

"Put it there," said Duggan, pointing to the place where the core was housed. "Commander McGlashan, please bring me up to speed with our situation."

"Sir, the enemy warship is tracking us and maintaining a distance of approximately forty thousand klicks. They have fired several waves of missiles at us. So far they have not hit us, though each miss is progressively narrower than the one which preceded it. We're going to need that core back in place if we're to give any sort of meaningful response."

"That's if it fits," said Chainer.

"What do you mean?" asked Duggan.

Then, he discovered what Chainer was talking about. Braler lifted the core from its pack and Duggan saw that one of the bottom corners was crumpled, presumably as a result of its unwanted impact with the ground. He wasn't happy the core had fallen and he didn't know why it had happened. There was nothing he could do to change the past and no angry words would fix it.

"Put it there," he said.

Braler lowered the core into place and stepped back.

"Thank you, soldier," Duggan said through the suit helmet's speaker, his tone making it clear he was referring to more than just the carrying duties performed by the Ghast.

"I will return to hear Lieutenant Ortiz' debriefing," Braler said, with the faintest hint of a smile. "She can be ferocious."

With the Ghast gone, Duggan activated the command to reintegrate the core with the ship. The metal cube remained stubbornly unmoving at the top of its shaft. Losing patience, Duggan pressed down on the two handles with his foot. He felt it slot into place and then it slipped away into its housing below the bridge. A slab of metal slid across to cover the opening.

"One of the enemy missiles has just missed us by a couple of klicks, sir," said McGlashan.

Duggan took stock – the *Crimson* was at a comparatively low altitude of twenty thousand kilometres above the planet Astorn. The enemy heavy cruiser was above and behind, currently thirty-eight thousand kilometres away. The tactical display showed three waves of enemy missiles were in flight, each consisting of exactly one hundred missiles. The first wave streaked by, this barrage even closer than the last.

"It's only a matter of time," said Breeze.

Duggan knew what he wanted to do. "I want the Planet Breaker," he said.

"It's not ready, sir," said McGlashan.

"The Dreamer core will take some time to re-establish its connections with the rest of the onboard systems," said Breeze. "There'll be a ramp-up, during which it will became steadily faster until it's operating at one hundred percent. Having said that, we may not be entirely in the clear."

"What do you mean?" asked Duggan.

"I have two amber warnings on the core, sir. I'd happily tell you what they mean, but I've not seen these ones before."

"I need more than that. What does it relate to? Weapons? Propulsion?"

"Sorry sir. When things are quiet I'll dig out the documentation and take a look."

Duggan wasn't happy. Although the enemy ship couldn't directly target the *Crimson*, it would get them eventually unless it happened to run out of ammunition. On top of that it seemed as if the *Crimson*'s AI had suffered some kind of damage and he didn't know if there was any significance to it, or indeed what else might be affected.

While he'd have dearly liked to destroy the communications hub planet, Duggan had to put his crew and their survival first. It was imperative they take the information they'd stolen from the transmission station back to Confederation Space.

"We'll give up on Astorn for the moment," he said. "The fifth planet has two moons – I'll try to get us there and see if we can lose the heavy cruiser."

He changed the *Crimson*'s course abruptly, pulling the nose up until it pointed directly away from Astorn. The enemy warship took a few seconds to realise what had happened and then it, too, changed course to follow. It was faster than the *Crimson* and closed the gap between them until it settled at forty thousand kilometres away.

"The core is at thirty percent of its usual output," said Breeze. "We should have countermeasures and targeting back to more or less full effectiveness."

"They've stopped launching missiles," said McGlashan. She looked worried rather than relieved. "Why on earth would they stop? They clearly have a pretty good idea of where we are."

"Don't knock it, Commander," said Duggan. "It's a long way to the fifth planet."

"Here we go," she said. "Another launch. A single missile this time."

"Just the one?" asked Chainer. "I can handle that."

Duggan watched the missile on his tactical display. This was something different to the smaller missiles used by the enemy. This one was slower and much, much bigger. "Don't be too pleased, Lieutenant. Whatever this is, it's something we've not seen before and I'm sure we're not going to like it."

He changed their course, taking them further away from the incoming missile's predicted path. To his horror the missile followed, swinging in a wide arc to pursue them.

"What the hell?" he said. "Can they target us now?"

"I think I know what's happening," said McGlashan in sudden realisation. "The missile is only following our approximate course. I think they have someone onboard controlling it manually."

"They haven't got a hope of hitting us like that," said Breeze.

"Unless they don't need to hit us directly," said Duggan, not liking this one bit.

He changed course again and once more, the missile clumsily turned to follow them. "Release countermeasures," he said. "And where are the Bulwarks?"

"The Bulwarks don't recognize it as a target, sir. Super Warblers on their way," said McGlashan. "The shock drones won't help if that missile really is under manual control."

"I know," he replied, not taking his eyes from the screen.

The enemy missile flew through the shock drones without any deviation in its course. It flew past the *Crimson*, several hundred kilometres to starboard and continued onwards.

"What are they doing?" asked Chainer.

Duggan had an idea. He threw the spaceship off to one side, hoping to escape what he suspected was coming. The missile turned as well. Then, when it was still a thousand kilometres away, it exploded.

CHAPTER TWENTY-SIX

THE DETONATION WAS cataclysmic in size. Duggan had no idea what kind of explosive the missile had been carrying, but it expanded at terrifying speed in a roiling storm of pale blue. It enveloped the *Crimson* and continued outwards, its force not yet spent. The power of the blast was such that it rocked the entire vessel and Duggan felt a juddering through the control bars.

"Hull at one hundred and forty percent of its design maximum temperature," said Breeze, his voice eerily calm. "Still climbing."

"We're going to melt," said Chainer. "I've lost one of the starboard sensor arrays."

The buffeting stopped and the blue fires withered until they were lost to the endless appetite of the vacuum.

"I calculate the diameter of that blast sphere at approximately five thousand klicks," said McGlashan in bewilderment. "That was crude as hell. If I had to guess, I'd say it's a weapon that's several generations old and likely one that's not intended to be deployed against spaceships. It could be a weapon they use to flatten ground targets when a Planet Breaker is too much."

"It made the blast radius of our biggest nukes look tiny in comparison," Duggan replied with a bitter laugh. "Why wouldn't the Bulwarks shoot at it?"

"The Bulwarks track the signals of electronic guidance systems, sir. Whatever the enemy fired at us, it can't have been fitted with an in-built targeting system, so our latest technology couldn't detect it."

"That's a big flaw in the design."

"They've launched a second," McGlashan said.

"What's our damage status?" asked Duggan.

"The hull temperature is down to one hundred and ten percent," said Breeze. "A lot of the heat dispersed through the engines. We're going to look like an overused candle if we get out of this."

"We're not going to make it to the next planet, are we?" said Duggan, as much to himself as the crew.

"I don't think we can ride many more like the last one," said Breeze.

"Those missiles travel at eighteen hundred klicks per seconds," said McGlashan. "If we could decloak for long enough to accelerate to our own maximum speed, we could outrun them."

"We can't outrun the warship," said Breeze. "As soon as we deactivate stealth, they'll be all over us and it'll take a couple of minutes before we can reactivate the modules. That's not a risk I think we should take."

"We're going back to Astorn," said Duggan. "I'm convinced they withheld those high-yield missiles until we were away from their hub. They didn't want to damage any of the transmitters."

"Missile number two will be within range in the next few seconds."

Duggan pulled the control bars hard to the left and the space-ship changed course, heading back on itself. In a split second, the pursuing missile was past them. Whoever was guiding it attempted to change course as well. The weapon wasn't very manoeuvrable and it needed a much wider arc to come back on course. Its controller decided to simply detonate it.

"The second missile has exploded," said McGlashan. "We're at the extremes of its blast sphere."

Once again, the blue flames washed across the spaceship's hull, pouring their heat into the already burning alloy. When they receded, the damage reports came in thick and fast across a multitude of status screens on the bridge.

"That's burned out a chunk of our gravity drive, and a few hundred tonnes of our rear armour plating has detached." said Breeze.

Duggan was only half-listening. His tactical display showed they'd caught the enemy warship unawares and they'd successfully doubled back past it. The heavy cruiser executed a rapid turn and resumed the chase.

"It's good to know you can trick a technologically advanced alien race," he said.

"They've fired a third," said McGlashan. "It'll detonate before we reach Astorn."

"We can't lose to something as old and slow as a remote control high explosive," said Duggan. "Commander, take manual control of one of the rear Bulwarks!"

"There's no chance I can hit something without the targeting systems, sir. It's slow by the standards of a Lambda, but it's still moving damned fast."

"I don't care. Try."

Someone brought up a feed from one of the rear sensors and put it on the main screen.

"Lots of stars and darkness," said Chainer. "We might see something."

"Here goes nothing," said McGlashan. There was a tiny,

analogue joystick on her console, which was rarely needed in this age of advanced targeting computers. The joystick combined with a small, razor-sharp vector screen to allow manual targeting of the warship's onboard weapons.

Streaks of white flashed off into space. The Bulwark quickly warmed up to its maximum output and the streaks became a solid line of projectiles. "Five hundred and thirty-two thousand rounds per minute," said McGlashan. "Come and get us."

Duggan clenched his teeth tightly together as he watched. The cannon wasn't designed to operate at maximum burst for longer than a few seconds. It would eventually burn out or explode, depending on how lucky they were.

Something else caught his eye and he swore. "The heavy cruiser has launched one hundred missiles," he said.

"We're more visible when we fire, sir," said Breeze.

"There's no damn choice," he replied.

The smaller missiles were much faster than the high-yield one. They overtook the larger weapon and sped by the *Crimson*, two of them coming within a few hundred metres. Up until now, Duggan had refrained from making extensive use of countermeasures when the stealth modules were active. With McGlashan's manual control of the Bulwark making them an easier target, it seemed a good time to change tactics.

"There's another wave of one hundred incoming," he said. "I've set our remaining Bulwarks to automatic. I'm releasing the shock drones."

He was none-too-soon. The Bulwarks opened up and the shock drones poured out. An inbound missile impacted with one of the drones just as it was leaving its launch tube. The drone was destroyed, but its job was done. The explosion barely warmed the damaged rear armour of the spaceship and then the blast was gone – left a thousand kilometres in their wake.

"Don't do that again please, sir," admonished Chainer, his voice pitched slightly higher than usual.

"I'll try my best, Lieutenant. Super-missile coming past us to the port side."

"Switching to forward port Bulwark," said McGlashan.

The switch was just in time – the second aft Bulwark changed to a flashing red icon on Duggan's screen. It would likely function again, as long as it was given plenty of time to cool down. The enemy cruiser continued to launch wave after wave of missiles and Duggan ejected the shock drones as quickly as they reloaded into their tubes. The drones were not one hundred percent effective, but they had decades of fine-tuning and development behind them. Wave after wave of the enemy missiles detonated fruitlessly in the cloud.

"Countermeasures down to twenty percent of capacity," muttered Duggan, releasing yet more of the drones. "I don't want to rely on Bulwarks alone."

"Switching to front Bulwark number one," said McGlashan.

"We don't have long," said Chainer.

"I know Frank, I'm trying my hardest."

McGlashan's best was good enough. The super-missile was close to its likely detonation range when she scored a hit. There was no explosion – one of the Bulwark slugs punched through the silvery metal of the missile's propulsion section and continued through the reinforced alloy box which housed the control unit. The missile was smashed into a hundred pieces, which separated and spun away.

"Yes!" shouted McGlashan.

"Nice shooting," said Breeze, wiping his forehead with a sleeve.

The *Crimson* was now only forty thousand kilometres above the planet Astorn. Duggan kept them pointing straight down, finally levelling them out at an altitude of five thousand kilometres. The enemy cruiser stayed behind, but fired no more missiles.

Chainer put his head in his hands for a moment. "Commander, I'd buy you a drink if it didn't come out of the replicator free of charge."

"You're not allowed to drink on duty," said Duggan, feeling a rush of good humour.

"How about I get you a coffee instead?"

"I think I'll pass, Lieutenant," McGlashan replied, slumping back, her hand still on the control joystick as if it had become glued in place.

The elation Duggan felt a moment before faded as quickly as it had arrived. They were effectively trapped here on Astorn, with the heavy cruiser keeping pace. The tactic of flying to another planet in the solar system had failed and there was no way he wanted to try deactivating the stealth modules in order to attempt a lightspeed getaway. On top of everything, their time was certainly limited – the enemy would surely have many ships heading this way. Cloaked or not, the *Crimson* would eventually be rooted out and destroyed.

"Commander McGlashan's done her bit, sir. Now it's your turn." The words came from Breeze and were intended as motivation, so Duggan took no offence.

"Is the Planet Breaker available?"

"No, sir. It takes almost everything from the AI to fire and we're not quite there yet. The core is clearly damaged – I expected to see full functionality restored by now."

"Never mind, Lieutenant - I have a plan. What's our hull temperature reading?"

"We've cooled down significantly, sir. The gauge is showing forty percent on the exterior. We're still hotter than we should be inside."

"It's going to have to be enough," Duggan replied. "They're faster than us, bigger than us and better-armed. The one thing the Dreamers seem to neglect on their warships is the armour. Let us see how they hold up to a few low-level, high speed circuits of Astorn."

He took the *Crimson* lower, until it was practically skimming the surface at an altitude of two hundred kilometres. As he'd hoped, the enemy followed suit, closing the distance between the two vessels to five hundred kilometres and remaining a little higher in the sky.

"Want me to nuke the transmitters as we go by?" asked McGlashan.

"Please hold, Commander. Nothing would give me greater pleasure than destroying this whole lot, but I'm aware the heavy cruiser is holding fire. If we start bombarding the surface, we can be sure they'll start up again."

"I'll hold until ordered otherwise," she said.

Duggan increased the *Crimson*'s speed, gradually at first, then at an increasing rate. The gravity drive had suffered damage in the missile blast and was also heavily burdened by the stealth modules. It didn't matter – this close to the planet, they could achieve more than enough speed to reduce the spaceship to molten alloy.

"What if they decide to sit off-planet and wait it out, sir?" asked Breeze.

"As soon as we lose sight of them, we're going to lightspeed, Lieutenant. Plus, I'm relying on the enemy captain being a sucker and following us to his own destruction."

"Unless we burn up first," said Chainer, unable to keep his mouth shut.

"That's the chance we're taking," Duggan replied, selecting a course that would avoid the main base on Astorn. The last thing he wanted was to be shot down by dozens of surface-to-air missile batteries.

The chase was on. The atoms of the planet's thin atmosphere collided with the *Crimson*'s hull at an increasing speed and the heat built up. The heavy cruiser remained behind, giving no sign it was willing to let the smaller warship escape.

CHAPTER TWENTY-SEVEN

THE HULL TEMPERATURE was soon at one hundred percent of its recommended maximum, producing a series of warnings on the bridge screens. Duggan ignored the alerts and turned the *Crimson*'s speed up another notch. The smaller installations on the surface flashed by underneath.

"One hundred and ten percent," said Breeze.

"Can you get a reading from their hull?" asked Duggan.

"Negative. I can tell you their approximate power consumption, but other than that, no."

"Our sensors can read heat," said Chainer. "I can give you a reasonably accurate estimation of their external temperature. The trouble is, the data will be next to worthless without knowledge of their heat dissipation technology, thickness of their hull, exact composition of their armour and so on."

"I get the idea, Lieutenant," said Duggan. "We're going to need to keep our fingers crossed on this one."

"Hull at one hundred and twenty percent," said Breeze.

"The enemy cruiser is maintaining a static distance," said Chainer.

Duggan fed more power to the gravity drives. He was aware that a warship could easily exceed its design tolerances for a short period – he'd done it on many occasions. It was the sustained heat he wasn't so sure about.

"One hundred and twenty-five percent."

"They're still with us."

"Our outer plates are beginning to soften," said Breeze. "Any more of this and you'll be able to stick your finger through the top few centimetres."

"We have to lose them soon," said Duggan. He didn't like to rely on hunches, but he had a very strong feeling they were going to see some additional company in the near future.

"One hundred and thirty percent."

"They're as hot as we are, if that's any help," said Chainer.

"I'm relying on them having a structural weakness that we lack," said Duggan. "If they're burning, that's good."

The hull of the *Crimson* had gone from a dull glow to a bright orange and then to red. It ignited the atmosphere's scant levels of oxygen as it went, leaving a trail of burning fire and smoke which stretched for hundreds of kilometres. The heavy cruiser burned as well. It wasn't as streamlined as the *Crimson*, and its external struts glowed white with the heat.

"They're melting," said Chainer.

"So are we," said Breeze. "That trail behind us isn't all oxygen. We're leaving our armour alongside it."

"They're not giving up," said Duggan angrily. He wanted the enemy captain to blink first and break off the pursuit. As it was, Duggan was left with no other option than to push his own space-ship to the point of destruction. *And beyond, if necessary,* he thought.

"One hundred and thirty-five percent," said Breeze. "The heat is pouring into the engines. We'll lose output soon."

"Two of the forward sensor arrays have alarms, sir."

"Several of our missile tubes have melted shut," said McGlashan. "We've lost those until we return to a shipyard for repairs."

"Engine output falling."

"I can feel it, Lieutenant. We need one last push."

"One hundred and forty percent. Six hundred tonnes of plating just fell away."

"The enemy ship is breaking up!" said Chainer excitedly. "They're leaving a trail of debris." His voice fell. "They're not slowing down."

Duggan held them at the same speed for a full minute. The hull temperature climbed another two percent and he realised the shape of the vessel must have been altered by the heat, making them less capable of cleaving smoothly through the air. It was now or never.

"Nuke them!" he said.

McGlashan gave the launch command, sending two of their nuclear warheads directly behind and four more into the surface below. Even in the low-oxygen atmosphere of Astorn, the warheads had a large blast radius. The enemy cruiser was engulfed in a mixture of white-hot fire and intense gamma radiation.

"I can't see it," muttered Chainer, peering at his screen to try and make sense of the garbled sensor feed. He gave a shout of excitement. "They're leaving a massive cloud of debris behind them! Their nose temperature is off the scale!"

"Are they following us?" asked Duggan, loud enough to cut across Chainer's words.

"They're falling back, sir! We'll be out of their sight in a few seconds."

Duggan didn't reduce their speed. The last thing he wanted was to misjudge the situation and have the enemy catch up again. He waited until they'd completed another quarter-circuit of the planet and then pulled back on the control rods. The *Crimson* climbed steeply away and the hull temperature started to drop.

"One hundred and thirty," said Breeze. "We're not out of the woods yet. There's been a chain reaction in one of the underside engine sections. It's going to burn itself out."

"Can you stop it?" asked Duggan.

"I'm trying, sir." Breeze grimaced to himself as he frantically issued commands to his console. "That's it," he said. "I've stopped it getting out of control."

When the *Crimson* had flown many thousands of kilometres away from Astorn, Duggan gave the order he'd been fearful to issue. "Disengage the stealth modules. Send us to lightspeed as soon as we're able. I don't care where or at what speed. Just get us away."

The power available to the gravity drives climbed to seventy percent, informing Duggan that the *Crimson* was no longer cloaked, whilst at the same time betraying the extent of the damage they'd suffered. If they'd lost much more of their engine output, the stealth modules would have failed. He accessed the full seventy percent in order to increase their distance from the planet.

"It'll be two minutes, give or take," said Breeze.

No one spoke on the bridge for a few seconds. Chainer was a man who saw silence as a challenge. "Those bastards are going to come racing out of orbit at two thousand klicks per second, aren't they? Then, they're going to launch six hundred missiles and a couple of super-missiles in our direction."

Duggan didn't have the heart to ask Chainer to shut his mouth, so he gave no response. The prophecy did not come to pass and the *Crimson* entered a medium lightspeed, heading in a direction that would take them to an unknown destination.

As he sat in his chair, Duggan closed his eyes and blew out the breath he'd been holding far longer than was comfortable. His emotions were mixed – there was excitement and there was also a trepidation which came with knowing how superior this new enemy had shown themselves to be. There was also pain – his spacesuit helmet was lying to one side. He couldn't remember when he'd removed it – certainly it wasn't easy to pilot a space-ship wearing one. The effects of decompression sickness crept into his joints and in his head, he could imagine them creaking as bubbles of gas expanded within his body. He looked his broken arm, still within the suit and tried to remember how long ago it had happened. It felt curiously pain-free, when he expected the painkilling drugs to have worn off.

"Where's Corporal Weiss?" he asked. "I thought Ortiz would have sent her here."

"She did, sir," said McGlashan, looking puzzled. "She gave you a booster jab only a few minutes ago when we were in low orbit. You told her to go away. You didn't tell us you'd broken your arm."

Duggan grinned. "Well I'll be," he said. "I didn't even notice her. I was too focused on what I was doing."

"It's the madness of command, sir," said Chainer solemnly. "It takes everyone, eventually."

"I can throw something at him if you like, sir," offered Breeze. "In case you don't want to risk further damage to your arm."

"Well, folks, we've done it," said Duggan, passing up on the opportunity to have Chainer struck by a flying object. "What exactly it is, I don't know."

"We stole a whole lot of data from them," said Chainer.

"Can we access it?" asked Duggan. "I mean, the damage to the AI core hasn't affected the integrity of the data, has it?"

"I doubt it, sir," said Breeze. "There's something wrong with the core, but I don't think it should affect the memory banks."

"Nevertheless, I want a copy made. Create a backup on the main data arrays. I'd rather have it twice than not at all."

"I'll do that at once, sir," said McGlashan.

"Let me know once it's done. I've got things to get on with," said Duggan.

McGlashan fixed him with a stare he'd seen before. "There's only one thing you have to get on with," she said, deliberately avoiding use of the word *sir*. "You need to get to the medical bay and get that arm properly looked at. And what's this I hear about a concussion *and* decompression sickness?"

Duggan could see the concern behind her eyes and he wondered if she knew just how close to death he'd come. Rather than making a flippant response, he met her gaze and nodded. "I got caught by surprise. I'll go and see Weiss now."

"What happens next?" asked Breeze.

"I haven't decided yet, Lieutenant. In truth, I'd like some time to consider our options."

"A few hours in the medical bay is what you need," said McGlashan, pointing towards the bridge doorway. "Now go!"

Duggan went. Events had moved at such a pace since the raid on the transmission building that he'd not been able to catch up with what was going on elsewhere.

The medical bay was cramped, with only six beds, each dressed in pristine blue sheets. Barron and McCarty occupied two of the beds. The former had taken a shot in the arm, which he dismissed as a flesh wound. It was patched up and the man looked as if he would prefer to be elsewhere.

McCarty was in a bad way – he'd been shot twice in the abdomen and was lying on his front, exposing the two exit wounds from the gauss projectiles. The holes had been sealed with artificial skin, but the real damage would be to his internal organs.

"Will he live?" asked Duggan.

"He won't die while he's attached to that medical robot and

nor will he wake up," said Weiss. "If we reach a proper medical facility he'll likely be fit to serve again in a few months."

"How did he get back to the ship?" asked Duggan incredulously.

"Painkillers, adrenaline and willpower," said Barron, his light tones concealing the pride he felt at the resilience of his fellow soldier.

Duggan sat himself upright on the third bed and remained still as a series of automated robotic arms began to poke at him. "Anyone not make it?" he asked.

"No, sir. This time we came back with the same number we started with."

"That's good," said Duggan. He closed his eyes for a moment. Needles jabbed him in several places. His arm looked surprisingly normal – he assumed the painkiller contained numerous other inhibitors to stop swelling and infection. The injections continued, most of them in his arm. He was faintly curious about what each one did, but was content to let Weiss and her medical robots continue their work in peace.

After an hour or so, his broken forearm was heavily strapped. Weiss told him it was broken in several places, though expressed confidence it would heal properly.

"Come back at this time tomorrow for a check-up, and you'll need to take it easy for a few days," she said. "I've attached several mesh accelerants to your bone, which should have you back to full strength within the week. We've flushed you clear, so the decompression sickness is gone and your concussion wasn't so bad – it won't be an impediment to your command."

In exceptional circumstances a Space Corps medical officer could temporarily strip a more senior officer of command. Duggan was glad he wasn't such a case. "Thank you, Corporal," he said.

"You'll need to eat as well – those mesh accelerants will burn through your energy reserves quicker than you can put food into your mouth to replace them. If you prefer, I can provide you with a high-energy paste." She wrinkled her nose, telling Duggan that he most certainly did *not* want to try the paste.

"I'll give the paste a miss," he said. "Am I free to go?"

"Whenever you're ready," she said. In the medical bay, Weiss was in charge and she had no need to call him sir.

Duggan rolled off the bed and stood upright. He half-expected to feel weak or giddy. In fact, he felt as good as new and he marvelled at the medical technology which could repair the human body so quickly and efficiently.

"Sir?" asked Barron. "Can I ask a question?"

"Anyone can ask me a question any time they please, soldier. You don't need permission."

"Where are we going to next?"

Duggan had made his decision not long before. "Listen," he said and then opened a channel to the bridge. It was McGlashan who answered.

"Sir?"

"Commander, please instruct Lieutenant Breeze to change course and point us towards the Helius Blackstar. We've got what we came for and now we're going home."

"Yes, sir," she said.

"I'll be back on the bridge in thirty minutes. Corporal Weiss tells me I need to eat."

With that, Duggan left the medical bay and headed for the mess room.

CHAPTER TWENTY-EIGHT

NEWS TRAVELLED fast and it would have been no surprise to Duggan if he'd found the soldiers already talking about the planned return home. As it was, he found McGlashan waiting for him. She was busy exchanging gallows humour with the few humans and Ghosts seated around the room. While he waited at the replicator for it to assemble a plate of hash browns and cheeseburgers, Duggan heard a noise he'd never heard before – it was a loud, rumbling sound. He wheeled about and saw that it was Braler laughing at something one of the human soldiers had said.

"There's hope for us yet," said McGlashan, when Duggan took his seat opposite.

"I'm pleased," he said with genuine feeling. "How long until we reach the Blackstar?"

"Forty hours, perhaps less. We've sustained a lot of damage. The AI can't reroute the gravity drives while we're at lightspeed. We're going to be slow when we arrive."

"What's the good news?" he asked.

"The Planet Breaker is back online, along with the disruptors. We could take another shot at the hub."

Duggan sighed. "It's too dangerous – they may have a dozen warships there already. We've got what we came for and it's time to go home."

"You won't get an argument from me. Getting home won't be plain sailing either."

"We may need to fight our way to the wormhole," he said in agreement.

"I asked Frank to start transmitting the data we stole from Astorn, in case we don't make it. We've had no time to sift through it so we don't know what's relevant and what isn't. He said we can only send it in tiny packets because we're on the backup comms."

"Didn't he say he had no idea where to direct the signal?"

"He's still not sure. I think he's guessing."

"It's usually better to do something instead of nothing."

"It could take years to reach Confederation Space."

"That'll be too late to have a significant bearing on the outcome of the inevitable war."

McGlashan smiled at him and Duggan felt his worries subside. "Hungry, huh?" she asked.

He looked at his plate and realised it was already half-empty. He pointed at his strapped arm. "Mesh accelerants. They like cheeseburgers."

"I couldn't stop eating when I was recovering from that shot I took in the stomach on Everlong," she said. "It felt good being able to eat what I liked without the guilt."

"We should be more like Frank," he said with a laugh. "I've never seen a man pack away so much food."

She lowered her eyes. "Do you still want that time away when we get back?" she asked.

They hadn't really spoken much since the start of the mission to traverse the Blackstar and he realised he'd been neglecting her. He was limited by the requirements of his duty, but he knew he should have paid more attention than he had.

"More than anything," he said. "I must be due about ten months of leave," he said.

"Me too." She looked wistful. "That would be nice, wouldn't it? Ten months away from it all."

"You'd be stir crazy inside two weeks," he joked.

"Probably. I won't know until I try."

"Anyway, I want you to know that nothing's changed," he said.

"There's another war to fight and it's coming," she said. "Let's hope there isn't an endless series of obstacles before us."

"We'll have to do the best we can with what we've got, Lucy."

One of the things Duggan most liked about McGlashan was that she was irrepressible. Her face lightened. "Since you've finished your nineteen cheeseburgers, how about we start looking through that data we stole? I'd like to learn a bit more about our enemy."

"There were only four cheeseburgers!" said Duggan in mock protestation. "And they were small ones."

"Never mind the details. Let's get to the bridge."

"Fine, I'm coming," he said. Something gurgled in his stomach and he raised an eyebrow. "Corporal Weiss was right about how many calories I'd need. I'll catch up once I've stopped off at the replicator."

"You can use the one outside the bridge, now come on!"

Duggan hurried after McGlashan, his anticipation building at what they might find amongst the transmission data. He remembered Chainer saying they'd intercepted it before encryption, but he still had no idea if the information would be easy to read or it if would need a team of Space Corps analysts to make sense of. *I won't know if I don't look,* he thought.

Once he was comfortable in his seat, Duggan accessed the memory arrays containing the transmission data.

"This isn't so bad," he said. "Every message is contained within its own discrete package."

"It's just a shame there are so damned many packages to open," said Chainer.

"There're only a few hundred thousand," laughed Breeze. "Enough to keep the Space Corps intel guys burning the midnight oil for a while."

"Some of these transmissions are enormous," continued Chainer. "The amount of traffic going through that hub was incredible."

"It's an ominous sign, if that's just one hub out of many. The Dreamers could have thousands of populated worlds."

"Subjos Gol-tur wasn't exactly forthcoming on the history of his former people, though his information is going to be somewhat out of date now," said Duggan. "Admiral Teron needs to pry the rest out of him."

"We could have everything we need here," said Breeze.

"Let's get on with it, then. If anyone has a bright idea about how we can separate the dross from the good stuff, I'm all ears."

Duggan opened a data packet at random. The contents were in an alien tongue and the *Crimson*'s language modules struggled to make sense of the characters. The Dreamers' language had deviated significantly from the version the Ghasts wrote and there were times the translation was clearly inaccurate. Some things were obvious – there were routing codes, along with various other tags from the sender such as their name and location. Without a way of putting these into context, they had little meaning and it would take perhaps weeks of cross-referencing to paint a picture of where and how the enemy lived.

It was tiring work and Duggan's concentration began to falter. Much of the data was nothing more than automated check-ins between computers to ensure they were online and operational. None of the messages were plain old person-to-person communications saying hello or inviting someone to lunch next week.

"They're a boring lot these aliens," said Breeze, his words echoing Duggan's thoughts. "I'd be happy to learn a few things about them, to see if there's anything in common between our two species. It doesn't seem like I'm going to find much of that in here."

Chainer, however, was far more enthusiastic. "I believe Astorn was at least partially a military comms hub," he said. "Some of the coding is similar to how we handle things in the Space Corps."

That got Duggan's interest. "If you're correct it means we've stolen some good stuff, instead of it being entirely civilian chatter."

"I believe I've also managed to identify their priority codes, sir."

"Now I'm *very* interested, Lieutenant. Can you sort the data according to its priority status?"

"I've just done it, sir. You'll see the updates on your screens in a few seconds."

"This is more like it!" exclaimed McGlashan moments later. "There's a transmission here that contains the coordinates of two more hub planets."

"That's a good start," said Duggan. "An excellent start, in fact."

With renewed enthusiasm, they got stuck into the task once more.

"I've archived the messages with priority codes seven and eight," said Chainer after a while. "That should help remove some of the clutter."

"Get rid of priority six messages as well," said McGlashan.

"I've opened dozens of those ones and I think they're network audit logs."

"Okay, I've hidden them as well."

"This is a gold mine," said Breeze eventually. "I've found what appears to be datasheets and specifications for spacecraft components being sent from one research facility to another."

"I've got the coordinates of a further three hub planets," said Chainer. "Alongside that, I've got what I believe to be an outline map of a place the language modules have translated as Sector-17."

"Show it on the main screen," said Duggan.

"Here you go. I don't think it's complete."

"If they have seventeen – *at least* seventeen – sectors like this one, humanity is properly screwed," said Breeze.

The bulkhead screen showed a map containing countless stars, spread across a huge distance.

"I'll highlight the solar systems I believe to be populated," said Chainer.

"Crap," said Breeze. "Dozens of them."

"That's assuming I've interpreted the data correctly."

"We can't get ourselves hung up on what we find," said Duggan. "I wasn't expecting our enemy to be confined to three planets adjacent to each other and I'm sure you weren't either."

"The bigger they are..." said Chainer.

"The harder they hit," finished Breeze. "And the more warships they have."

"Here's something else," said McGlashan. "I don't think we're the only species fighting against them."

"What have you found, Commander?"

"One of these transmissions is a requisition order, demanding six Class-8 and nine Class-15 vessels, whatever they are. Apparently, they are to replace losses in Sector-23."

"Do you ever get the feeling that the Confederation is really,

really insignificant?" asked Chainer. "I've spent my entire life thinking I'm a speck amongst the billions, and then I find out that the Confederation is no more than a speck of its own."

"I'm not sure I approve of the word *speck* when it comes to a description of the Confederation," said Duggan drily. "Nonetheless, it does appear that other species have expanded significantly further than we have."

He opened the next transmission on his list and scanned through the contents. Then, he blinked to be sure his eyes weren't deceiving him and he read it again, this time with great care. "You need to read the details of data package 62534A," he said.

There was a period of quiet, before Breeze spoke. "I don't know if this is very, very good or very, very bad."

"If I understand this correctly, that installation on Frades-2 was a slingshot?" said Chainer.

"That's how I read it," said Duggan. "Designed to fire a spacecraft up to lightspeed through the Helius Blackstar."

"Then the affected vessel activates its own fission drive as it emerges," said Breeze.

Chainer looked puzzled. "But they're sending warships through anyway," he protested. "Why do they need this slingshot?"

"We have no idea what modifications their spacecraft require in order to make a successful transit," said Duggan. "We know they keep trying and they've failed a few times with it."

"But the *Crimson* is using one of their very own cores," said Chainer. "If we can do it, why can't they?"

"We've done it only once, Lieutenant."

"It makes you wonder about the risks," said Breeze.

"I wouldn't spend too long thinking about it. We've got no choice other than to attempt a second journey through the Blackstar," said Duggan. "We know it's coming and we can't allow ourselves to fear it."

"Doesn't this mean we've scuppered their plot for a while?" asked Chainer. "The Frades-2 installation won't be doing many lightspeed catapults after Commander McGlashan got her hands on it."

"What they built once, they can build again, Lieutenant. When it's working, they can throw their ships towards Confederation Space at will, except this time it won't be a mothership and a smattering of others. They'll be able to send whole fleets through. We'll never defeat them."

The situation was about to get a whole lot worse.

"Sir?"

"I don't like it when you start off a conversation like that, Commander. It means there's bad news ahead."

"They have another installation close to the first – the same thing as they had on Frades-2."

"Where is it?" asked Duggan, crossing to look at her screen.

"I don't know, sir. They use their coordinates and we use ours. We haven't yet been able to tie them together. That isn't the worst part of it."

Duggan read the rest of the details over her shoulder. He swore loudly.

"They've got a fleet ready," he said. "Eighteen warships waiting to be sent through the wormhole."

"Damn," said Chainer.

CHAPTER TWENTY-NINE

DUGGAN PACED UP AND DOWN. "I need every scrap of information we can find about this second planet," he said. "I want to know where their fleet is located and when they plan to launch it. Lieutenant Chainer, I need you do everything you can to tie our coordinates with theirs, so we have the same points of reference. You have my permission to drink as much coffee and hi stim as you require, but I want those coordinates!"

"What're we going to do, sir?" asked Chainer.

"I don't know, Lieutenant. I really don't know."

Duggan took his seat and resumed his search through the Dreamers' transmission data. He uncovered much that would be of interest to the Space Corps, but he didn't have time to look at it in detail – there were other, more pressing concerns. A fleet of eighteen ships would represent a significant incursion into Confederation Space, especially since they would be free to travel wherever they chose and destroy whatever they wished.

The search proved fruitless and they found no more details relating to the capabilities of the assembled Dreamer war fleet, nor anything which would allow them to pinpoint the location of the second ground installation. They'd stolen a large quantity of data, but it was after all only a snapshot of events taking place within the enemy's territory and it was naturally going to have many gaps. As time passed and fatigue crept in, Duggan felt a growing certainty about what they had to do.

"We have to destroy that installation and hope they haven't already sent their warships through the wormhole," he said.

"I think I can offer something positive," said Breeze looking up. "There are time stamps on each of the transmissions. They mean nothing to us, of course, except as a list of numbers. However, we can translate into something we know by deducting the time stamp on the earliest transmission from the time stamp on the latest one."

"What does that give us?" asked Duggan.

"If you look at the transmission which mentions their war fleet, you'll notice a time reference that's later than anything on our stolen data. It could be their planned time to launch."

"It may be nothing relevant," said Duggan. "The arrival of a nineteenth ship or the time of a drill."

"This is what we have, sir. If this is their departure time, it's approximately five hours after we reach the wormhole."

"If only we knew where to find them," said Duggan.

"It's down to you, Frank," said McGlashan.

"Great! Thanks, Commander."

"Maybe we can help," said Duggan. "While Lieutenant Chainer does his thing, we can look at the data from our first scan when we came through the Blackstar. There might be something that gives us a clue as to where the second installation is. We need to look for similar planets to Frades-2, which are a similar distance away from the wormhole."

"You may be disappointed, sir," said Chainer. "It takes a long time for the super-fars to interpret distant data. You may recall there wasn't a great deal of time to spend map-making."

"I understand, Lieutenant, but we have to do something."

Chainer's assessment of their chances proved to be an accurate one. The *Crimson*'s sensors had picked up numerous solar systems in the vicinity of the wormhole, without gathering much in the way of additional details. The end result of the crew's search was eleven separate planets, any of which might be home to a second enemy installation.

"There's no time to check out eleven planets," muttered Duggan.

"Let's face it. We need the coordinates of the enemy fleet and the target planet," said McGlashan.

"I'm not planning to attack the enemy fleet, Commander – just the installation."

"If they're stationed close by, we could emerge from light-speed only to find two thousand missiles coming our way."

"It's unlikely," said Duggan.

"Not as unlikely as you might think, sir," said Breeze. "We can assume their fleet is somewhere near to the catapult. Unless we arrive many hours away, there's a chance one of them will see our fission signature. If we know where they are, we can tailor our approach. I'd far rather arrive undetected so that we can take a look about in comparative safety."

"Fine, fine, I acknowledge the necessity," said Duggan.

The minutes and hours ticked by. Duggan, Breeze and McGlashan were able to take breaks, but Chainer seemed like a man possessed. He drank coffee after coffee while he stared at his console screens, muttering words to himself that the others couldn't quite hear. His hands never stopped as they punched up lists of data for his eyes to read.

"We might have to get you that third hand after all, Lieutenant," said Duggan at one point.

"I'm feeling pretty worn out, sir. The caffeine isn't working anymore."

"Want me to see if Corporal Weiss can fix you up with something stronger?"

"Not a chance, sir. I don't want her putting any of that medical crap into my body."

Duggan looked sideways at McGlashan. Her mouth was half-open in shock from hearing Chainer's words.

"Frank, you eat and drink crap every single day," she said at last.

"Yeah, but it's healthy crap and I won't hear another word said on the matter."

McGlashan sat down with a shake of her head and a bemused expression on her face.

"Anything you want, Lieutenant, let us know," said Duggan.

Chainer was already lost to the world and his lips moved in time with his thoughts.

"Ten hours until we break from lightspeed," said Breeze. "I've chosen a place that's two hours out."

"What if we can't translate the coordinates of this second installation, sir?" asked McGlashan. "Are we going to wait around until we find it?"

Duggan chewed on his lip. "No," he said. "I don't like the odds if we have to search randomly. We'll need to jump from planet to planet, each time taking the risk of our fission signature being seen. If I'm not confident it'll be an in and out raid, we'll go through the wormhole. The second installation is a target of opportunity – an important one, but not enough to attack at any cost."

Ten hours became five and Duggan took himself off for a walk through the confines of the spaceship's interior. Inevitably, he found himself at the mess room, where all corridors seemed to eventually lead. The room was three-quarters full, the soldiers in high spirits and exchanging wisecracks. Duggan counted four Ghasts in the room, their grey-skinned heads easily visible above the others. They seemed at ease with their human counterparts.

He took a seat opposite Lieutenant Ortiz. "Thirty years of fighting and now this," he said.

"Most of us have no reason to hate the Ghasts, sir. They're the same as us, they just fought for a different bunch of politicians."

"Practical to the last, Lieutenant."

"I'm not saying it's all handshakes and smiles. I can see it in the eyes of a few of our troops."

"As long as they keep it to themselves."

"I'll make sure they do, sir." She sighed. "If everything goes to plan and our alliance with the Ghasts remains strong, it could be generations until the war is forgotten."

"There's a new war to help them forget. It's hard to hold a grudge against the man or woman who just saved your life."

"The Ghasts don't let their women fight, sir. I twisted Red-Gulos' ear about it and I finally managed to wring an opinion out of him. Apparently, the women are the artists of the species, while the men go to war. It sounds a bit Neanderthal if you ask me."

"We can't expect them to have identical values to us."

"I know sir, but can you imagine me writing poetry or playing a harp?" She smiled at this alternative vision of herself.

"Don't knock it until you try it, Lieutenant. I'm convinced everyone has more than one talent."

"So what's yours, sir?"

Duggan tried to come up with a response and couldn't immediately think of one. "I don't know," he said.

This time Ortiz laughed, with no trace of mockery in the sound. "How's about you take up the harp and I'll try my hand at poetry?"

"That's a deal," he said. "Let's wait until we get back to base before we take up any new distractions."

"We're not going straight home, are we?" she asked.

He suppressed a look of surprise at her intuition. "How the hell did you figure that out?"

"You always come to the mess room when you're searching for something to take your mind off your duty."

"You've got me there, Lieutenant, and you're correct. We've discovered evidence of a second enemy base near to the wormhole, along with a war fleet. If we can nail down exactly where they are, we're going to take a shot at them."

"Need me to prep the boys and girls?"

"There'll be no troop deployment this time, Lieutenant. We're going to nuke the crap out of them and fly away through the wormhole, giving them the finger as we go."

"Sounds like a plan."

"It might not come off, in which case we'll simply leave this area of space, taking our stolen data with us." A clock on the mess room wall told him it was nearly time to get back to the bridge. "I didn't thank you for sealing up my suit helmet on Astorn."

"That wasn't me, sir. It was Lieutenant Chainer – he was first down the shaft to see what was wrong."

"He never said."

"Did he need to?"

"I guess not," he replied.

He left the mess room and took a longer route to the bridge. He stopped briefly at the medical facility and looked inside. Barron was gone, leaving McCarty as the sole occupant of the room. The man was still attached to the medical robot and it was only the steady beeping accompanying his heartbeat which told Duggan he was alive.

Back at the bridge, there was a change.

"Where's Lieutenant Chainer?" Duggan asked.

"I was just about to message you, sir," said McGlashan. "You must have missed him by about twenty seconds. He found what we wanted to know and I gave him leave to take a nap."

"He'll never sleep. I've seen how much caffeine he's taken today," said Duggan, hurrying to his seat. "What've we got?"

"The second base is only a few minutes' high lightspeed away from the first one, sir, and it's about the same distance away from the wormhole."

"Was it one of the eleven planets we'd narrowed it down to?"

"Nope – it's in an entirely different area."

"That figures," he said. "Where's their fleet?"

"This is the part you might not like so much – they're parked right off the wormhole. The coordinates are quite precise."

Duggan sighed. It was the second most logical place to leave the warships after the planet itself, but the exact last place he wanted them to be.

"Could the catapult pick their warships up from that that range in order to launch them?" he asked.

"I don't know, sir," said Breeze. "The target vessel might need to be within a few thousand kilometres or it may be that the installation can perform its function from a great distance away. The first base had colossal reserves of power."

"Did the super-fars get anything on this planet?"

"Nothing of great significance. It's the sixth planet out and far larger than average."

"How long until they're due to launch?"

"Four hours."

"And we're two hours away ourselves," Duggan mused. "That doesn't give us a lot of time to play around."

"What sort of playing around did you have in mind?" asked McGlashan.

"I'm not sure," he hedged. "Eighteen warships clustered around the Blackstar limits our chances of escape somewhat."

"I could aim to get us close to the wormhole, sir and we could try to activate the launch sequence. The trouble is, we're heading into the unknown. We can't go straight to lightspeed after leaving it and you're aware the stealth modules take some time to reactivate. If luck isn't on our side, we could find ourselves right in the thick of it."

Duggan felt the beginnings of a plan forming. He had no idea if it would work or not and he turned the possibilities over in his mind. If it came off, they could accomplish a significant victory as well as escaping. If it failed, they would be just as dead as if they tried to escape and something went wrong. After ten minutes of weighing up the odds, he decided to speak to his crew and see what they thought of it.

CHAPTER THIRTY

"THAT'S why he's captain and I'm only a lieutenant," said Breeze. "There must be a test you need to sit in order to see how many crazy ways you can think of to get your crew killed."

"If it works, we'll find it significantly easier to reach the wormhole and we'll have reduced the enemy's capability to strike at the Confederation."

"I understand the positives, sir."

"Can you modify the launch sequence that we used to get through the wormhole?"

Breeze huffed and puffed. "I couldn't reprogram it, but I could modify it to do what you want easily enough."

Duggan turned his attention to McGlashan. "We'll have a tiny window during which we can launch. Do you think you'll be able to pull it off?"

"It's going to be tight, sir."

"That's not what I asked."

"I'll give it my best shot." She smiled. "No promises."

At that moment, Lieutenant Chainer walked onto the bridge. He looked pale and haggard. "What do you know? I feel

exhausted but my brain won't shut down. No sleep for me."
Something in the tableau caught his attention. "What?" he asked,
patting himself down in case his dishevelled appearance had
caused the scene.

"Captain Duggan is asking if we wish to face eighteen
Dreamer warships head-on."

"Oh. I thought it was something serious," said Chainer, dropping into his seat as if nothing untoward had happened.

"Fine," said Breeze. "Don't come running to me when we're
all dead."

Duggan filled Chainer in on the details.

"That sounds like an excellent plan, sir."

"Has everyone lost their mind?" asked Breeze, aghast.

"I'm trying to be more positive in my outlook," said Chainer.

"You've picked a funny time to give it a go," Breeze replied.

"If I'm going to die, I might as well have a smile on
my face."

Duggan was beginning to wonder if Chainer's lack of sleep
was affecting him adversely. "Are you ready for duty,
Lieutenant?"

"Definitely, sir."

They sat quietly until Breeze announced there were only
thirty minutes until they entered local space. Duggan busied
himself with a few final checks.

"What's our weapons status following the damage our hull
suffered at Astorn?"

"Two of our nuke tubes were permanently disabled and three
of our Lambda clusters, sir. That leaves us with six nuclear
launchers, twenty-one fully operational conventional clusters and
two Shatterer tubes."

"I'd like double the number, but it's going to have to be
enough," he said. "Lieutenant Breeze, are the modifications
completed yet?"

"That they are, sir. I'll have to leave the timing with the AI, since this is way beyond the capability of my reactions."

Duggan walked over until he was standing at Breeze's shoulder. "You're comfortable with what we're doing?"

"Of course I am, sir. I just needed to make sure everyone was aware of what we're getting ourselves into."

"Nothing worse than any other choice we could have made."

"No, I suppose not. When it comes to judging risk, there's always going to be guesswork involved and I trust you to make those guesses more than anyone else."

Duggan stepped away. "Is everyone ready?"

"As I'll ever be," said McGlashan.

"Five minutes," said Breeze after a time had passed. "At thirty seconds before we exit lightspeed, I'll activate the wormhole launch sequence. We're going at lightspeed anyway, so we won't notice anything. The AI will need to work at double speed to prepare for the immediate re-launch, so there're going to be a few alerts on your screens. When we arrive at the wormhole the real fun and games will start."

"I'll blow as many of the bastards up as possible," said McGlashan.

"Then the second lightspeed jump will activate after a second or two," confirmed Breeze.

Duggan spent the next five minutes suppressing the urge to ask his crew if they were ready. They were professionals and they'd have raised any uncertainties already. Nevertheless, he found it difficult to remain quiet and he recognised it as a symptom of his nervousness. They were coming to the end of the mission and now they were so close to home, the final hurdle seemed to be the highest.

"Thirty seconds," said Breeze. "Launch sequence activated."

The utilisation on the AI shot to the end of its gauge and remained firmly in place. A figure beneath it showed the usage at two hundred and thirty percent of its intended maximum. Duggan couldn't help but look at the hatch by his feet and he wondered how hot it was getting in there.

"Fifteen seconds."

"Three hundred and twenty percent on the core," said Chainer in amazement. "It's going to burn out."

"No it's not," said Duggan through gritted teeth.

"Here we go," said Breeze. "Arrival."

The external sensor feeds winked into instant focus. Duggan saw the slab side of something vast and metallic, barely ten kilometres away. The port-side feeds showed seven or eight of the enemy warships, including three battleships and two of the same heavy cruisers they'd encountered near to the planet Astorn. To the front, the remainder of the enemy fleet was visible, their warships gathered together with hardly fifty kilometres between each.

"Launching," said McGlashan.

Something flashed white, completely obscuring the main screen. Then, the sensor feeds went blank and the *Crimson* entered lightspeed once more, less than two seconds after it had arrived at the Helius Blackstar. This second jump was a short one and the spaceship returned to local space almost immediately.

"They didn't have their energy shields active," said Breeze. "On the other hand, one of them managed to hit us with a particle beam on our way out. It's knocked a few million tonnes of our gravity drive offline."

Duggan looked at the power gauges. "Forty-five percent."

"Say goodbye to stealth – the modules have shut down," said Breeze. "We might be in a position to activate them in an hour or so when things have cooled off."

"This will have played out long before then," said Duggan.

"The target planet is dead ahead, sir," said Chainer. "Someone give it a name for me."

"Glisst," said Breeze promptly.

"On we go," said Duggan, accelerating to maximum velocity.

"It'll take ten minutes to reach high orbit at this speed," said Chainer.

"Commander McGlashan, please report."

"We entered local space nine kilometres from one of their battleships. I hit it with three nukes and seventy-two Lambdas. The rest of our missiles were distributed amongst the remainder of their vessels. You're aware our homing systems don't work against the Dreamer warships, but we were close enough that I'm confident we scored a high number of hits. I was unable to launch from five of our Lambda clusters because they lacked a line-of-sight path."

"What about the Shatterers?"

"I targeted one of their other battleships, sir. I can't confirm if they successfully impacted – we know they'll target the bastards, so I'm hopeful."

"It's the best we could have done in the circumstances," said Duggan, running high on his body's natural adrenaline. "That's not something they'll forget. Lieutenant Chainer – have you located the enemy installation on Glisst?"

"Negative, sir. You're going to have to come around the planet until I can see it. The coordinates were for the planet, not the location of the installation on the surface."

"We need to find it while they're still pissed enough to act in haste."

"There might be a problem," said Breeze, his voice loud enough to make it clear it was something important.

"What's wrong, Lieutenant?"

"Check out the AI core, sir. It's not cooling down."

"Three hundred and ten percent," said Duggan. "That's lower than its peak."

"I know. It should be closer to one hundred percent by now.

I'm not an expert on Dreamer tech, but I doubt it's meant to be performing so many cycles for so long."

"What's making the demands on it?"

"I can't be sure. If you made me guess I'd tell you it's a bug in the programming of the launch system, keeping it running instead of letting it slow down."

"Do what you can, Lieutenant and keep me informed."

"It might stop us doing what we came to do, sir."

"It can't."

The news about the AI core wasn't good. Even so, Duggan couldn't let it distract him and he left the worrying to Lieutenant Breeze. Chainer provided a new course to follow that gave the greatest chance of locating the installation on Glisst in the shortest amount of time and Duggan piloted the *Crimson* directly along this trajectory.

Five minutes passed until Chainer shouted in excitement. "Got them!" he said.

"I need to be sure it's the same as the one on Frades-2."

"It is, sir. Four towers, one huge central pyramid and lots of smaller buildings in between."

"That's what we want," said Duggan.

He took the *Crimson* straight towards the installation. At first glance, it looked identical to the previous one and for all he knew, it may well have been so.

"There is no sign of surface-to-air defence batteries," said McGlashan.

"If they've got some hidden away, this plan is going to go wrong pretty quickly, Commander."

They came to forty thousand kilometres without encountering a hostile response. Duggan took them to twenty thousand and then ten. Still nothing was fired towards the spaceship.

"That settles it – this base is as vulnerable as the last one," he said.

By the time Duggan brought the *Crimson* to a halt, they were only five hundred metres above the corner towers. The spaceship hung in the air, promising death to everyone who saw it.

"The core is at two hundred and ninety percent," said Breeze. "It's definitely something in the launch sequence program."

"Can you fix it?"

"I don't have a choice, do I?"

"None."

Duggan closed his eyes and lay back in his chair.

"How long?" asked Chainer.

"Your guess is as good as mine. We'll wait here and see what happens."

"I hate waiting."

"It won't be long."

In his mind, Duggan counted the seconds.

CHAPTER THIRTY-ONE

DUGGAN HEARD Chainer stringing together some guesses.

"Ten seconds for the Estral below to realise we're not one of their own, plus twenty seconds to recover from the panic. A further minute to act upon the information and let their war fleet know we're here."

"Let's call it forty seconds for the war fleet to coordinate and a further fifteen seconds to set Glisst as a destination," said McGlashan, joining in.

"With an additional thirty to forty seconds for fission drive warm-up," said Duggan, his eyes still closed.

"That's a total of three minutes and five seconds if we assume the quickest response," said Chainer. "How long have we been here?"

"We've been above the base for about one minute," said McGlashan. "They'll have detected us before then, so I don't know when the timer will have started."

"We could be down to thirty seconds already," said Chainer.

It turned out they'd overestimated the response time.

"Six big fission signatures," grunted Breeze. He was too busy working on the core to elaborate.

"Those will be the battleships," said Chainer. "They'll have the fastest response times."

Duggan looked at the gravity drive and saw it was stuck at forty-five percent. Whatever was burning the core, it was also preventing the AI from realigning the atoms in the engines.

"There are seven more fission signatures, sir," said Chainer, covering for Breeze. "Most of the enemy war fleet will arrive somewhere close to Glisst in the next few seconds."

"Lieutenant Breeze, I need the core back."

"I'm working on it."

"We have no time left. Get the fission drives ready – we're leaving. Take us anywhere."

"We can't, sir, the core will burn out."

"There's no alternative, Lieutenant! Do it immediately!"

"Fission drives warming up. They'll be five minutes and twenty seconds – the AI is busy on other things."

"Two more fission signatures," said Chainer. "That makes fifteen of their war fleet."

"I need specifics on their locations, Lieutenant. Is there a course that will allow us to avoid them until we can go to lightspeed?"

"There are a few choices, sir. None of which will allow us to avoid destruction for five minutes. In fact, their closest vessel will be in a position to launch missiles at us in approximately ninety seconds."

Duggan realised he'd led them into a dead end. There was no hope of escape from here and it appeared as though it was down to nothing more than a bug in the launch sequence coding. He was calm and his brain continued to evaluate the possibilities, but the best result he could imagine was mutual destruction. It wasn't something he wished to contemplate. Deprived of choice, he gave the order.

"Get the Planet Breaker ready," he said. "If we're going down, we'll take their fleet with us."

"I'm unable to access it, sir," said McGlashan. "It takes a lot of processing power to fire."

"We're to be denied even this one opportunity to fight?" he said.

His tactical screen showed the approaching enemy warships. The first few to arrive had exited lightspeed at the far side of Glisst. The red dots which represented the battleships moved at incredible speed and would soon emerge above the horizon. After that, a torrent of warheads would rain down upon the *Crimson*.

"Perhaps they'll hold fire while we remain above their base," said Chainer hopefully.

"They may do just that Lieutenant, but as soon as they realise that we're about to escape into lightspeed, they'll have no choice other than to destroy us. They can't permit us to roam through their territory. Whatever it takes, they'll want to stop us right here."

From the corner of his eye, Duggan saw an electronic needle flicker and jump. "The core..." he began.

"I think I've done it," said Breeze, his voice laden with a mixture of stress and relief.

"It's dropped to two hundred and sixty percent already," said Duggan. "Two hundred, one-eighty."

"It should have gone straight to about sixty percent," said Breeze. "There's still a problem."

"What's the fission drive timer?"

"Fifty seconds, sir. It's falling."

"I can access the Planet Breaker!" said McGlashan. "I'm powering it up."

"The fission warmup time is falling quickly now that the core is closer to its usual operating parameters," said Breeze.

"Will it be soon enough?"

"Maybe."

"Sir, the closest battleship has launched," said McGlashan. "You were right, they're taking no chances."

"I don't need to know how many missiles there are," Duggan replied, looking at the sea of red circles on his screen. "We're back on the plan. Do what we agreed."

"This one is going to be tight," said Breeze.

"You did well to fix the core," Duggan told him.

"It's not fixed. If by some miracle we get away from here, it's still got to get us home."

"Ten seconds until the enemy missiles reach us, sir."

"The Planet Breaker is online and available," said McGlashan. She took a deep breath. "Firing the Planet Breaker at Glisst."

"The fission drives have engaged," said Breeze.

The *Crimson* exited local space. At the same moment in time, Glisst was broken apart by the weapon carried somewhere deep in the spacecraft's hull. The wreckage of the planet burst out from the centre, engulfing the fifteen enemy warships and destroying them within moments. The installation on the surface fared no better and it was hurled into space at several thousand kilometres per second, before it broke into progressively smaller fragments which would be forever lost.

Those on the *Crimson* didn't witness the death. Duggan stared straight ahead, with no desire to see the aftermath of another planet's destruction.

"Another one bites the dust," said Chainer. "It doesn't get any easier."

"We're in charge of a terrible weapon," said McGlashan. "It would be better if it had never been invented."

"Yeah. What sort of bastard sets out to create something that can do so much damage?"

"I do not wish to empathise with our enemy, but we don't know what drove them to it," said Duggan.

"It's because they're warmongering swine, sir."

"We don't know what their motivations are, Lieutenant and we can only guess." Duggan sighed. "As I told you, I don't want to sound like I need to understand their reasons. At the moment, I only wish they had never come through the wormhole and we knew nothing about them."

"It was easier when it was only the Ghasts."

"The AI core is holding at a steady one hundred and twenty percent," said Breeze. "That's higher than it should be, but I'm a lot more comfortable with how it is now."

"Where are we going?" asked Duggan, remembering there were still urgent matters to attend.

"I have no idea, sir. I just plugged in some numbers and set us on our way. We'll exit lightspeed in about five minutes. I didn't think you'd want us to go far."

"Indeed not. We'll take stock and consider the best way to proceed."

"The way it's going, we'll surely appear in the middle of seven of their combined fleets," said Chainer. "Anyone want a coffee?"

"I'm beginning to have serious concerns about the state of your mental health, Frank," said Breeze.

"Really?"

"He's speaking for everyone," said McGlashan.

"We need to calm down, folks," said Duggan. The thought came to him that the crew were high on battle – it was a buzz that could make men and women act differently to normal. *We've been out here for too long. It's time to fix that.*

He stood up and faced the others. Chainer was halfway to

the doorway in his hunt for coffee and Duggan motioned for him to sit again.

"These have been trying times for us," Duggan said. "I realise we've not been here for anything like an extended period, but there's hardly been a moment where we've been able to sit back without the threat of death hanging over us. We've far exceeded my expectations and I'm sure we've far exceeded anything Admiral Teron wished to come from this."

"If we get back alive and nothing else, I'm sure he'll be surprised," joked Breeze.

"I've no doubt that's true, Lieutenant. Think of what else we can tell him – not only have we got enough data to map out this area of enemy space, we've also obtained technical specifications on their warships, details of their comms hubs and some of their home worlds. If those things alone were not enough, we've knocked out two of their lightspeed catapults and surely reduced most of those eighteen warships to wreckage."

"Not bad for a few days' work, sir," said Chainer.

"We'll exit lightspeed in about twenty seconds," said Breeze.

"Get yourselves prepared," Duggan ordered, hurrying to his station. He hadn't intended his pep talk to last quite so long.

"We have entered local space."

"Nothing on the fars," said Chainer. "I'll have the results from the supers shortly. Other than that, we're pretty much nowhere."

Duggan was relieved. It would have been tremendously bad luck if their randomly-chosen trajectory had exposed them to an immediate hostile encounter.

"Give me the run-down," he said.

"The core is still churning over something," said Breeze. "It's going at a near-constant sixty percent utilisation. If the Dreamer tech is anything like our own, it'll run for decades at eighty or ninety percent without problems – anything much over and you start to run into problems."

"Why is it still running so hot?"

"I'm not sure, sir. I shut down each of the remaining process threads from the wormhole launch sequence program and that's what brought the utilisation down. I'm out of ideas when it comes to getting it to its expected level. If you think about it, the core fell most of the way down a thirty-metre shaft onto a hard metal surface. We should be thankful it's working at all."

"Will it get us back to Confederation Space?"

"I don't know. My honest opinion is that we're in real danger of being stranded here."

"There's nothing stopping us activating the launch sequence is there?"

"No, sir."

"If we make it through the wormhole, it doesn't matter if the core burns out."

"Aside from the fact that it's an irreplaceable piece of hardware."

"I'm more interested in getting everyone home alive. Admiral Teron can worry about what comes after."

"In that case, we need to do the same as we did on the first transit – point the *Crimson* towards the wormhole and activate the double-jump at the last possible moment, hoping we don't get crushed by gravitational forces or blown up by an enemy warship."

"We did it once and we'll have to do it again," said Duggan. "We'll head towards the Blackstar as soon as we've got our stealth capabilities and sufficient spare gravity drive power to manoeuvre."

"The gravity engines are on forty-seven percent. The core is repairing slower than usual."

"An hour or two won't make a difference."

"The super-fars have come back clear," said Chainer. "Unless a Dreamer ships decides to come sightseeing in this precise location, we've got the time we need."

"Remain on high alert. I'll let you know when we're going for our second traversal of the wormhole."

The others fell into a silence that spoke of concentration and trepidation. For his part, Duggan watched the progress of the AI core on the engine re-routing. Staring at a gauge occupied his eyes, while his mind searched ahead, trying to weave future possibilities into something he could grasp and mould.

Whatever happened, they had to risk the dangers of travelling through the Helius Blackstar. That was an unavoidable fact. There was much he didn't know and it was the uncertainties which he hated. There had been only fifteen fission signatures at Glisst. Fifteen out of eighteen enemy warships had succumbed to their desire to pursue the much smaller Space Corps vessel and been destroyed for their rashness. That left three unaccounted for. It was likely they'd destroyed one of those three, but that left two remaining which may or may not have been knocked out of action. The sensor data from their recent lightspeed jump to the wormhole was inconclusive and there was no way to be sure how many spaceships had been wrecked or rendered inoperable.

The end of a mission is always the hardest part and we always pull through, he told himself.

On this occasion, the words brought no comfort.

CHAPTER THIRTY-TWO

"THE GRAVITY DRIVES are at seventy-five percent," said Breeze. "The core utilisation is creeping up again."

"Is that expected?" asked Duggan.

"It happens at times. If the core hits a particularly difficult run of realignment choices, it can go up. Given our current situation, I view every deviation as a cause for concern."

"I'd like to wait until at least eighty percent," said Duggan. "That'll give us some flexibility if we need to take evasive action."

"You're looking at another hour or so."

"We'll wait. Is everyone aware of what we're going to do when we reach local space around the wormhole?"

"Keep our fingers crossed," said Chainer.

"We need a bit more than fingers crossed, Lieutenant."

"Yes, sir. I understand what lies ahead of us."

After what felt like an interminable wait, the gravity drive reached eighty percent of its maximum theoretical output. Duggan gave it an additional five minutes for luck and then informed his crew it was time to be on their way.

"Lieutenant Breeze, take us back to the wormhole."

"Am I aiming for close in or far out, sir?"

"I want caution. We'll aim for a good distance out, which should give us time to activate the stealth modules. I'd like a chance to scout the area first – we've seen first-hand that the enemy visit the place with regularity. We may need to wait for our opening or we may not. Either way, I don't want to be dodging missiles at any point if I can avoid it."

"The fission drives are building up. We'll only be at light-speed for a few minutes."

"We could be in Confederation Space in three or four hours," said McGlashan.

"It's just as cold and dark as it is in Dreamer Space," Chainer replied.

"It's still home."

"That it is, Commander."

"We're at lightspeed," said Breeze a short time later. "I wonder what fun and games lie ahead."

There wasn't much chance to ponder it further. With barely a murmur, the *Crimson* switched to its gravity drive and entered local space, three hours out from the Helius Blackstar.

Duggan called for updates.

"There isn't anything close to us," said Chainer. "The fars and super-fars are updating slower than normal, but so far there's nothing highlighted as a possible risk."

"That's what I like to hear. Lieutenant Breeze, I want you to activate the stealth modules the moment they become available."

"Yes, sir. That should be two minutes, give or take."

The *Crimson* was enveloped in its cloak minutes before Chainer had completed his area scan.

"It's amazing how much less vulnerable I feel when the modules are running," said McGlashan.

"This is the best technology we've come up with in decades," Duggan replied. "Give me a ship-mounted cluster of miniaturised Shatterer missiles to go with it and I'll be a happy man."

"I can't give you miniaturised Shatterers, but I can give you some good news," said Chainer. "The fars and super-fars have come back with negatives. There are no enemy warships in the vicinity."

"What about somewhere behind the wormhole?"

"Yes, there could be something I can't detect from here. Other than that, it's clear."

"I'm going to take us in," said Duggan. "We're three hours away – that's ample time for an orbiting spaceship to show its face. Lieutenant Chainer, can you look for any signs of wreckage that might tell us what happened to those Dreamer spacecraft we attacked when we did our double-jump into this area?"

"I'm doing so right this moment, sir. I don't expect it to take long, given the size of the vessels."

As he waited, Duggan brought up an image of the wormhole on the main screen. It looked no more inviting than it ever had, though it was now a gateway to what felt like freedom. Duggan had gone into this mission with open eyes, yet he'd been in no way prepared for what was to come. *That's the nature of the beast.*

"There are floating scraps close to where their fleet was positioned, sir," said Chainer. "There is also radiation in the form of gamma rays. They're dispersing but they're easy enough to detect, especially on the wreckage."

"Can you confirm the kill?"

"With confidence, sir. We took out one of their battleships."

"There are two more unaccounted for."

"There's other wreckage. It's drifting away in a different direction, with the large bulk of it spiralling towards the wormhole. There'll be nothing left of it in a day or two."

"Is that the wreckage of three separate vessels?" Duggan persisted.

"I do believe it is. One of them hasn't broken up entirely – there's a kilometre-long section, close to another piece of a similar size. They're drifting slowly and in parallel."

"Show me the coordinates," said Breeze.

"There you go."

"That's a lot of their hull," mused Breeze. "There's something still active onboard – the power output is rising and falling. It's decaying slowly, but there's plenty going on."

"I've heard it said Gallenium reactions can continue for what is effectively an eternity," said McGlashan.

"You could power a few big cities from what's left of that warship," said Breeze.

"I'll try not to crash into them," said Duggan. "We'll need to deactivate stealth in order to launch into the wormhole and I'd prefer to do it at the last possible moment."

"I've got an eye on the timings," said Breeze. "We launched at sixty thousand klicks on the way here and it seemed to work. I'll assume we're doing the same thing this time."

Duggan nodded his agreement and turned his attention to the course leading towards the Helius Blackstar. During the following two hours, he spoke little, other than to check for updates from the crew. With the inevitability of death, the wormhole beckoned the *Crimson* onwards.

"Even if we don't make it, I'm glad we came," said Breeze, when they were less than thirty minutes away.

"Me too," said Chainer. "It was a once-in-a-lifetime experience."

"It'll have shown our enemy that we're not going to be a pushover in the coming conflict," said McGlashan. "I'm sure we took them completely by surprise. Their defences were poor and they have been slow to react to the threat of our presence."

"I don't want to be the voice of gloom, but for all we know, this could be a tiny, near-forgotten corner of the great, eternal Dreamer Empire," said Chainer.

"I'll speak to Subjos Gol-Tur when we return," said Duggan. "This time I'll get answers."

At ten minutes away, the signs of nervousness were clear. Chainer fidgeted and drummed his fingers, Breeze cleared his throat constantly, and Duggan felt a sheen of sweat prickling on his forehead. Only McGlashan appeared unaffected and she smiled at Duggan when he looked at her.

"We're going slower than usual owing to our reduced engine output," said Breeze. "Assuming we experience a modest acceleration when we're closer, we'll need to activate the launch sequence approximately forty seconds out. On top of that, we should deactivate stealth an additional three minutes away, which gives us room for manoeuvre if we need to make any last-moment alterations."

"How is the core activity?" asked McGlashan.

"Elevated," said Breeze.

"Succinct," she replied.

"There's nothing else to say, Commander."

With five minutes remaining, Duggan spoke to Ortiz on the internal comms. "We're going to attempt the second and final transit in a few minutes. Let the troops know."

"It won't be the final transit, sir. Even if we don't make it, there'll be another bunch of us ordered through from the other side at some point," she said, without apparent rancour.

"No doubt," he said. "If it goes wrong, I want you to know I'm proud of everyone who came."

"This won't be your last voyage, sir. There's always another."

"We'll see, Lieutenant. Over."

"We're coming up on some of the larger pieces of wreckage, sir," said Chainer.

"There's plenty of gamma radiation and I can see a few

plasma craters," added Breeze. "We hit them pretty hard, considering how little time we had to do it."

"The risks of war," said Duggan.

"Indeed."

They flew by the wreckage and Duggan checked the sensor feed. It looked as though one of the enemy's mid-sized cruisers had been torn in half and the pieces placed side-by side. The overall shape of the vessel had not been altered by the damage, though many of the delicate structures which the Dreamers attached to the hulls of their spacecraft were missing, presumably knocked away by the *Crimson*'s missile barrage. Here and there, anomalous pockets of excess heat showed up on its outer plating.

"We're three minutes away. Stealth modules deactivated," said Breeze. "Preparing for the final run home."

"Good luck to us all," said Duggan. "Hold the launch until sixty thousand klicks as agreed."

"Yes, sir. I'm getting it ready to go. We're about to see some extra burn on the core."

"Sir?" said Chainer. "That's not all we're about to see. There's movement along the closest flank of the Dreamer wreckage."

"What do you mean, *movement*?" asked Duggan.

"Crap, I think I know what it is," said McGlashan. "They've opened their missile ports. They're preparing to fire!"

"The Commander is correct, sir," said Chainer. "The enemy vessel has opened fire on us!"

"Shit."

Whatever damage the enemy cruiser had suffered, there was evidently sufficient command and control remaining to order the launch of exactly one hundred missiles. Duggan didn't know if there was a crew left alive on the cruiser or if this was an automated response from the warship's AI. It didn't make a difference which it was.

"Will we be in a position to launch into the wormhole before those missiles impact?" he asked.

"Negative, sir. Even if we take into account our increased acceleration as we get pulled in."

Duggan swore again. "Prepare countermeasures," he said. "And blow the crap out of that cruiser."

CHAPTER THIRTY-THREE

"COUNTERMEASURES LAUNCHED," said McGlashan.

"Again."

"We're nearly out of drones."

"It doesn't matter now. Release more."

"Done. I've fired two Shatterers, but only sixty Lambdas – we still can't target the bastards and that's all we have pointing their way."

"What's our distance from the wormhole?" asked Duggan.

"One hundred and thirty thousand klicks, sir. Ninety seconds."

"Enemy missile impact in thirty seconds."

"We're not going to make it," said Chainer.

"Not without taking damage," said Breeze.

"We'll have to activate the launch sequence early, Lieutenant. Do it at eighty-five thousand klicks."

"That'll reduce our chances of a successful transit."

"It'll be an improvement over our deaths."

"Yes, sir. I'll initiate the launch sequence at eighty-five thousand."

"The shock drones have taken out sixty-three of the inbound," said McGlashan.

"There's a spike on the core, Lieutenant," said Duggan. "Is that part of the launch?"

"No, sir. There shouldn't be that much of an increase."

"Two hundred and thirty percent already."

"Launching at the wormhole in fifteen seconds," said Breeze, his stare fixed on his screen. The timing was critical.

"We've scored four hits on the enemy cruiser, sir," said McGlashan. "It won't put them out of action. The last of our shock drones are away, along with another sixty Lambdas. They've fired another salvo."

"Five seconds."

"The core is at three hundred and ninety-five percent," said Chainer. "Oh shit."

"Rear Bulwarks firing."

"First missiles incoming."

"Launch sequence aborted! The core is shutting down!"

"We've taken two missile strikes aft, sir!"

Red alerts appeared across a dozen separate displays. The control bars juddered in Duggan's hands as the spaceship rocked beneath the force of the high-yield missile impacts. The walls of the bridge creaked and the bulkhead display split down the middle, whilst smaller stress fractures appeared around the edges. A violent, rumbling vibration shook the crew.

"We're being crushed," Duggan said, raising his voice to be heard.

"Our structural integrity was reduced by those plasma strikes," said McGlashan.

"The gravity drive is failing."

"You have to pull up, sir!" said Chainer.

"We have another hundred missiles coming after us!"

For the first time in his life, Duggan understood what utter helplessness felt like. In moments, the *Crimson* would be crushed by the overwhelming gravity of the wormhole. The engines had plummeted to twenty percent and continued to fall. Behind, the wave of missiles raced towards them and there were no shock drones left.

"The aft Bulwarks are in a state of catastrophic failure," said McGlashan.

At that point, Duggan heard Breeze speak, the words forced grimly from his mouth.

"I've got this."

A wave of incredible nausea rolled through Duggan's body, forcing him to curl up in his chair. His body felt as though it weighed a thousand pounds and the agony of it made him shout out with bestial anguish. The sensation lasted for only a few seconds and then, when he thought the worst of it was over, it returned, as bad as it had been before. He blacked out.

He had no way of knowing how long he'd been unconscious, but he awoke to the blaring of the bridge siren. His joints ached and his broken forearm throbbed deep inside. *Got to get moving,* urged a voice in his mind.

With a groan, he sat forward. The screens on his console were a mess of failure warnings, a mixture of minor, major and critical. The tactical display was still operational and it showed there were zero potential threats in the vicinity.

"What the hell?" he muttered.

He turned as best he could to see if his crew were still out cold. "Any of you awake?"

"Just about," said Chainer. "I wish I wasn't."

"Commander McGlashan? Lieutenant Breeze?"

McGlashan grunted something to reassure him she was alive. Breeze snored gratingly in his seat, his head tipped back and his mouth open.

"What happened?" asked Chainer.

"I think Bill managed to pull us out of the fire," Duggan replied. "He got us to lightspeed somehow, before the core shut down."

"Are we home?"

"I don't know, Lieutenant - you tell me. I've got almost zero left on the gravity drives and just about everything else is offline or failing."

"Wherever we are, it isn't home, sir."

"Damn."

Additional alerts came onto one of his screens, giving him warnings he couldn't ignore.

"I need to set us down, Frank. It has to be soon."

"We're in a solar system with three planets. The middle one is the closest."

"I see it. I'm setting us on a course towards it. Someone get Lieutenant Breeze awake. I need to see where he's taken us."

Breeze didn't want to be woken, though he eventually came to with a snuffling intake of breath.

"What?" he asked, his brain clearly uncertain what was going on.

"I need you alert, Lieutenant. What happened and where are we?"

"I don't know where we are, sir," he mumbled. "Everything was failing, so I punched in some coordinates and sent us into lightspeed before the core stopped working entirely. There was no way we could have managed a double-jump, else I'd have attempted to get us through the wormhole."

"You did well, Lieutenant," said Duggan. "We'd have been crushed on the far side if you'd sent us into the Blackstar. You saved us all."

"And brought us to what?" Breeze asked, clutching his head and grimacing.

Chainer's mind was surprisingly sharp, given what had

occurred. "I've located us!" he said. "We're a short lightspeed distance from the wormhole. It appears as though Lieutenant Breeze's randomly-selected destination was somewhere about eight months away from here, but we've suffered so much damage that we came back to local space after only a short time. Once the AI shut down, we got dumped here."

"That'll be why it felt like I was put through the mill twice," said Duggan. "Once on the way in and once on the way out." He knew what that meant. "The life support is damaged," he said.

"Along with everything else."

"We need to get to this planet."

"Nistrun," said Breeze.

"Eh?" said Chainer.

"That's what it's called," Breeze replied with a weak smile. "Planet Nistrun."

"We'll reach it in approximately twenty minutes," said Chainer.

"Will we be able to land?" asked Duggan. "The gravity engines aren't looking good for it."

Breeze pulled himself together. "They're failing at a reducing rate, but the eventual trend is for them to end at zero output."

"What can we do to maximise our chances? And will someone shut off that damned alarm?"

"There's little we can do but hope, sir. I could attempt to take the gravity engines offline in the hope it'll reduce the rate at which the output is falling, but there's no guarantee they'll come back when I try to restart them."

The alarm stopped and its sudden absence made Duggan realise what a distraction it had been. "Keep the engines warm and I'll try the landing."

"We've got a couple of nice craters towards the back of the ship," said Breeze. "I'm glad our armour plating is thickest there.

If we'd been hit somewhere else, I don't think there'd be much left of the *Crimson*."

An image of Nistrun appeared on the bulkhead viewscreen, distorted by the cracks. They were approaching from the day side and the surface was hot from the scouring heat of the sun. It wouldn't have been Duggan's ideal destination, but the planet was no more or less hospitable than countless others in the universe.

"I'm going to try a quarter orbit and put us down. If the life support isn't able to sustain us, expect it to get bumpy." He opened a channel to Lieutenant Ortiz. "If there's anyone alive down there, tell them to remain seated and strapped in."

"Sir," she responded with noticeably less enthusiasm than usual.

The gravity drive output registered as hardly a flicker on the needle. The spaceship rumbled and shook as they approached, reminding Duggan of a trip he'd once taken on an ancient transport shuttle that had run into severe high-altitude turbulence on New Earth. The *Crimson*'s approach wasn't a quick one, sparing the battered hull much of the heating effect of a rapid entry into a gaseous atmosphere. Even so, the alloy glowed and its temperature soared far quicker than he expected.

"Coming in too fast," he said through gritted teeth.

"We'll impact with the surface in twenty seconds," said Chainer, the use of the word *impact* not lost on Duggan.

"We've got nothing left, Lieutenant."

The altimeter dropped like a stone, numbers blurring with the speed of their descent.

"Landing gear down, we can make this," said Duggan, as if the force of his will alone could make it happen.

The *Crimson* smashed its way through the peaks of a high mountain range, sending countless tonnes of rubble into the valleys, or far away across the surface. The spaceship was so heavy its course remained unaltered by the collision and it streaked onwards, still falling in half-controlled flight. At the last moment, Duggan shut down everything on the spacecraft apart from the life support and one front sensor array, freeing up a fraction of the engines' output.

With a howl of displaced air and a screech of tortured metal, the *Crimson* hit the surface. One of the forward landing legs bent and snapped away, clattering beneath the still-moving spaceship and tearing a deep gouge through the underside plating. The life support struggled to keep the occupants alive against the thundering contact with the solid rock and the men and women onboard felt a renewed nausea.

"Come on!" Duggan roared.

The *Crimson* skipped up once and threatened to flip over entirely. Instead, it slowed and then it stopped, leaving a wide furrow through many kilometres of the surface behind.

"Are we alive?" asked Chainer.

"For the moment," said Duggan. "I know we're screwed, but you might as well give me a status report."

"Well, sir, we're screwed," said Breeze, attempting humour. "We have less than one percent of the gravity engines, the fission drive is offline and the Dreamer core is completely inaccessible."

"Can we repair it?"

"I really don't know, sir."

"We're stuck here, then."

"For the time being."

Duggan closed his eyes and pressed his fingers against them. Things weren't going to get better.

"I think I detected something on the way in, sir," said Chainer. "Right on the cusp of the horizon when we came down."

"Come on, Lieutenant, give me the bad news."

"I think the enemy have a base on this planet. I don't have

much information on it, since you shut off most of the sensors to get us safely down. I'll be able to make some educated guesses once I've enhanced the recorded feed."

"It can't get much worse than this," said Duggan, expecting one of his crew to volunteer something which would prove him wrong. They did not.

"We're alive, sir," said McGlashan. "That's something."

"Marooned in hostile space with a heavily damaged warship, near to an enemy installation." He shook his head bitterly. "With no way to get home."

"We've come through worse," said Chainer, repeating the old mantra.

"Only a couple of times," said Breeze.

Duggan forced a smile to his face that he didn't feel inside. "And we'll damn well get out of this one," he said.

He'd never been a liar, but he knew this was going to be the hardest promise to keep. The hopeful faces of his crew roused him to action and he got to his feet, determined he wouldn't let them down.

———

Look out for more books in the Survival Wars series, coming soon!

Follow Anthony James on Facebook at
facebook.com/anthonyjamesauthor

THE SURVIVAL WARS SERIES

Printed in Great Britain
by Amazon

60239157R10158